FINISH THE GAME
THE CITY OF LIGHT

IAN JOLLY

Pen Press

© Contento de Semrik 2013

All rights reserved

No part of this publication may be reproduced, stored in a retrieval system, or transmitted in any form or by any means, without the prior permission in writing of the publisher, nor be otherwise circulated in any form of binding or cover other than that in which it is published and without a similar condition including this condition being imposed on the subsequent purchaser.

First published by Contento de Semrik

All paper used in the printing of this book has been made from wood grown in managed, sustainable forests.

ISBN13: 978-1-78003-556-7

Printed and bound in the UK
Pen Press is an imprint of
Indepenpress Publishing Limited
25 Eastern Place
Brighton
BN2 1GJ

A catalogue record of this book is available from
the British Library

Cover design by Jacqueline Abromeit

"Finish the Game" is dedicated to my beautiful wife Jan and my children Camille, Anthea, Briana and Marcus. They patiently endured the time I spent typing up the story and the numerous requests I made for them to read it as each edit was completed.

PROLOGUE

Rosie and Marcus entered a tunnel formed by a thick mat of twigs, vines, branches and leaves. Continuing for well over one hundred metres, the bushes and vines grew right up to the edge of the path but not on it. Some strange, powerful and invisible force seemed to stop them from growing on the path itself. As they walked slowly through the leafy tunnel, the darkness closed in on them. The thick leafy wall and roof of the tunnel filtered out most of the light. Rosie, now frightened by the cold, damp darkness, grabbed Marcus' hand.

Marcus felt the same, "This is getting scary. I feel as though someone is watching us."

"Yeah," she whispered back. She sensed a spine-tingling feeling, like a spider running up her back. Her voice trembled, "Did you hear that?"

Marcus felt the vibration before it increased in volume, filling the twins with absolute terror. Rosie squeezed her brother's hand tightly and drawing closer to him yelled, "It sounds like someone screaming."

The branches, vines and leaves of the tunnel brushed up hard against them. A musty damp smell inundated the tunnel and the terrible screaming hurt his ears.

"Let's get out of here," Rosie shouted out over the appalling screams. Turning around to go back the way she had come in. Terrified, she screamed, "The entrance. It's gone," and stood, thoroughly hypnotised by the sight of the moving vegetation.

Marcus twisted around when she screamed. He watched in complete astonishment as the branches and vines grew, before his eyes, across the path.

"That's not possible," he shouted.

He saw quickly what Rosie meant about the entrance. There was now only one thing to do. "Run!" he yelled over the noise, as the screams from the tunnel intensified further. Rosie didn't seem to hear so he pulled her along to escape the rapidly growing vegetation. Vines with razor sharp thorns reached out, clawing viciously at them, tearing deep into their arms and legs as they sprinted down the tunnel...

CHAPTER 1

THE COMMISSIONERS

The warm yellow light of the afternoon sun filtered through the massive stained glass windows into the Great Hall. In the middle of the hall stood a young man, his thick, long, shoulder length black hair hiding much of his face.

With each passing moment, the young man was becoming noticeably more agitated. He glanced impatiently at his watch and swore, "Damn. Not again." The Commissioners were late again. This was the second time this week and this delay wasn't helping his frame of mind or his temper. Today's meeting was vitally important. He smiled for a brief moment, as he reflected on his wife's words to him, 'Don't lose your temper. Be patient. Remain calm,' and stretched out, taking in several long deep breaths to do so.

That's when he first became aware of the tiny particles of dust floating aimlessly through the coloured shafts of light. He watched with interest as the dust drifted without purpose or direction. Recognising the similarity between the dust and the directionless leadership of the City of Light changed his frown to a wry grin. The current Chairman didn't have a clue and the others followed like lost sheep. He couldn't say a good word about any of them.

Putting these thoughts out of his mind, he concentrated on what he had to say. Deep in thought, his mind was a thousand miles away when a shrill screech took him by surprise. Instinctively, he turned his head towards the source of the noise and watched as the heavy wooden door, to his right, opened. The metal hinges squealed as the door moved at a snail's pace, finally stopping when it came to rest against the wall.

Loud enough for the nine Commissioners to hear, he said, "About time." However, they paid him no attention as they entered the Great Hall in single file. They strode towards the end of the room where nine beautifully carved marble chairs sat waiting for them. High above and behind each of the chairs, thick tapestries hung from the ceiling to the floor. Each had its own distinctive symbol. The nine tapestries clearly identifying each Commissioner's seat on the Council of the City of Light.

The Commissioners' ceremonial robes matched the colours of the tapestries. A large hood covering their heads created dark shadows hiding their faces. They stood in front of their chairs. Then, with a slight nod from the Council Chairman, they sat down together. Proceedings were about to commence.

Commissioner Dagar rose to his feet. Without a word of introduction, he started the meeting. "So

Dalastar, you think Lord Theda will attack the City of Light?"

This surprised the young man but he didn't show it. He had thought the Council Chairman would commence proceedings, not Commissioner Dagar. It was widely known this Commissioner was a hard, ruthless man. Anyone who crossed paths with him usually came off second best. Dalastar had a feeling that something was wrong. Terribly wrong. He had had his suspicions for a number of weeks. Until now, he had never had enough evidence to prove anything. Dalastar desperate to speak his mind fought hard to rein in his temper and answered calmly, "Yes Commissioner, I do."

Commissioner Dagar asked, with a slight hint of sarcasm in his voice, "And what have you seen to suggest this will occur, Dalastar?"

Dalastar, despite feeling angry with the Commissioners, maintained his composure, "As you are no doubt aware, Commissioner Dagar, the dark army has become increasingly active. We have received numerous reports of destroyed and plundered villages on the verge of the areas affected by the eclipse. Hundreds are missing from their homes. With Lord Theda as their leader, the creatures of the dark army are now bolder and more ruthless than ever before." He paused for a few seconds before continuing, even more fervently than before, "We must put plans in place to protect the City. If we..."

Commissioner Dagar interrupted, "But you have no physical proof to suggest Lord Theda will attack the City of Light. Do you?" Commissioner

Dagar paused a moment, glaring at Dalastar, to make his point. "A city," he continued, "...which has never, in its long history, Commissioners... suffered an attack from the dark army. Nothing. You have nothing. We will not allow you to create panic in the City. The..."

"With respect, Commissioner Dagar," said Dalastar with great conviction, clenching his fists tightly by his side, struggling to control the anger rising up from within.

"Dalastar, we will not tolerate you interrupting Commissioner Dagar while he is speaking," commanded the deep authoritative voice of the Council Chairman.

Now Dalastar was annoyed. He had always thought the Council Chairman was a weak, pathetic little man, and nothing he had seen today caused him to change his mind. However, Dalastar stood quite still in the middle of the room. The warmth of the afternoon sun wasn't the only thing heating up the room, as beads of sweat trickled down his back. It was obvious the other Commissioners were acting against their better judgment. He knew they should be protecting the City of Light from Lord Theda. Clearly, Commissioner Dagar was in control. Dalastar knew he had to try something.

"Thank you, Chairman Dioti," said Commissioner Dagar as he turned his attention back to Dalastar. "As I was saying you have nothing..."

Dalastar tuned out to what the Commissioner was saying, when he saw a flash of coloured light from under the darkness of Commissioner Dagar's hood. Everyone in the room heard Dalastar swear under his breath, as he once again scrutinised the dark shadow hiding the Commissioner's face. Everything became perfectly clear when he caught, for the briefest of moments, sight of the coloured flash for a second time. The shock of his discovery worried him. Now he was alone, "It's now or never," he whispered and lunged towards Commissioner Dagar. The speed of Dalastar's attack surprised the Commissioner, forcing him to step backwards. Commissioner Dagar stumbled slightly, but it was enough to force the dark green hood to slip from his head.

The Council Chairman rose from his chair and, pointing his finger at Dalastar, roared in anger, "I command you to leave this chamber immediately! This behaviour is not acceptable and will not be tolerated."

Dalastar lost his temper and ignored the command. Furious, he shouted back, "I will not listen to this nonsense any more. Can't you see who this is?"

He stared angrily at each of the Commissioner's but their faces remained hidden in the dark shadows of their hoods. "Cowards, you are nothing but cowards," he yelled at them. Dalastar looked directly into Commissioner Dagar's eyes. The eyes were cold and steely black, revealing the sinister green and red firestorm of energy burning within the Commissioner. Only one creature in the known universe displayed these characteristics.

Dalastar had seen this twice before. His father had caught one of these creatures many years ago. A chilling sensation ran down his spine as he recalled the horror of the most recent encounter, which was only a few months ago. It was something he would never forget. They were a vile parasitic race from the furthermost part of the universe. With no physical form, they invaded and possessed the bodies of other life forms. Over several months, they consumed every ounce of energy their host produced. Eventually the host died and the creature moved on to another. Lord Theda must have taken over Commissioner Dagar's body months ago. Many who'd known the Commissioner had noticed the changes in his behaviour. No one knew why, until now.

"It's you. Now all this makes sense," whispered Dalastar. He was acutely aware this creature would not surrender easily. They were stubborn, proud creatures who rarely made mistakes, and they possessed great powers. Dalastar was determined this destructive, evil creature would not have this world — his world.

"So, Dalastar. You have finally unravelled the mystery," as Lord Theda's face broke into a sinister smile. "But you are too late."

"It is never too late, Lord Theda. You will not win," said Dalastar defiantly. When he raised his right arm in the air to throw, a brilliant bright blue ball of fire burst into existence around his hand.

Lord Theda was quicker than Dalastar and flung a death arrow at the Council Chairman. "This is outrage ..." was the last thing the Chairman said, before the arrow hit, and he vanished in a bright green flash.

Then quicker than the eye could see, seven more arrows, thrown by Lord Theda, rocketted across the room towards the remaining Commissioners. The arrows flew straight towards their targets, stopping suddenly, hovering and quivering just millimetres from each of the Commissioners' noses. They all froze in shock, no one dared to move.

Lord Theda smiling victoriously, turned to Dalastar, "Very good. You have seen right through me. However, as you see, I am the one in control. The lives of the Commissioners are in your hands," his right arm extended out, pointing at the trapped Commissioners. "Put away the fireball, otherwise you will be responsible for their deaths."

One of the Commissioners, recognising his mistake by supporting this monster, called out bravely, "We have been tricked gentlemen." Then speaking directly to Dalastar, "get away from ..." Lord Theda clicked his fingers, freeing the arrow to complete its deadly journey. The Commissioner died quickly, vanishing in a bright green flash.

"Well. What is it to be? It is your decision," said Lord Theda, taunting his opponent.

Dalastar already knew the fate of the remaining Commissioners. With great power and accuracy, he threw a blue ball of fire directly at Lord Theda. A red shield, emblazoned with a depiction of a green dragon, appeared in Lord Theda's hands. The green dragon flashed brightly in the afternoon light. With a flick of his wrists, Lord Theda deflected the fireball with the shield, where it exploded loudly yet harmlessly in the far corner of the room.

Lord Theda laughed loudly, "You will have to do better than that, to defeat me."

Dalastar surveyed the room and swiftly considered his limited options. Having entered through the main front door, Lord Theda was most likely to have soldiers waiting for him that way. The massive stained-glass windows were on his left, and trying to crash through any of them could cause him to be seriously injured. The Commissioners' entrance to the Great Hall was his only option.

Dalastar knew he would need to time his escape perfectly. The first thing he wanted to do was distract his opponent. With all his energy, he unleashed a fireball, directly at Lord Theda. He threw another fireball in the same direction just before he dived for the entrance. Landing on his side, he slid quickly across the polished stone floor, making himself a difficult target to hit. Lord Theda flung three death arrows towards him. At the speed Dalastar was moving, the arrows smashed into floor behind him, blasting out chunks of stone.

The explosions created hundreds of deadly bright green sparks that hissed viciously around the room, leaving whorls of putrid smoke hanging in the air.

Reaching the safety of the Commissioner's room, Dalastar leapt out through an open window. Landing safely in the alley below, he raced through the back streets to return to the others.

The fireballs thrown by Dalastar thundered into Lord Theda's dragon emblazoned red shield. The powerful blows knocked Lord Theda off his feet. A cloud of red sparks and blue flames blossomed outwards and the deafening boom blasted the stained glass out of all the windows. Furious his young opponent had upstaged him, Lord Theda took out his anger on the trapped Commissioners, shouting, "YOU SHOULD HAVE LISTENED TO HIM!" Turning his back on them, he clicked his fingers. Six green flashes flared up behind him, creating a brief, eerie shadow as he walked towards the front door of the Great Hall.

On the way back to his friends, Dalastar stopped to peer around the corner from across the road from the Great Hall.

Citizens and travellers from all over the universe gathered around, staring up at the damaged windows of the Great Hall, wondering what had happened.

Lord Theda pulled his hood over his head and appeared at the main door in front of the crowd. Raising his hands in the air, he called for quiet. Eventually the citizens stopped talking, turned, and listened to him speak.

CHAPTER 2

DALASTAR STANDS FIRM

Dalastar didn't wait to hear what Lord Theda had to say to the huge crowd who had gathered at the bottom of the stairs outside the Great Hall. He raced off to be with his three friends, who were waiting at his apartment. The survival of the City and this world were far more important.

His wife, Phoebe, slightly shorter than her husband, was greatly relieved to see him safe and wrapped her arms joyfully around his neck. "What happened?" she asked. "We heard the explosions from the City Centre."

"The news is not good. Lord Theda is in control, and…," Dalastar sighed, "he killed all the Commissioners." He gave them a brief account of the events in the chamber of the Great Hall. Alexandria, his sister and Lucian, his trusted friend, listened intently.

Dalastar felt his wife's slight frame shiver, as tears ran down her small round face. He stroked her long black hair, kissed her on the forehead and held her closely.

"You knew something wasn't quite right about Commissioner Dagar," said Lucian.

"Yes. But, I was too late."

Phoebe, feeling his anger and frustration, let Dalastar go and watched as he walked out onto the balcony. Resting his hands on the parapet, Dalastar looked out over the city.

Dalastar heard the others come up behind him, and turned to face them.

"The city has no leadership," he said. "Unless we act now, he will destroy everything. We are the only ones left who can stop him from taking the energy crystals. We cannot fail."

The other three were staring up in shock at something behind him.

Dalastar's heart missed a beat when he saw the reflection of green light in his wife's eyes. He spun around as Phoebe cried out in horror, "Look up there!"

Hundreds of green sparkling lines filled the sky, green trails from deadly projectiles.

Dalastar shouted to the others, "DEATH ARROWS! GET INSIDE NOW!"

Reacting immediately his white shield appeared beside him. On his command, the shield filled the doorway, protecting the four of them from the deadly onslaught. At least a dozen arrows slammed into the shield exploding on impact. Green and white sparks spilled over the balcony on to the street below. The noise was deafening.

Absolute chaos reigned throughout the streets of the City of Light. The screams of hundreds of terrified people rose up from below, as wave after wave of death arrows rained down on the citizens. Forgetting about his own safety, Dalastar raced out on to the balcony to investigate. Pointing to the road below, he called out to the others, "There are survivors. They're all heading towards the gatekeeper," desperately hoping they would make it. He thought about the gatekeeper and his family, confident they could deal with the great numbers of people who would soon be on their doorstep. They welcomed and farewelled all the visitors and travellers to this world through the gateway to the universe.

There was one thing they had to accomplish first. He asked the others "Are you ready?"

"Yes," came the collective reply.

Looking at his watch, he said, "Good. Let's get to the tower. We must put our plan into action."

The apartment was a good five minutes from the Central Tower.

Dalastar warned everyone, "This will be dangerous and you will need to be careful. His soldiers will be everywhere."

The others acknowledged Dalastar, and then together, rushed down the stairs and out onto the street. It was crucial they reached the tower standing in the middle of the City of Light before five o'clock. Hurrying through the streets, they looked around as they ran; ready to hide in the shadows at a moment's notice, from the soldiers of the dark army.

When they arrived, the four of them hid in the entrance of an apartment just across the courtyard from the tower entrance.

"We've only got a few minutes left," said Dalastar, worried about being late. "Go now."

Alexandria and Phoebe sprinted across the courtyard first, disappearing safely into the tower.

Dalastar grabbed Lucian by the shoulders. "When you get inside the tower, seal the entrance with your shield, and protect them. I must see to Lord Theda myself."

Lucian couldn't believe it and said, "No. You can't. That's not part of the plan."

"I know," he said, thinking back to his father's death. "I must do this for him Lucian. Now go."

Lucian nodded. He understood why his friend wanted to do this. "Take care, my friend," and scooted across the road and dived into the tower. His shield filled the entrance just as Lord Theda came into the courtyard.

Dalastar stood up, sucked in a deep breath, and strode out to face Lord Theda by himself.

Lord Theda watched the sole figure striding towards him and smiled. "So we meet again."

"Yes," said Dalastar. "And this will be the final time."

Lord Theda scoffed at his opponent, "You are so confident young man — so much like your father. What do you have that I don't know about? Look around. You are outnumbered and surrounded by over a hundred of my soldiers."

Dalastar thought of the others, hiding in the Tower above him. All we need is time, just a couple of minutes. "You know the power of this shield. You cannot hurt me", he said.

Lord Theda laughed, "That is what your father said before he died."

Dalastar had vivid memories of that day and hurled a fireball towards Lord Theda. Lord Theda returned the attack. Each successfully deflected the attack of the other.

The two combatants circled around each other, now only twenty metres apart.

"I do know about the shield Dalastar, but I also know about your wife and the others who are now in the tower. You four ... bring them to me," he ordered his troops. The soldiers obeyed at once and ran towards the tower. They were only five steps away from the tower when the town clock struck five o'clock. Within a matter of seconds, the yellowish glare of the late afternoon changed unexpectedly to an intense bright blue light. The change took Lord Theda by surprise. He roared out in anger, "What is this?"

The bright blue light blinded the soldiers of the dark army. Another powerful wave of light burst outwards in all directions from the top of the tower. It struck down the soldiers of the dark army in a vicious but brief attack, leaving them lying dazed and disorientated on the ground. Dalastar's confidence reached new heights. Armed with the knowledge the weapon had worked, he taunted Lord Theda, "What is it I have, that you are not going to like? You will not have this City nor will you escape again."

Another even more powerful wave of light pulsed out from the tower. This time like an enormous wall of water, it swept the dazed and fallen soldiers away, cleansing the courtyard of their presence.

Lord Theda still in control of Commissioner Dagar's body, stood alone in the courtyard. He was livid, which fuelled his defiance. "I have underestimated you again, but you will not take me alive."

Dalastar had convinced himself he could stop this monster and said, "That is what you think. You will not be allowed to escape."

Lord Theda's arrogance hadn't diminished, "I will escape."

Both continued to circle around each keeping a distance from each other.

Dalastar tripped on a cobblestone and stumbled. For a split second, he lost eye contact with his enemy. Lord Theda saw his opportunity and attacked by hurling his shield with incredible power and accuracy at his opponent. Dalastar never expected Lord Theda to use his red shield as a weapon. He cursed himself for making such a stupid mistake. When the two shields collided, the deafening boom echoed off the buildings around the courtyard. The red shield split in two and released a powerful pulse of electromagnetic energy. Dalastar staggered backwards with the force of the blow. It felt like someone had whacked him with a sledgehammer. The red shield hadn't finished its task and wrapped itself around Dalastar. His arms and legs were immobilised. Even though his shield protected him, he found himself lying flat on his back, unable to move. The powerful binding forces lasted for a minute or two. Then the red shield vanished and returned to its master. Dalastar picked himself up off the ground and went in pursuit of Lord Theda.

Lord Theda took the opportunity to flee, running off towards the Gate, the entrance to the rest of the universe. In sheer desperation, Dalastar fired off two arrows, which left trails of white sparkling light behind. They landed well short of the mark. Three or four times he had to take cover behind his shield as Lord Theda fired off death arrows to try to slow down Dalastar's progress.

With their task on the tower completed, Phoebe, Alexandria and Lucian raced down the staircase and dashed out into the courtyard.

Alexandria slipped a sapphire pendant and chain over her head. She caught sight of Dalastar in the distance, "There they are," she said, pointing in Dalastar's direction. "They're headed towards the gate to the universe."

Lord Theda finally reached a courtyard above the gate to the universe. Everyone who'd travelled through here knew it as the gatekeeper's courtyard. Right in the middle stood a building with a domed roof. Six carved marble columns held up the roof, which covered the long spiral staircase to the gate itself. Without slowing his pace, he climbed down the stairs. At the same time, he hurled a red and green fireball upwards at the domed entrance. The fireball rose, exploding under the centre of the domed roof. A great cloud of smoke and flame billowed outwards as the roof lifted up and twisted around. Four of the marble columns fell outwards as the remaining two columns collapsed inwards. The roof crashed down on top of them.

Lord Theda's shield protected him from the falling rubble as he continued down the staircase. "That will slow Dalastar down," he said, laughing all the way to the bottom.

Now he had time to regroup and plan another attack.

CHAPTER 3

DEATH AND DESTRUCTION

Dalastar reached the path leading into the gatekeeper's courtyard just as the domed roof exploded skywards. A great cloud of smoke and flames followed the path of the roof upwards. Dalastar stopped and stared in utter astonishment and disbelief as the whole building collapsed in front of him. The building had been there for thousands of years. He couldn't see the sense in such wilful destruction and was further outraged by Lord Theda's actions. A strong breeze cleared away the dust and smoke. Dalastar walked around the collapsed structure. Halfway around, he discovered a hole beneath the dome where the roof remained intact and rested on a marble column. Just as he was about to climb in, he heard Lucian call out to him, "Wait. You need to see this."

Annoyed by the delay he looked back at the others, "What is it?"

"It's very important," Lucian replied solemnly. Dalastar trusted Lucian and from the tone in his voice, knew it must be serious.

Phoebe and Alexandria stood next to each other, staring at the ground on either side of the path leading into the gatekeeper's courtyard. There were hundreds of small circles clearly etched on the ground on both sides of the path. The circles, once green grass, had instantly withered, turned brown, and died, a little puff of icy coldness rising from the centre of each one.

Alexandria squatted down, reaching out to touch one of the circles.

Seeing what his sister was going to do, Dalastar yelled, "DON'T TOUCH!"

Alexandria reacted to the urgency in his voice and pulled her hand back.

"If you touch that the same will happen to you. Watch this," as Dalastar broke a branch off a small shrub and threw it into the middle of one of the circles. When the branch hit the ground, it shrivelled up and vanished.

Alexandria was horrified.

Dalastar sank to his knees, "Damn. I didn't see these when I came through here." He had never expected Lord Theda would go this far. "Each one of those," he said, waving his hand at the circles, "is where a death arrow has hit a citizen or visitor to our city. Their souls will lie there forever."

Dalastar stood and said solemnly, "That's not all that happens. Stand back and watch."

The others stood beside him in absolute silence, each feeling the loss of so many citizens and trying to understand the—annihilation, which had taken place here only less than half an hour earlier.

What happened next surprised all of them, even Dalastar who'd seen this once before.

Alexandria cried out, "That's not possible!" she said, pointing to the ground as seedlings popped out of the ground from the dead centre of each circle.

"That's amazing. I've heard about it but never seen it," said Lucian.

Phoebe asked, "What is it?"

"When a death arrow hits you, the ground beneath you swallows up your soul," explained Dalastar. "Plants grow in the circle and take the place of the fallen souls. They seek revenge on the one who killed them. In certain circumstances, because of the anger within, their judgement is impaired and sometimes, these plants will attack anyone or anything that comes anywhere close to them."

"How could someone do something like this? It's terrible," said Phoebe as tears streamed down her cheeks.

"Yes it is. So is Lord Theda, let's not forget that."

In just a few minutes, the seedlings had grown into a wide variety of small trees and thorny vines, as the four onlookers watched on in complete astonishment.

"Come. We don't want to be their first victims," said Dalastar, his heart heavy with a combination of anger and sadness as he walked slowly back towards the collapsed building. "There is nothing more to be done here."

Dalastar showed them the hole under the dome, "This is the only way to get through."

Phoebe dropped down on her hands and knees and stuck her head in the hole. All she could see was darkness. Standing up, she said, "We'll need some light"

He acknowledged her by holding out his hand and ordered, "Illuminate." A small ball of blue light burst brightly into existence in the palm of his hand.

"I'll go first," he said, and wriggled down through the hole.

Lucian allowed Phoebe and Alexandria to go before him. Before climbing down after the others, Lucian looked across at the entrance path and swore under his breath. The trees and vines had formed into a thick, impenetrable wall of vegetation around the courtyard. Over the gravel path, which led into the courtyard, the vegetation had formed an arch over the path creating a dark tunnel of vines and branches. I hope I'm not the next one to walk through there, he thought. He then wriggled down through the hole and caught up to the others.

The four of them half-ran and half-walked down the long circular staircase.

Dalastar pushed open the wooden door at the bottom of the staircase and entered an empty octagonal room. On the opposite wall, a large octagonal steel door hung wide open. The light in Dalastar's hand shone brightly in the darkness.

A voice called out from the darkness above, "What is it you want?"

Dalastar asked, "How many travellers left here today?"

"One hundred and fifty one," said the voice from the darkness above them.

Dalastar needed answers urgently and asked, "Can you tell me what happened with the survivors?"

Delostyek the gatekeeper remained hidden in the darkness above. He told them everything, from the time when the surviving travellers and citizens rushed through here to escape, right up to when the last visitor left. His voice started to break as he began to describe the final visitor to the chamber.

Phoebe, more sensitive and perceptive than her husband, heard the hurt and sorrow in the gatekeeper's voice, and said softly, "Please take your time."

"Thankyou," he replied, taking a few moments to steady himself before continuing.

The story the gatekeeper told them was full of sadness and horror, "... and then he stole the key and vanished," he finished abruptly.

The sombre atmosphere in the small room weighed heavily upon them all. Phoebe could see the anger in her husband's face as Delostyek told them about the death of his family at the hands of Lord Theda.

Lucian, aware of the others' feelings, put his hand on Dalastar's shoulder and said quietly, "We must find him."

"Yes, we must," said Dalastar looking up in the direction of the gatekeeper, "I am truly sorry for your loss. We must leave this place and find him before he destroys any more lives."

"I understand," said the gatekeeper, who remained hidden in the darkness. "What would you have me do?"

"Close the door behind us and lock it."

The gatekeeper was horrified and said, "But you will not be able to return unless I have the key. No one will be able to enter this world."

"We understand, but Lord Theda cannot be allowed to return. His sole purpose is the destruction of this world. We cannot allow that to happen. Never give up hope for we will return. Stay and guard this place until then."

Beyond the octagonal doorway, lay the tunnel travellers used to visit and leave this world. It was the entrance gate to the universe. The four said their farewells to the gatekeeper, stepped into the tunnel and then, in a bright flash they were gone.

In the darkness of the room, the octagonal door slammed shut. The gatekeeper slipped the locks through the lugs. Two loud metallic clicks echoed around the room closing the locks, locking the door securely.

The energy within the tunnel propelled them forward at great speed. Without any warning, they stopped and found themselves standing on the verandah of an old derelict house.

The roof had collapsed, all the windows were smashed and the timber boards hung loosely on the wall buckled and twisted beyond any hope of repair. The pitch-black darkness of this strange new world surprised them. Dark clouds covered the sky blocking out any light from the moon and stars behind. Dalastar wasn't worried about the darkness. Their light tunics were no match for the bitter cold. The icy coldness attacked their exposed skin and chilled them right through to the bone. Within a few seconds, they were all shivering. Dalastar called out quietly, "Illuminate," and a small ball of light appeared glowing brightly in his hand

The doorway through which they had entered this new world leaned forward at an angle of forty-five degrees.

Lucian after examining the timber frame said, "We're lucky we were able to come through here. It's only just holding together."

Phoebe stood shivering, her teeth chattering, "It's very cold here."

Dalastar grimaced and put his arm around her shoulder, "It certainly is."

The combined effects of the cold night air, the darkness and the sudden creaking and groaning of the house as the wind picked up, distracted them from the impending danger.

"We need to find somewhere warm to stay," said Alexandria, who'd jumped off the verandah and walked down the overgrown path at the front of the house. She turned around to look at the house, "It must be ready to fall..." when she disappeared in a flash of green light, a green trail leading back to her killer.

The shields of the others appeared just in time as three more death arrows rocketed into them.

"Damn you!" Dalastar cursed loudly, overcome with anger. All he wanted was to destroy Lord Theda for killing her.

Lord Theda, who lay hidden in the darkness laughed at them, "So Dalastar, you decided to follow me."

Dalastar couldn't control his anger. Wanting to go after the creature and kill it, he yelled, "You, gutless, cowardly..." when Lucian grabbed him from behind.

Lucian had seen the expression on Dalastar's face. He had anticipated what his friend was going to do and restrained him for his own safety. Once Dalastar lost his temper, he was like a bull at a gate and stopped thinking about the consequences of his actions. Alexandria was gone. Lucian didn't want to lose someone else close to him. Dalastar struggled to break free, cursing Lord Theda's existence.

"That's exactly what he wants you to do," shouted Lucian, trying to talk sense to his friend. "We can't afford to have you killed as well."

Dalastar struggled to break free from his friend but Lucian held firm.

"You've got to control your temper," Lucian yelled into his friend's ear. Dalastar's efforts to break free weakened as he realised his friend was right. Anyway, Lucian had lost someone dear to him tonight as well. Dalastar yelled out, "We will never give up until you are caught and punished."

Lord Theda laughed loudly, taunting them. With great accuracy and power, he hurled three reddish-green fireballs in quick succession.

The first struck Phoebe's shield. The force of the blast lifted her off her feet, propelling her backwards off the verandah. As it struck the shield, the fireball turned into hundreds of fiery fingers that clung to the side of her shield, trying their best to kill her. Her shield wrapped around her like a bubble, protecting her from the tiny aggressive fingers of death. She landed in the long grass at the side of the house with a thud. The thick grass broke her fall but she lay motionless, stunned and winded, her shield still wrapped around her.

Lucian managed to deflect the fireball and fired one back in the direction of Lord Theda.

It fell short and the resulting explosion covered Lord Theda in a layer of mud. It was enough to make him race off into the darkness of the night.

Dalastar also managed to fend off Lord Theda's fireball. The deflected fireball slammed into the old house where it exploded with tiny sparks of fire flying in all directions. The force of the explosion lifted Dalastar and Lucian off the verandah throwing them into the overgrown garden at the side of the house, where they landed heavily. Numerous chunks of timber, debris and splinters flew in all directions, narrowly missing the three travellers. The dry timber in the old house offered no resistance to the intense heat and ferocity of the fireball tearing into it, and like a ravenous beast, it consumed everything in its path.

CHAPTER 4

LORD THEDA STRIKES

Lucian crawled over to Dalastar, and they helped each other to their feet. Stunned by the blast, they watched helplessly as the fire spread rapidly through the house.

Phoebe stood up slowly and groaned, "Ouch. That hurt". For a few moments, she stood there like the others staring at the flames and enjoying the warmth, as she came to her senses. The others, she realised were watching the fire take hold of the house. She shouted, "What about the doorway?"

Dalastar heard her call out and cursed himself, "Damn. Why didn't I think of that?"

It was their only link to their own world. He leapt up on to the verandah. The intense heat of the fire pushed him back but he had no choice. He had to save the doorframe; it was their only hope of returning to their own world. Fortunately, the force of the blast had knocked it over onto the verandah where it lay in four pieces. The scorching heat singed the hairs on his arms as he picked up the pieces and hurled them, one by one, towards Lucian. Lucian caught them and placed them carefully on the ground.

Meanwhile Phoebe walked around to the path where Alexandria had perished and sat down next to the circle of dead grass on the ground.

Dalastar jumped down off the veranda and spoke briefly with Lucian, finishing with, "Be careful." He watched as Lucian disappeared into the darkness to go after Lord Theda. Dalastar was far more concerned for Phoebe and anyway Lucian was capable of completing what he had failed to do himself. Sitting down next to his wife he said, "At least you were thinking clearly."

"Well, with what we've been through it's a wonder we're still alive," Phoebe whispered unsteadily, and then started sobbing uncontrollably.

Dalastar held his wife closely and whispered, "You are right, we have been lucky. Alexandria should still be here with us. I am the one who should have been more careful. I promised my father I would protect her, but I've failed."

Dalastar sat with his arm around his wife's shoulder. The heat from the burning house warmed them physically but Alexandria's death left them feeling cold, empty and miserable.

Behind them, in the middle of the circle where Alexandria had died, a tiny green shoot popped up out of the ground.

Meanwhile, Lucian had found it easy to follow Lord Theda. He had fired off dozens of fireballs, leaving a trail of blazing houses behind him.

The residents fled in terror, forced out of their homes into the cold night air.

Lord Theda stood admiring his handiwork and the terror he had created. He wondered what this world was. It appeared he had incredible power over it. However, Lord Theda didn't realise that Lucian was not far behind him.

Lucian raced down the lane towards the town, which he had seen in the distance. He would have missed Lord Theda had he not heard a hideous laugh off to his right. Steadily and quietly, he crept up on Lord Theda who was only twenty metres away. Lucian's bow and arrows appeared at his side. Quietly he loaded up the bow, took aim and fired. The arrow flew straight towards Lord Theda, leaving a glistening white trail behind it.

Lord Theda didn't see the arrow until the last moment as he stood gloating over the destruction he had caused. His shield reacted quickly but it wasn't quite fast enough. The arrow deflected upwards off the shield, hitting him squarely in the shoulder.

Lord Theda fell to the ground screaming and contorted with agony. There was no explosion this time, just a terrifying high-pitched scream that shrieked out into the darkness. A white haze surrounded Lord Theda as he thrashed about in pain. He knew this body was finished and he needed to find another.

Lucian ran over to Lord Theda. After the attack at the house, Dalastar had given him a brief description of what to expect. What he saw was horrible and much worse than he had expected. An eerie reddish-green fog emerged from the pain-racked body writhing about on the ground. The horrible screaming continued unabated. If that wasn't enough, a vile stench, filled the air around him, forcing Lucian to take several steps backwards. A unique bright red outline started to form around the foggy, shapeless creature emerging from the Commissioner. Hundreds of thousands of tiny concentrated red and green flaming balls of fire blazed fiercely within it.

In view of the awful stench and remembering his friend's words, Lucian decided it was time to move further away from Lord Theda.

A long skinny lick of flame spurted out from the creature trying to grab Lucian's leg. Lucian saw it just in time and moved his shield swiftly to form a protective sphere around himself.

Lord Theda grew rapidly and towered above Lucian. The creature hissed venomously, spurting out tiny deadly flames of green spittle. Once again, Lucian's shield protected him. He drew in a deep breath, thankful he had escaped unscathed.

The terrible screaming stopped at the same time Lord Theda vanished into the darkness.

Commissioner Dagar lay sprawled out on the cold ground. After the intense physical agony of the last few months, his body was finally pain free. He knew the end was near. Lucian knelt down beside the critically injured Commissioner. The bloodshot eyes focused on Lucian. He grabbed Lucian's hand and pressed a small object into it. Lucian guessed what it was and opened it to check. The gatekeeper's purple key sat in the palm of his hand. He wasn't entirely surprised, "Thank you, Commissioner," he said softly.

The Commissioner, struggling to speak, said, "Take this and... give it to... Dalastar. You... must stop... Lord... Theda..." This time the Commissioner grabbed Lucian's shirt and stared desperately into his face, "Promise me... please."

Lucian put his hand on the Commissioner's undamaged shoulder, "Yes Commissioner, we will stop him. I promise."

"Good. Tell Dalastar I'm sorry," he gasped with his last breath. The Commissioner's body glowed white for several seconds, and then vanished in a puff of white smoke.

Lucian ran into town searching desperately for Lord Theda. He heard one hideous scream in the distance but after about forty-five minutes, gave up the search. There wasn't any trace of him. Lucian, cold and tired, walked dejectedly back to the others. The trip back took longer than expected. On several occasions, he had to hide in the shadows, to avoid detection, as people ran from burning house to burning house checking on their neighbours and friends.

Finally, when Lucian arrived back at the glowing remains of the derelict house he saw Dalastar and Phoebe hadn't moved from the spot where they had first sat down.

Lucian called out to make sure the others knew he was back, "You two. You need to look behind you."

Twisting around at the sound of Lucian's voice, they couldn't believe what they set their eyes on.

They hadn't heard a thing while they had been sitting grieving about Alexandria's death. Phoebe leap to her feet, and backed away. Dalastar stood and whispered to her, "Look," pointing towards a sapphire pendent hanging from a branch of the tree.

Phoebe recognised it straight away. It was Alexandria's. Moving forward carefully, she reached out and gently removed it from the branch. "It can't be," she whispered in shock. The tree, pleased with itself, swayed and twisted as though blown about by a strong wind. A long slender branch swept down towards Phoebe, stopped, then reached out with its leafy fingers, touching her softly on the cheek. That's when the tears flooded down Phoebe's face and the leaves lovingly wiped them from her wet cheeks. Dalastar reached out as well, letting the small branches and leaves stroke his fingers. They wrapped gently around his arm and squeezed tenderly, "Thank you Alexandria," said Dalastar, who had tears running down his face. "We will make sure he is punished for what he has done today."

CHAPTER 5

THE TWINS

Peter Saunders sat huddled over the keyboard reviewing the opening scenes of the new game he was developing. Leaning back in his chair, he scratched the side of his head, wondering about the tree scene at the end. He pondered over it for a few minutes then decided to leave it as it was. There was still a fair bit of work needed to tidy it up, and he still had to complete the last fight scene. He was happy with the way it was going when he heard his wife calling the kids. It was time to finish up, so he quickly scribbled some final comments in his handwritten notes, slipped them into a purple plastic folder and put them in the top drawer of his desk.

"Rosie and Marcus, wake up. It's time to get ready for school," called Helen Saunders, the twins' mother from the top of the staircase. Rosie sat up in bed, pulled back the curtains and peered out the window.

The leaves of an enormous redwood tree growing in the front yard seemed to reach out and wipe the water from the window, "I wish Dad would have that tree trimmed," Rosie mumbled to herself as she looked out the window. "And it's raining again." She was worried the teachers would cancel the school archery competition, as she was hoping to beat her friend Isobel this time.

Disappointed, Rosie jumped out of bed and dressed herself in her school uniform. She ran a brush through her long black hair and tied it up neatly into single ponytail.

Her twin brother Marcus, on the other hand, was looking forward to tomorrow. Hamish, his best friend, was having his thirteenth birthday party. He was two months older than Marcus and they did everything together. Hamish was good at everything he did. He was always top of his class at school, and excelled at sport. There were times, however, when Hamish just made silly errors of judgement, for absolutely no reason at all. Hamish's mother had described him on a number of occasions as, 'accident prone,' and his father said that Hamish had 'pokey fingers'.

Anyway, Marcus liked him and made a mental note to ask his mother to buy a present.

"Come on you two. Hurry up," called their mother again. "We haven't got any time to waste this morning." Their father was going to their school today to give a talk about computer games.

Peter was still in his office when the twins descended the stairs.

As they reached the bottom, a loud buzzing sound attracted them towards their father's study. This was something new, and they were interested in what he was doing. The twins looked at each other.

"Probably Dad trying something on his new game," said Rosie. Just as they were about to walk away, a bright flash of purple light burst out from underneath the door, lighting up the hallway for a brief moment, before fading away.

"What was that?" Marcus whispered excitedly.

Rosie shrugged her shoulders, "How should I know? He'll be trying something we're not supposed to know about," she said, trying to mimic her father's voice.

"Yeah. You're probably right, Sis," he said, as he walked into the kitchen.

Rosie continued down the hallway towards the dining room, where a one thousand-piece jigsaw puzzle lay half completed on the dining room table. Rosie loved puzzles, particularly difficult ones. She loved reading mystery novels, and her bookcase was full of all the classic thrillers. She always seemed to be able to put the clues together and work out who the villain was before all her friends could.

Her mother called, "Rosie, you won't have time to work on your puzzle this morning. Now come and eat your breakfast."

"Coming," she said, as she carefully pressed another couple of pieces into the puzzle and then walked casually into the kitchen and sat down next to her brother.

The twins didn't hear the door of the study open and close. Their father hummed to himself as he sauntered down the hallway from his study. Coming up behind them, he touched them on the back of the neck. They yelped in surprise as a small purple spark jumped from their father's finger and arced across onto their necks.

Rosie squealed, twisted around and whacked her father on the hand. "Ouch," she grumbled. "That hurt!"

"Oh, stop it. It's only a bit of static electricity from the carpet in the hallway."

Rosie was angry with her father and told him so, "Well don't do it again. It's not funny."

Marcus didn't know what to think. For a brief moment, he saw a reddish-green ball of fire hurtling towards him. It came closer and closer, then completely disappeared from his mind. He shuddered and shook his head, frowning at his father, saying, "Dad, that's not funny."

Peter rested his hands on Marcus' shoulder. The vision returned. This time he saw it more clearly. A reddish-green ball of fire flew directly at him. It exploded in front of him. Just as quickly as it had come into his mind, it vanished. Bewildered, he looked up at his father only to catch a glimpse of tiny purple flashes around his father's face, just before they vanished.

"Come on Marcus, surely you've done this to your friends at school before?"

"Sometimes but that really hurt," he said, rubbing his sore neck.

The twins were both upset and sat quietly eating their breakfast. Eventually though, Rosie turned and asked her father, "What are you going to talk about today?"

Marcus asked before he could answer, "Are you going to talk about the new game you're working on?"

"How do you two know about that?"

"Oh. Come on Peter," said his wife. "You spend most of your time when you're at home working on it in your study."

Peter knew she was right, shrugged his shoulders and said to the twins, "Now look you two, you can't talk about it yet. It's not finished and there's a lot of editing I need to do. So promise me you won't say a word about the game outside the house." Their father became even more serious and leant closer to them and said sternly but quietly, "and I don't want you playing it either. Do you understand?"

It was more of a statement than a question, and without looking away from their father, they replied as one. "Got it, we promise not to tell anyone about it," the twins said, crossing their fingers and nodding their heads together in agreement.

"Good," said their father. "That's the end of that."

Rosie and Marcus glanced at each other and smiled wickedly, and without saying a word, knew what they were going to do.

The trip to school took just over half an hour. It was located right on the fringe of town and had many tall shady trees planted in the grounds. The gardens were in immaculate condition, with a wide variety of plants and colourful flowers planted throughout. Certainly what you would expect for the fees I'm paying, thought their father.

The schoolteacher, Miss Spencer welcomed the twins' father into the classroom. "Good morning, Mr. Saunders," said all the children.

Peter spoke for just over thirty minutes and had his audience completely captivated. He told them stories and how he developed ideas into successful computer games. Most of the kids in the room had played many of the games he had produced and eagerly asked questions about them.

The twins sat listening to their father. Even though he was home every now and then, they really hadn't seen much of him lately, as he spent a lot of time in his study or away travelling for weeks at a time. At home, he had installed all the latest and greatest systems and software, a large plasma screen, and the best quality sound system. Their father said he had the seventieth fastest computer in the world and it could process over a billion bytes in a second. Anyway, it was fast.

Miss Spencer stood up in front of the class, "Thank you Mr. Saunders your talk was very interesting and informative." She turned back to address the class, giving them specific instructions, "Class, while I show Mr. Saunders out, please start reading your local history books from page four. We are going to be doing a project on the anniversary of The Great Fire that almost burnt the town down nearly one hundred years ago. I'll be back in a minute."

"Saunders," called a voice from the next aisle.

"Oh no," sighed Marcus. "It's that pest Billy and his stupid friend Fred."

Marcus tried to ignore the interruption but they kept flicking paper balls at him. Finally, he turned around to face the school bully. Billy pointed at Marcus, then thumped his right fist into the palm of his left hand, "I want to see you after school, you little freak," Billy threatened.

Marcus now worried, muttered, "Oh great. I hope Mum's on time today."

Fortunately, Billy and Fred were in detention during lunch for fighting with another student and Marcus didn't see them at all. The rest of the day went rather slowly. Marcus and Rosie didn't get a chance to talk even after they jumped into their mother's car after school.

"Hello, you two. What did the other kids think of your father's talk this morning?"

"Hamish thought it was great. You know how much time he spends playing games," said Marcus.

"Yes," replied his mother. "And so do you two. Anyway I have some news for you."

The twins spoke together, "What is it?"

"That always amazes me with you two, the way you always answer at the same time. You are twins, I suppose. Your father is flying up to the company's interstate office tonight to have some more discussions about his new game," said their mother.

"We thought the game was supposed to be a secret," Rosie replied, "and today's Friday."

"It is," answered their mother quickly to both questions, "and I expect you two will try and keep it that way." The twins glanced at each other mischievously.

Marcus lent across to his sister and whispered, "We'll have to be very careful." Nothing was said during the rest of the journey home.

When they arrived home, their father, bags packed, stood ready and waiting on the verandah. As the car pulled up alongside the house, he picked up his bags, jumped down from the verandah and threw them into the boot of the car.

"I won't be long," said Mum. "I'm taking your father down to the airport bus terminal and on the way back I'll buy some groceries. There's some afternoon tea ready for you on the kitchen bench."

"See you later," the twins called out to their father from the verandah. Marcus headed inside while Rosie watched as her father ran his hands through the leaves of the enormous old redwood tree growing in the front yard. A small branch appeared to wrap around his arm and another brushed lightly against his face as he climbed into the car. She thought, that's strange, but didn't think any more about it after he called out, "See you on Sunday afternoon."

Rosie waved, and watched her parents drive off down the tree-lined driveway and turn left into the street.

"Well there he goes again," she mumbled. "But why on a Friday night?" Rosie knew he was a very successful executive, creating and developing computer games and making a lot of money from it, but secretly wished he would spend more time at home. She followed her brother inside.

CHAPTER 6

THE GAME BEGINS

The twins sat at the table eating the afternoon tea their mother had left out. Just as they finished and were about to go and watch television, they heard a strange noise coming from their father's study.

Rosie turned to Marcus with a puzzled look on her face, "Did you hear that?"

"I did" said Marcus, just as intrigued. "Let's check it out."

BANG, BANG, BANG, BANG! It echoed up the hallway.

"It's getting louder. It's giving me goose bumps," whispered Rosie. The closer they moved towards the noise the more frightened she became.

"I know," said Marcus. He wasn't quite sure what to do. They had now slowed down to a crawl and inched their way along the hallway. The walls of the hallway shook with each bang.

"It sounds like someone smashing a hammer against a piece of steel. It's hurting my ears," said Rosie.

"Me too, and it's getting louder as we get closer," said her brother, now almost shouting to be heard.

They peered around the corner into the study. They couldn't see anything in the darkness, so

Marcus reached around the doorway with his right hand quickly flicking on the light switch. Everything appeared to be in place. They could feel the vibrations as the noise grew louder. Marcus raced into the room and switched off the stereo system connected to the computer. The noise stopped immediately.

"That's better," said Rosie.

"Ymmm," replied Marcus as a green flash of light caught his attention.

Securely mounted on the wall behind the desk hung a huge plasma screen, and in the bottom right hand corner, a green icon flashed.

As their father had spent the afternoon working on the game he had been interrupted by a phone call and forgotten to switch off the computer before he left.

"Dad's left the computer on. That's not like him. He must have been in a hurry to leave this afternoon. Let's have a look," as Marcus sat down in his father's chair as Rosie stood behind him.

"We shouldn't be doing this. You know we're not allowed to touch Dad's computer," Rosie whispered.

"I know," he whispered back. "But he has left it on."

"Just because he left it on doesn't mean we should use it."

Marcus had been wondering for ages how he could get in here to play and said, "Now's our chance." His hand came down on the mouse and he guided the cursor down to the green icon. The rest of the screen was blank.

"Well here goes nothing," he said, clicking on the icon.

The screen filled with a beautiful picture of a heavily grassed clearing in the middle of a forest. Tall trees swayed in the breeze and the twins could see birds sitting in the trees and animals of all sorts grazing on the forest floor. In front of them, the clearing sloped away steeply. All around them colourful wildflowers dotted the landscape.

"That's not a computer image," said Rosie. "That's like a DVD. It's so amazing, Marcus. It's so real." Rosie stood in silence, absorbed with the fantastic picture in front of her.

After a minute or so, she asked her brother, "What about the noise? I wonder if it has stopped now the screen has changed."

Reaching across to the stereo, he hesitated for a moment before switching the speakers on again. The horrible noise didn't restart. The twins were astonished to hear the wind rustling through the leaves of the trees and the insects chirping away in the background. Another icon appeared in the bottom right hand corner of the screen. "Are you ready to play the game?" it prompted in bright green writing. Underneath the icon were two coloured boxes flashing brightly. One box flashed green for 'Yes' and the other box blinked red for 'No'.

Marcus was excited and said, "Let's see what happens." He moved the cursor to the Yes icon and, without hesitating, clicked the mouse. A chilling scream echoed throughout the forest, "Let me out. Let me out. Get me out of here!" it screamed.

Rosie jumped in fright and moved closer to her brother, Marcus looked up at her, feeling very unsure about what to do next.

"Hang on a tick," said Rosie, her expression a combination of fear and surprise. "That voice sounds familiar."

"Don't be silly," said Marcus, when the twins heard the garage door open.

"Oh great, Mum's home," exclaimed Rosie. "You switch it off right now because if we get caught in here we'll be grounded for weeks." She ran up the hallway to head off their mother in the kitchen while Marcus hurriedly escaped from the game. He stopped to think for a moment. His father would probably have passwords on his files and he was not coming home until Sunday night. If he switched it off now then he was not likely to get a chance to try this again. The decision was easy; he reached around and pulled out the leads to the speakers and the power cord to the screen, thinking, that should keep it safe until the morning. On the way out Marcus switched off the light and closed the door behind him.

When Rosie reached the kitchen their mother asked, "What have you two been up to?"

She looked sheepishly at her mother, "Oh, nothing."

"Where's that brother of yours? I want him to unload some groceries from the car."

Rosie called out, "Marcus! Mum wants you."

Marcus walked slowly up the hallway and brushed past Rosie, "That was close," he whispered. "What do you think that noise was all about?"

"It's probably some part of Dad's game," she said, just loud enough for him to hear.

"You could be right Sis," he replied, as he walked out to collect the groceries for his mother. Reaching in to the boot of the car to pick up the shopping bags, a strange purplish coloured light attracted his attention.

Placing the shopping bags on the ground, he stretched in and picked up the tiny glittering object. It looked like a tiny charm about the size of a small coin. Holding it up to the light, it gave off a strange purplish glow. He wondered if it was a piece of jewellery, or maybe part of an earring.

He jumped nervously when his mother called out, "Marcus where are you? I want to start dinner."

Putting the strange object into his pocket, he shut the boot and carried the groceries into the house.

Just as Marcus walked into the kitchen, the phone rang.

Rosie answered it, "Hi, Isobel." There was a brief, silent pause as Rosie listened, "Yep — right. Okay I'll ask. Mum, can I go over to Isabel's tonight?"

"Yes," she said. "But I want you two to tidy your rooms before dinner. Rosie, I'll take you over to Isobel's place after that."

"Mum. Not now. It's Friday night," she complained then spoke briefly with her friend and hung up.

"Do it now," their mother growled. "I'm not in the mood to argue."

Marcus caught his sister's attention and moved his head in the direction of their rooms. "Come on, let's go," he said softly. They walked slowly up the stairs.

When they reached the top Marcus grabbed Rosie by the elbow, "Look what I found in the boot of the car," he said, taking the tiny object out of his pocket. The tiny piece gleamed in the light as Marcus held it in his hand.

Rosie picked it up and examined it closely. "Wow it's so tiny. It looks like a tiny key."

"Are you sure it's not a piece of your jewellery? It might be a charm from one of your bracelets"

"No, I've never seen it before," she said.

"Here. Give it back. I'll keep it safe in my room," he said.

Taking the tiny object back from Rosie he slipped it into his pocket. They moved towards their own rooms when Rosie turned and said, "Don't you go anywhere near Dad's game until I get home, will you?"

"No way," answered Marcus. "I don't think there'll be a chance of that happening with Mum around. Besides, I'm going over to Hamish's house tomorrow afternoon for his birthday party. We'll probably play plenty of games there anyway."

CHAPTER 7

ALONE IN THE GAME

Straight after they had arrived home from driving Rosie to Isobel's house, Marcus decided to hop into bed early. He set the alarm on his mobile phone to wake him up at half past five the next morning. Pulling the doona up over his head, he tried to go to sleep, but lay in bed thinking about the game in his father's study below. He finally dozed off, but tossed and turned all night. The loud noises filled his dreams and the voice called out, over and over again. When the alarm went off the next morning, it was a relief to wake up. Reaching over to his bedside table, he grabbed his mobile phone, stuck it under the doona, and fiddled with the buttons to turn off the alarm. Marcus lay staring at the ceiling. In the quiet of the morning, he heard the rain falling on the roof and hitting the windows of his bedroom. That meant Hamish's party would be indoors. Climbing sluggishly out of bed, he changed out of his pyjamas into a pair of jeans and a T-shirt his mother had bought earlier in the week. It was half-blue and half-white and embossed with a black panther. Pulling on a pair of white sports socks, he slipped into a pair of old shoes he kept for wearing around the house.

Sneaking out of his room, he crept down the carpeted stairs, walked noiselessly along the hallway and opened the door to his Dad's study.

Closing the door quietly behind him, he knew he had to be careful. After plugging the headset into the socket on the stereo, he made doubly sure he had turned the speakers off. Reaching around the back of the computer, he reconnected the cables he had pulled out the night before.

Slipping the headset over his ears, Marcus reached down with his right hand and quickly moved the cursor onto the icon and clicked the mouse again. All was quiet and the screen filled with the forest scenes he had seen the night before. He waited for the bright green writing to appear. "Are you ready to play the game?" it prompted in bright green writing. He clicked on Yes and the game began. The desperate call for help they had heard last night didn't start again.

Sitting on the bookshelf next to the screen were his father's PC controllers, all numbered one to four. Marcus picked up the controller marked number 'One.' After settling himself into the comfortable office chair his father used, he looked up at the screen. His eyes nearly popped out of his head. Right in the middle of the screen was a figure. It was a perfect image of him; it was even wearing his T-shirt, jeans and old sneakers. Marcus couldn't believe his eyes and dropped the controller on the desk in front of him. The image disappeared. Standing up he walked away from the screen to calm down a little, saying, "Wow. That's awesome." He certainly hadn't expected anything like that to happen and felt his heart racing as he sat down to try again. Picking up the controller, he kept his eyes firmly focused on the middle of the screen. As his fingers touched the controller, his mirror image re-appeared on the screen. Breathing heavily in anticipation, Marcus still expected something else to jump out at him.

Marcus muttered, "What's going on here?"

"Why don't you ask me?" asked the figure on the screen.

Marcus practically jumped out of his skin and swore in shock, "Who the hell are you?" Shaking his head, he wondered how he would tell Rosie about any of this.

"Who's Rosie?" asked the image. "Ah, so she's your sister," answered the image.

"How do you know that?"

The image looked at Marcus "I am you, only I'm in the game and you are there in your world."

"I know that," said Marcus with a sarcastic tone in his voice.

"Well you did ask. Anyway if you want to play this game you will need to concentrate and control your thoughts," said the image.

"You haven't told me your name."

"You haven't asked me yet," the response came quickly, surprising Marcus.

"Okay then, what's your name?"

"Imagen," the image replied.

Marcus found talking to himself felt weird. He couldn't explain it so he moved the joystick on the controller to make the image move, but nothing happened.

"All you have to do is use you thoughts and think about what you want," his image said patiently.

"Fine," said Marcus and closed his eyes to concentrate.

"What is it you want? All you have to do is concentrate your thoughts and let them tell me what to do. Don't speak, just think," said Imagen.

Marcus closed his eyes to concentrate, "Open your eyes and see what you have achieved," said the image on the screen.

Marcus opened his eyes, to find three paths had appeared. The paths snaked off in different directions, disappearing off into the distance.

"Awesome. Where do they go?" he said excitedly.

Imagen's answer was immediate, "The one on the left goes down to the beach, the one in the middle runs deep into the forest and the last one leads up to the mountains. Which one do you choose? Ah that's good, so you want to go down to the beach."

Marcus nodded. He found it so much harder than using the game's controller with his fingers. Just to make Imagen walk down the orange-grey gravel pathway required a massive amount of concentration. He heard his feet crunch on the gravel path with every footstep he took; with every breath he took, he smelt the fresh clean air of the forest and shivered ever so slightly with the chill of the early morning air, "This is so unreal," he said.

"Well it is," said the image. "You have so much to learn about the game you are about to play."

Marcus asked, "Where do you come from?"

"I don't come from anywhere, I'm here all the time and whenever you hold the controller I will appear, and whenever your thoughts tell me to do something, I will complete that task."

Marcus looked around, focused his thoughts and commanded, Go and climb that tree.

The image ran over and scampered up the nearest tree. It wasn't easy and every time the image stretched out to grab another branch, Marcus felt it. His breathing increased with the effort as the image climbed higher and higher. When the image slipped, scraping its knee on the rough bark of the tree, Marcus groaned as his own knee started to hurt. Looking down, he was surprised to see graze marks from the bark appear on his jeans.

"Stop," he instructed Imagen. "This is too much."

Looking back at the image on the screen Marcus found it sitting on a branch a couple of metres above the ground.

Without saying anything, Marcus commanded, Jump.

Marcus felt himself falling and gasped in surprise. A sharp stabbing pain shot up through his legs as Imagen landed on the ground. He had learnt the real consequences of the game the hard way. Lifting his legs off the ground Marcus curled up like a ball in the chair, rocking back and forth in agony. He wanted to scream out loudly but that would have woken up his mother, and he didn't want that. Instead, he held onto his legs tightly, grimacing in pain silently. Tears ran down his face until, after a minute or two, the pain started to subside. Even though his own legs hurt, he asked Imagen if he was okay.

"Oh, I'm fine. It hurt me less than it did you. If you want to play this game you need to think about what you do, for there may be consequences for you and others."

Marcus heard footsteps upstairs from his mother's bedroom and he knew he had to escape from the game.

"You need to go now," said Imagen. "There is someone coming."

He placed the controller on the desk just as Imagen said, "Farewell Marcus."

The image vanished, as did the pain in his legs and the scratch marks on his jeans. "Rosie is never going to believe this," he said to himself as he quickly disconnected the cords and cables. Before leaving the room, he made sure everything was back in place and switched off the lights. Just as he was closing the door, a purple glow in the top drawer of his father's desk caught his attention. He wondered what it was. With his mother walking around upstairs, he knew he didn't have a lot of time. Stepping over to the desk, he pulled open the drawer. Purple light flooded the room then quickly faded away. After his initial surprise, Marcus saw a purple folder marked

Instructions to
Finish the Game. DRAFT COPY

Picking up the folder, he pushed the drawer shut

and closed the door. He decided to walk up to the TV room at the other end of the house rather than go back to bed.

Meanwhile, in the same clearing where Marcus' image had been only a few minutes before, a loud sizzling noise replaced the sound of the wind blowing through the trees. A strange purple mist appeared mysteriously, swirling around in the middle of the clearing, and then silence. Ten creatures emerged from the mist. The creatures were Imitators, able to appear in any form they wished. Now they took the form of black panthers, sleek powerful animals, with piercing green eyes. The panthers formed a circle around Imagen.

Their leader, Electra, asked Imagen, "What happened with the human child?"

"He has a sharp mind and a keen sense of adventure. The boy is very inquisitive and demonstrated certain skills, but will need much training. Most importantly however, he has found the key just as our master informed us. I could feel its energy when I was with him. He was also thinking about his sister. There appears to be a strong bond between them. I know both of them will return to the game."

"Good," said Electra. "All is going according to plan. Copia, you will accompany Imagen when the children return, and remember your roles are to train and guide them."

"Yes we understand," Imagen and Copia, responded together. The meeting finished and the creatures vanished.

In a different part of the game, another ruler prepared his army. He appeared as a dark black shadow, his silhouette highlighted with a green and red glow. His commanders stood in front of him, covered in black robes, their faces hidden from view.

In a deep authoritative voice he asked, "Are you ready to carry out my plans?"

"Yes, Lord Theda. We are in the final stages of preparation and will be ready to move at the designated time," answered the highest-ranking commander.

"Good. I will be with you soon. Be ready for my return," and with a slight crackle and a flash of reddish-green light, he disappeared from sight.

CHAPTER 8

THE EXPERIMENT

Peter Saunders had flown up to the northern office the previous evening. He'd had meetings with his marketing partners to discuss the progress of his latest game. Today, however, he was here for a completely different reason.

"Good morning Mr. Saunders," said the security guard at the front desk.

"Good morning, Sam," he replied politely. "Is Andrew in yet?" he asked.

"Yes Mr. Saunders he's just in his office. I'll give him a buzz." Before Peter could say, 'don't worry', Sam had dialled Andrew's office.

"Mr. Saunders is here in reception for you."

"Thanks, I'll be right up," the muffled reply came over the phone.

"He's on his way, Mr. Saunders," said the security guard.

"Thanks," Peter read the newspaper on the front desk for a couple of minutes. Just as he decided to walk down to Andrew's office, he heard someone approaching.

Andrew greeted Peter, "Sorry about that. I was just reading my emails before we start. How was the flight this morning?"

That's strange, thought Peter. Why is he wearing sunglasses? "Good, but I actually arrived last night and stayed at the Airport Hotel."

"Oh I didn't know," said Andrew uneasily, "If I'd known we could have caught up for dinner."

"That's all right. I had another appointment," Peter said, patting Andrew on the shoulder.

Peter, concerned about his friend asked, "Is everything all right?"

"Yes. Why do you ask?"

"You're wearing sunglasses," said Peter.

"Oh you mean these?" Andrew reached up with his hands, readjusting the glasses. "Yes of course. Sorry, completely forgot to mention it. I've had some minor eye correction surgery. My eyes are extremely sensitive to light. The doctor said a couple of days and it should be fine." Andrew saw Peter didn't believe him, and said, "Seriously."

Peter didn't push it any further but had a strange feeling it was something far more serious.

Together, he and Andrew had set up a games development company ten years ago. The early years were tough but they had managed to build the business up and it was finally making a handy profit. About five years ago, Andrew moved to the current location in the north whilst Peter ran the original company down south. Peter hadn't been able to put his finger on it but something had changed in the last couple of months. Andrew's marriage had fallen apart and he wasn't talking to the rest of his family. Peter, without wanting to pry too much had been trying to find out what it was going on.

Anyway, Peter didn't want to waste time and said, "Come on. Let's get this meeting underway."

The two men walked down the long corridor to the boardroom. When they opened the door, two other people were already sitting at the table.

"Hello Zig. Chloe." Peter shook hands with both of them, "Thanks for coming in on a Saturday morning," he said. "All right, let's get down to business."

Peter sat down and looked across the table at Zig.

Zig had been engaged to be married to Peter's sister, who'd died tragically many years ago. Zig and Peter had been close friends now for many years. He trusted Zig more than anyone else he knew. Sitting next to Zig was Chloe. She was in her late twenties, intelligent and attractive, as Zig had reminded him on a number of occasions. There was no doubt she was the driving force behind this project. No one knew more about the science involved. Best of all, Zig and Chloe worked extremely well together and were the main reason the project had developed so quickly.

"This is your baby Chloe. Where are you up to with it?"

Peter was anxious to know how it was progressing as he had put a lot of his own money into the project over the last couple of years.

Chloe spoke first, "As you know, a wormhole is like a tunnel that connects two different points in space and time. It's the quickest way to travel to different points around the universe. Now this is important. Wormholes are unstable and usually crush any object going into one. What we have been able to do is develop software that calculates the exact amount of positive energy required to protect the object, so the wormhole doesn't crush it. In other words, we coat the object with positive energy to protect it from the negative energy created by the wormhole. Wormholes exist in the universe. In addition, they have an entry and exit point. Our software also allows us to enter the co-ordinates of both these points, create a wormhole and pass matter through it."

She paused and took a sip of water from her cup, "Zig's going to show you our fifth trial. We completed it early this morning. This is very exciting but as you already know, we've had a few mishaps. Our first four trials ended with massive explosions. This experiment shows we are getting there. It's just a little unstable, at the moment."

Zig opened the file and pulled out a DVD from a plastic holder. Standing up, he inserted the disc into the DVD player on the wall opposite the table, and pushed play.

The picture on the screen showed two plasma screens marked entry and exit sitting on a table facing each other. Nothing else was in the room. The digital clock started ticking down: five-four-three-two-one. What happened next was amazing to watch. On the entry screen appeared a bright flash of swirling blue light, with a fast spinning centre of intensely bright white light. It was a whirlpool, not of water, but of extremely high energy light. The exit screen was exactly the opposite, and the bluish-white vortex burst out of the exit screen like a soap bubble, extending about a metre into the room. Zig pushed the pause button on the DVD, and turned to face the others, "We thought we'd achieved our goal but then this happened," and pushed play. The exit screen exploded, breaking up into thousands of pieces, which instantly disappeared, sucked into the whirlpool of light and energy. Finally, the entry screen imploded in a great flash of blinding light, consuming itself, and then exploded in a force so strong, it cracked the armour plated glass windows of the secure room. Then silence. Apart from the table, the room was completely empty.

Peter looked up at his colleague, smiled and half jokingly said, "Well Zig, it certainly goes off with a bang." Everyone in the room, except Andrew, laughed, but became more serious when Peter asked, "Now can you get it to work properly?"

Andrew turned to all three of them and in an unexpected outburst, yelled angrily, directing his fury solely at Chloe. "What are you talking about, a little unstable? Last week you destroyed the experimental computer with your technology." Andrew looked over his sunglasses, his piercing glare aimed directly at Chloe. A chilling shiver went right through her as she looked into the steely, cold, black eyes. For a brief moment, she witnessed something horrible and evil, just catching the green and red flashes in the darkness of Andrew's eyes. She shuddered.

Andrew pushed the glasses back up his nose with his finger and continued, "That little experiment of yours cost us over one hundred thousand dollars to repair. Come on Peter. This is madness. It doesn't work and I will not be part of it anymore," and stormed out without saying another word, slamming the door behind him.

Peter looked at the two programmers, "How do we fix this problem?" Peter's thoughts briefly focused on Andrew. That sort of behaviour was completely out of character. Although over the last few months, everyone had found Andrew's behaviour had become more erratic. I'll sort this out first and then find out what's going on with him, mused Peter.

The three of them brainstormed all the options open to them, and after a couple of hours of solid discussion, Peter called an end to the meeting, "So from what I understand you should be ready to try it again next week."

"Yes. Another week's work and we should have a much better result for you," said a very determined Chloe.

"Good. I'll look forward to it."

CHAPTER 9

LEARNING THE HARD WAY

When Marcus arrived home from Hamish's party at around six o'clock on Saturday evening, he went straight up to his bedroom. He flopped onto his bed and from under his pillow, pulled out the purple folder he had found in his Dad's study. Undoing the clips, he carefully removed the handwritten document from the folder. Marcus flicked through the pages but found he couldn't decipher his father's handwriting. After a couple of minutes, he gave up, slipped the notes back into the folder and slid it back under his pillow. He was planning to return them to the top drawer tonight. Reaching under his bed, he pulled out his favourite book, 'A Greater Understanding of Rocks and Crystals.' On the bookcase opposite his bed, stood his personal pride and joy ¾ his crystal collection. He had started collecting them about three years ago. Most of his collection had come from picking up bits and pieces around different locations when the family had been on holidays, together with him saving his pocket money and buying special pieces. The centrepiece was a rare specimen of blue fire agate, given to him by his parents last Christmas. Carefully cut, the fine layers within the rock reflected the light, giving the illusion a fire burnt within. Marcus had read that the stone had a deep calming energy that brought safety and security. His books said it represented 'absolute perfection and instilled fortitude', whatever that was, he thought.

He had been reading for around ten minutes or so, when out of the corner of his eye he thought he saw the specimen of fire agate glow brightly. Blinking then rubbing his eyes, he had another look and this time everything appeared normal again.

Thinking, that was strange; he hopped up and walked over to have a closer look—everything seemed okay. Then he heard their car coming up the driveway and he raced downstairs to greet his sister.

"Rosie, Rosie," he whispered excitedly, as she walked in the door.

"Not now, let's go upstairs and we'll talk up there," she said. They climbed the stairs and went into her room. Marcus closed the door behind them and turned to speak to his sister.

Before he could say a word, Rosie asked him, "Have you played the game?"

Marcus smiled just a little too much and nodded his head guiltily.

"I thought so. I can tell. Why didn't you wait until I got home? You promised me." She sat down on her bed in a huff, arms folded, "I'm really upset," she said, glaring angrily over at her brother.

Marcus waited a few moments before saying anything, "Well, you weren't here were you? Do you want to hear what happened or not?" he said with one hand on the door handle, ready to walk out of her room.

She looked up and sighed, "Oh. All right, tell me what happened."

He walked over and sat down next to his sister. Rosie listened for several minutes, hardly breathing as Marcus excitedly told her about the morning's events.

She was still somewhat sceptical but asked, "What are we going to do next? Dad'll be home tomorrow afternoon."

"We'll have to get up tonight and play it, after Mum goes to sleep. Then I'll show you what I found."

"Good," she said. "I want to see this for myself."

Later that night Marcus hopped into bed fully dressed, ready for the night's adventure. He struggled to stay awake and just after nine o'clock, fell asleep. Waking up early that morning, coupled with Hamish's party, finally took its toll.

Rosie's alarm beeped and woke her right on eleven o'clock. She slipped on a gown and pink ugg boots, and then sneaked into her brother's bedroom. Shaking Marcus, she whispered in his ear, "Come on, sleepy head. Wake up. It's eleven o'clock. Mum's finally gone to bed."

Bleary eyed, Marcus dragged himself out of bed and slipped on his old sneakers. Reaching under his pillow, he grabbed his father's purple folder. They crept down the stairs and felt their way along the dark hallway, into their father's study. Marcus closed the door quietly, found the light switch and turned it on. He sat down in his father's chair and returned the folder to the desk drawer. Rosie dragged another chair over to the desk and sat down next to Marcus. After plugging in all the leads, he passed a pair of headphones to Rosie and then slipped some over his own head. "Ready?" he asked.

"Yep."

They prepared themselves for the hideous noise but it didn't start.

In one smooth motion, Marcus moved the cursor onto the green icon, clicked on the mouse and grabbed his game controller.

His image appeared up on the screen.

"Hello," groaned Marcus, as the soreness returned to his legs from jumping out of the tree that morning. The graze marks reappeared on his jeans. He pointed this out to Rosie, who shook her head in disbelief.

Imagen responded, "Hello Marcus and Rosie. Are you ready to proceed?"

Marcus turned to his sister. "See. I was telling the truth."

Rosie couldn't contain her excitement and knowing she had to keep quiet, whispered, "That's incredible!"

The moment she touched the second controller, her image appeared on the screen. She just couldn't believe it. It was wearing the same pink floral pyjamas, covered by the thick pink dressing gown she wore. It was even wearing her pink ugg boots.

Marcus looked at her image on the screen and laughed loudly, "Next time you'll have to get dressed properly."

"Shush, you idiot. Otherwise you'll wake Mum up," she scowled.

He pulled a face and said, "Oh stop complaining and watch this. Paths." Three paths appeared on the screen as they had earlier that morning.

Rosie, excited, asked, "How did you do that?"

"All you have to do is hold the controller and think about what you want. Watch this, Sis." The hill was very steep and Imagen, his image, lay down on the edge of the slope and rolled down the hill through the thick green grass. Marcus felt every bump on the way down as the grass brushed against his arms and face. When he reached the bottom, Marcus' image stood up and looked back up the hill. Rosie stared at her brother, her mouth wide open, particularly when she saw the grass stains on his T-shirt and jeans.

"This is very strange. What's going on?"

"Don't be silly. Can't you see? This is an interactive game. It uses our thoughts. Dad's been working on it and that's why he didn't want us in here."

Rosie's image took over the conversation. "Hello, my real name is Copia," it said, "and I will help you enjoy the game. All you have to do is think about what you'd like to do."

"Come on, give it go, Sis" said Marcus.

Reluctantly at first, she thought about running downhill towards Marcus' image. Her image took off downhill, running quickly. At first it was fun, she felt the wind blowing her hair about, and she found it difficult to run wearing ugg boots.

Marcus watched his sister, running downhill. Her pace quickened, "You're going too fast," he called out. "Slow down or you'll fall over."

Marcus's warning came too late. Rosie's image tripped over a small rock hidden in the long grass and she flew through the air, landing heavily on her right wrist. Rosie and her image groaned in unison. Rosie, sitting in her chair, grabbed her wrist as it began to throb with pain. Marcus reached over to take the controller out of his sister's right hand. The images on the screen called out together, "No, don't do..." but Marcus didn't hear them. He was more concerned about his sister and grabbed her controller in his left hand. Immediately Rosie's image disappeared from the screen. The impact of the powerful forces emanating from two Imitators was too much for Marcus to handle and he found he couldn't let go of Rosie's controller. What started as a slight tingling sensation in his hands, quickly flowed up through his arms and into his shoulders and head. A blue haze covered him from head to toe as he felt a sharp burning pain in his head which made him light headed and dizzy and he knew he was about to pass out. He cried out feebly, "help me, help me please, please... help me," before his eyes closed and his head rolled forward.

Rosie sat next to him in a state of shock. Before her brother had grabbed her controller, all she remembered was the severe pain in her wrist and throbbing in her foot after falling heavily. Now it was gone, and something bad was happening to her brother.

"We should never have started this," she cried out to Marcus. Rosie really started to worry when a blue haze surrounded his body but the desperate cry for help made her act quickly. Without understanding why, Rosie knew she had to get the controller out of Marcus' hands. She put both hands around her controller that Marcus clutched tightly with his left hand. The pain in her right wrist returned immediately. A tingling sensation surged throughout her body. Ignoring the pain and pulling with all the strength she could muster, she finally managed to free the controller from Marcus' grip. Marcus sat bolt upright in his chair and turned to Rosie, "What happened?" The last thing I can remember was the pain after I grabbed your controller."

Rosie's fear quickly changed to anger as she turned to the images on the screen and demanded, "I want to know what happened to Marcus, and I want to know NOW!"

The images looked at each other and Imagen responded, "When Marcus was holding both of the controllers he took on the energy from both our bodies. I would advise that that never happens again. We can help you within the confines of the game but we cannot protect you in your world."

Rosie was a little confused and asked Imagen, "What about my sore wrist and foot? The pain disappeared when I let go of the controller and came back when I picked it up again."

"That is part of the game. You seek adventure, and if you take the risks, you will suffer the consequences. Play the game carefully, because as you have already discovered, it can be painful."

Rosie asked, "But why does it disappear when we let go of the controllers?"

"Those controllers you have are not ordinary game controllers. The special wiring in the controller picks up the electrical impulses from your mind. This means you can make us do certain things. The electrical impulse returns to your mind in the same way and you will feel the pain of your misadventure, hear the noises you make and even breathe in the smells of wherever you are. Therefore, once you break the connection, you are safe from the game. Remember this, if you hurt yourself in the game the pain will return at the same level when you pick up your controller again. You need to know three things. Firstly, as you have just learnt, you can only use one controller at a time. Secondly, now you have started playing the game you must use the same controller every time you play the game. Finally, you must return to this place before you leave the game."

Copia asked, "Do you two understand these things?"

"Yes," said Rosie, with a puzzled expression. Marcus agreed by nodding his head, as he was ready for more.

"Wait a minute," said Rosie. "I thought if we broke contact with the controller, we were supposed to be safe."

"You will be Rosie. To exit the game safely you must return to this place. If you don't, the game will continue without you."

"Okay. Now I understand." Then she asked, "What are you?"

"We are Imitators," said Imagen. "We have one preferred physical form ourselves, which we will show you shortly. We can be described as a collection of high-energy light particles, which can take the form of any creature we desire. At this moment we are taking on your appearance." Imagen paused, allowing the twins to think about this for a moment. "We will show you what I mean."

A purple haze appeared around the two images on the screen and a bright flash blinded the twins for a moment. Their eyes eventually refocused on the screen. Much to their surprise, the images had changed shape. Two great black panthers, sleek and powerful animals, with green piercing eyes and razor sharp teeth, replaced the images of the twins.

The twins' jaws dropped in unison and they stared in total amazement, whilst Imagen continued. "We copy how you look and what you wear and the way you speak. We will take you anywhere you want to go and do just about anything you want us to do. But, we will not hurt other creatures unless you are in danger, nor will we keep you from danger. We will make suggestions on what to do, but only if you seek our counsel. At the end of the day, as you already know, you make the choice. Choose wisely the course you wish to take." Then, in another brilliant flash of purple, the images changed back into the shape of the twins.

Without speaking, Marcus tapped Rosie on the arm, and then directed her to put her controller down on the desk. She understood straight away and the twins placed their controllers down on the desk at exactly the same time. They were now alone in the room.

CHAPTER 10

TERROR IN THE TUNNEL

"Wow," exclaimed Marcus. "What do you think?"

"I don't know," she replied quickly. "I know this is amazing but it could be really dangerous."

"How dangerous can it be? Whenever you let go of the controller everything returns to normal."

"Well, you couldn't, could you?"

"No. You're right. I couldn't let go of it, probably because I was holding both controllers at the same time. Maybe that's why. Who knows?"

"Could be, but you have to admit, it was pretty scary." Rosie wasn't sure what to do next. Marcus felt the same, but didn't want to admit it. Although shaken by the incident with the two controllers, his eager sense of adventure and curiosity compelled him to continue. For Rosie this was like a puzzle with no pieces and she was keen to work it through to the end.

Marcus suggested to Rosie, "It might be better if you get changed into some other clothes. I'll go grab something to eat and drink."

"Great idea," she agreed. Tiptoeing quietly up to her room she changed into some jeans and her favourite pink top, pulled on a light pink floral jumper, pink socks and some comfortable walking shoes. She felt a bit weird getting into comfortable clothes to play a computer game and shook her head at the thought. By the time she sat in her seat again, Marcus had raided the fridge and brought enough food back for both of them.

Marcus waited a few moments before asking his sister, "Ready to go?"

"Ready when you are Sis."

She picked up her controller first, followed by Marcus. The twins found themselves concentrating so hard on the screen they didn't notice the edge of the screen slowly fade away. As the edge of the screen disappeared, the walls and the ceiling of the study disappeared and the forest spread swiftly throughout the room, invading every corner. Then the screen vanished completely.

Marcus led the way, "Let's keep following this path—if that's all right with you?"

"That's okay with me." replied Rosie enthusiastically.

When they started out there were vast open spaces of lush green grass to the north with wildflowers of all different varieties and colours. Several tall trees dotted the countryside, swaying in the gentle breeze. To the south, the stands of trees thickened, into a dark, heavily treed forest.

Rosie was enjoying the walk and the serenity of the forest. Leaving the path, she bent down and picked a handful of flowers. Lifting them up to her nose, she breathed in the sweetest and most intense fragrance she had ever experienced. It was intoxicating and she felt as though she could stay here forever.

Marcus moved closer and caught the scent from the flowers, "Wow. That's really strong."

She laughed and threw the flowers high in the air, "Isn't this fantastic?"

Marcus watched as the smile disappeared from her face and asked, "What's up?"

"The room's disappeared. I know I'm holding my controller, I can feel it, but I can't see it."

Turning right around, he said, "Awesome, the whole room's disappeared. We must have been concentrating on the game so hard we didn't see it happen. Stay here. I'm going to try something."

"What are you going to do?"

"I'm going to drop my controller. Just stay put and I'll find out what's going on."

"All right then," she replied, worried about what might happen.

Marcus consciously dropped his controller. The forest disappeared and he found himself back in the computer room. Rosie sat in her chair perfectly still, eyes closed, head tilted forward and hands resting in her lap holding the controller. She appeared to be asleep.

"Hey, Sis," he said. "Can you hear me?"

Rosie remained quiet and motionless in the chair.

Rosie's response came from up on the screen, "Yes, but I can't see you. Where are you?"

"I can see you. You're up on the screen. Awesome!"

"Where are you?"

"I'm sitting in the chair next to you in Dad's study."

"Really?"

"Yes. I'm coming back now."

"Good," said Rosie, greatly relieved.

Marcus found himself back in the forest standing next to his sister as soon as he touched his controller. Rosie grabbed onto his arm and squeezed firmly, "I'm so glad you're back."

"Told you it would work, didn't I?"

"Well sort of," answered Rosie.

Marcus, quite happy with his discovery, said, "I think you should go back, just to see."

"Okay, I will." She, like Marcus, dropped her controller and found herself back in the room with Marcus. He was sitting perfectly still in his chair, hands resting in his lap holding the controller, and looking as though, he too, was sound asleep.

"It's true. I can see you on the screen."

The knowledge she was safe gave her renewed confidence. Reaching down she picked up her controller. Straightaway, she found herself with Marcus, back in the forest.

"We're really part of this game now. You know that, don't you?"

"Yes," said Rosie. "Come on. Let's keep going."

The path they followed weaved through thick clumps of trees and open grassland, down small valleys and up gently sloping hills. They had been walking for a while when they arrived at a fork in the path. The path on the left continued on, winding through the trees and open grassland. The other one turned sharply right, and ran through a dense stand of trees and undergrowth.

Rosie turned to her brother, "Which way?"

Scratching his head, he said, "I don't know." Guessing, he suggested, "This way looks interesting," and pointed to his right.

"Okay. We'll try your way," said Rosie.

They entered a tunnel formed by a thick mat of twigs, vines, branches and leaves. Continuing for well over one hundred metres, the bushes and vines grew right up to the edge of the path but not on it. It was as though some strange, powerful and invisible force stopped them from growing on the path itself. As they walked slowly through the leafy tunnel, the darkness closed in on them, the thick leafy wall and roof of the tunnel filtering out most of the light. Rosie, now frightened by the cold, damp darkness, grabbed Marcus' hand. Marcus was thinking exactly the same thing as his sister and said, "This is getting scary. I feel as though someone is watching us."

"Yeah," she whispered back. She sensed a spine-tingling feeling, like a spider running up her back. Her voice trembled, "Did you hear that?"

Marcus felt the vibration before it increased in volume, filling the twins with absolute terror. Rosie held her brother's hand tightly and drawing closer to him yelled out, "It sounds like someone screaming."

The branches, vines and leaves of the tunnel brushed up hard against them. A musty damp smell inundated the tunnel and the terrible screaming hurt his ears.

"Let's get out of here," Rosie shouted out over the appalling screams. Turning around to go back the way she had come in. Terrified, she screamed, "The entrance. It's gone," and stood, thoroughly hypnotised by the sight of the moving vegetation.

Marcus twisted around when she screamed. He watched in complete astonishment as the branches and vines grew, before his eyes, across the path.

"That's not possible," he shouted.

He saw quickly what Rosie meant about the entrance. There was now only one thing to do. "Run!" he yelled over the noise, as the screams from the tunnel intensified further. Rosie didn't seem to hear so he pulled her along to escape the rapidly growing vegetation. Vines with razor sharp thorns reached out, clawing viciously at them, tearing deep into their arms and legs as they sprinted down the tunnel. When they reached the end, they kept running out into the open space of a large courtyard, breathless, their lungs burning from the sudden and panicked exertion. They collapsed onto the grass, relieved it was over. The screaming stopped. Marcus looked back in horror, "It's still growing. And the tunnel's gone." Branches and vines entwined tightly together, rapidly filling in all the spaces. As it grew, the twins could hear the wall of branches and vines creak and groan under the effort.

Rosie, breathing heavily, sat up. Her arms and legs ached. Blood trickled down her arms and legs and dripped onto the dark green grass of the courtyard. She had never been that afraid before. Now in the aftermath of the tunnel attack, she sat there completely devoid of emotion.

Marcus lay flat on his back staring at the bright blue sky. His whole body was sore. An irregular pattern of red sticky spots appeared on his clothing as the blood soaked through the torn material. He was truly thankful that that was over. Like Rosie, he lay there feeling completely exhausted.

Rosie glanced across at Marcus. "You okay?" she asked.

"Yep," he nodded. What about you?" he asked.

"Well," she replied. "I never want to do that again. What are we going to do now?"

CHAPTER 11

SPIRALLING DOWNWARDS

Marcus stood and surveyed their surroundings. The tunnel had been the only entrance into the huge grassed area, which was the size of a hockey field. A thick impenetrable hedge of vegetation, at least three metres high grew round the edge of the courtyard. The tunnel had vanished. There was no way out. Rosie had suggested dropping their controllers to exit the game. She changed her mind when she remembered the Imitators warning to them, 'You must return to the clearing to exit the game.' Marcus knew there had be a way out and was determined to find it first.

In the middle of the courtyard lay the remains of a very old building. Two white marble columns lay broken under the collapsed roof of the building, while the other four lay intact in the thick long grass.

Marcus sat down next to his sister, and asked, "I wonder what this place is?"

"This is the gatekeeper's garden," said a voice out of nowhere. "You must meet him before you can go any further."

The twins sprang to their feet, searching around for the source of the voice.

Rosie couldn't speak and Marcus asked the question.

Trying to sound brave, his voice squeaked out, "Who are you?"

"Stay calm and we will reveal ourselves to you."

A swirling purple mist appeared, followed by a blinding flash of light.

Imagen and Copia appeared before the twins, in the form they had seen once before, black panthers.

Clearly relieved, Rosie said, "Why didn't you just tell us who you were in the first place? Anyway, I thought you two were supposed to be imitating us."

"We were initially. You didn't need us for long. You are truly part of your father's game," said Imagen.

"What about ... I mean our bodies. They're sitting in the chairs at home. How does that work? It looked as though we were sleeping."

"To be here takes an enormous amount of concentration and energy on your behalf. Your bodies are not resting. They are working hard to convey your thoughts here, into the game. You are here as yourselves. You truly are a figment of your own imagination."

Rosie asked, "So we aren't controlling you any more, is that right?"

"That is correct. We didn't think you would become part of the game so quickly, but you did."

Marcus was far more interested in exploring his surroundings, "What is this place... I mean, what happened here?"

"This is the gatekeeper's courtyard and garden. You will have to ask him yourselves, for it is his story to tell," said Copia.

Walking around the collapsed building, Marcus stopped half way and pointed at a hole between the ground and the roof where the roof was resting on the two columns.

"Come and have a look, Rosie."

She really wasn't in the mood and sat down on the nearest marble stone to rest.

Looking across at her brother she said, "I've had enough. This is all a little too much. I'm tired and I just want to go home."

Marcus ignored her and dropped down onto his hands and knees. Brushing away a thick layer of cobwebs covering the entrance he stuck his head into the hole. Peering into the semi-darkness, he could just make out a circular staircase, which appeared to spiral down around the edge of the hole and disappear into the darkness below. After backing out of the hole, he found himself covered from head to waist in a light grey dust and couldn't hold back his excitement. Exploring under the dome had now become his first priority.

"Hey Sis, there's a staircase under here. Wish I had a torch," he said.

"You can make your own," Imagen suggested.

Marcus was sceptical and asked, "Out of what?"

"First you need to find a small rock about the size of your fist."

Shrugging his shoulders he searched around until he found one about the size of a tennis ball, "Now what?"

"All you have to do is concentrate on creating light. You will really need to focus your thoughts for this to work. Just call out, 'Illuminate'. Are you ready?"

"Yep," replied Marcus, closing his eyes to concentrate.

"Illuminate," he called out. The rock in his hand started spitting out blue sparks. The rock began to glow a pale yellow colour for a few moments, then went out.

Rosie couldn't believe what she saw and encouraged her brother, "Try it again."

"Illuminate," Marcus called out, more confidently this time, concentrating harder than before. Bright blue sparks discharged out from the rock and after a couple of seconds, the rock burst into a brilliant blue light.

Marcus turned to his sister and said, "Rosie, let's just have a quick look before we call it a night. What do you think?"

"Okay," she agreed reluctantly. "Just down the stairs and nothing else, all right?"

"Awesome," he said enthusiastically, and waited for her to walk around and join him.

"I'll go first," said Marcus, passing the glowing rock to Rosie. The warmth generated by the rock light eased her uncertainty as Marcus wriggled his way through the hole; feet first, until he could feel the floor beneath his feet. The low ceiling height made him crouch over at first, but he could see that in a couple of steps he would be able to stand up properly. Marcus put his hand up through the hole and Rosie passed down the light. She copied his method of entry and was soon standing beside her brother.

"Can I carry the light?" she asked, "That way you can use both your hands to explore."

All Rosie really wanted was the warmth of the glowing rock, and to be able to use her other hand to hold Marcus' hand. Marcus didn't really mind either and passed the light to her, happy to have her company, because in reality he was afraid of the dark. Initially they descended the stairs carefully but after a couple of minutes, when they felt more confident, they increased their pace. Enormous blocks of white marble lined the stairwell. Smooth to the touch, a thick layer of dust clung to the walls, hanging like a fine, delicate, black curtain covering a white background. The stairs, covered with a thick layer of dust, were made of marble slightly rougher than the walls. Rosie held the rock out in front of them, the bluish light guiding their every step. They didn't dare go near the edge of the staircase because it disappeared into a black and bottomless pit, into which they had no intention of falling. Rosie, who was nearest the wall, had a coating of dust all down her left side. Stopping for a moment, she held the rock up high above her head and looked back up towards the top of the staircase. All she could see was a white circular trail of marble showing through the dust where she had rubbed up against the wall on her descent.

"Look at that," she said softly, pointing upwards. There about thirty metres above them was a small bright spot where they had entered the staircase.

Marcus bent down and picked up a small stone sitting on the next step.

Reaching across to the edge of the stairs, he dropped the stone into the darkness. After about five seconds, they heard a clunk as the stone hit the bottom.

"Good," said Marcus. "Not far to go." Before he had finished speaking the stairs above their heads started to creak and groan.

Rosie, now frozen in absolute fear, said, "You idiot. What have you done now?"

"Nothing... stay here and give me the light," said Marcus, ignoring her jibe. "I'll be right back," as he darted off up the stairway. He was only away for about thirty seconds but Rosie was shaking like a leaf by the time he returned.

"Come on Sis, we have to go down."

"Why?" she whispered back at him, fearing the answer.

"Because we can't go up—the staircase is disappearing into the walls. If we don't move now there'll be nothing left to stand on."

Rosie looked in horror at her brother when she felt the steps start to move sidewards under her feet.

Handing the light back to Rosie, he grabbed her other hand and for the second time today told her to run for her life. He dragged her down the stairs as the deafening grinding sound became unbearable. It sounded like some one running their fingernails down a blackboard, only a thousand times worse. The noise wasn't their only problem. One hundred years of dust started falling from the top, completely obscuring the entrance they had passed through. It fell all the way to the bottom like heavy rain in a thunderstorm. They were too busy running to see the great cloud of dust following them. After a quick descent, they reached the bottom. Rosie held the light up and immediately saw a doorway in the wall ahead.

"Come on!" she cried out leading him into the open doorway. The shower of dust reached the bottom of the staircase just as she shut the door. Resting her forehead on the door, relieved to have escaped the disappearing staircase, she sighed heavily. Turning to speak to her brother, she found he had disappeared.

Meanwhile Marcus was so thirsty he had decided to stop for a drink and have a brief break from the game. Without speaking and using his thoughts alone, he told Rosie he was returning to the study. Thinking she had understood, he simply dropped his controller. Instantly, he was back in the computer room, sitting in the chair next to his sister, clean and free of all the aches and pains of the game.

Rosie sat in her chair perfectly still, covered in dust, eyes closed, head tilted forward with her hands resting in her lap holding the controller.

This time, tears flowed down her face. Worst of all she was visibly shaking. Reaching across he went to grab Rosie's controller but an enormous spark zapped him viciously.

Realising now that she hadn't understood him, he reached down, grabbed the controller off the floor and returned to the game.

Rosie, who was just relieved to be safe from the disappearing stairs hadn't recognised her brother's thoughts and was now on the verge of screaming when he reappeared in the game behind her. Instinctively, he covered her mouth, stifling the scream, and then caught her as she fell backwards. Dust covered her from head to toe. Little tracks ran down her face where her tears had washed away the grime. Sitting down on the floor, he held her in his arms. "Rosie, Rosie," he whispered softly. She was coming to. "Rosie, it's all right I'm here." Marcus said quietly but firmly. "Drop the controller. Drop it now."

Eventually she did as her brother asked, and found herself sitting back in her father's study. Marcus joined her a few seconds later. The cuts and scratches disappeared from their arms and faces, and the dust vanished from their clothing.

"Thanks. I feel so much better." She paused for a few moments then said angrily, "Why didn't you tell me? When you disappeared, I thought you'd been taken somewhere and I was going to be left in the bottom of that horrible hole by myself."

"Sorry Sis," Marcus said sheepishly. "I was thirsty and came back for a drink. I did try to tell you."

"Next time make sure I hear you because if you do it again you can forget about me playing this stupid game any more," Rosie shot right back at him.

"All right, settle down. I'm sorry. I didn't do it on purpose. I promise I won't do it again."

"Good."

Sitting in their chairs, the twins nibbled on the food Marcus had brought down earlier on in the night.

After a couple of minutes, he was surprised to hear his sister say, "Let's have one more go at this before we switch it off and go to bed."

"All right. You realise we're going to get dirty again and the scratches and cuts are going to come back straight away," he reminded her.

"Yes. Well I was trying to forget that part, but here goes," Rosie said as she gathered the courage to start again.

"I'll go first if you like, so you won't feel as though you are there by yourself," said her brother.

"Thanks."

"When I get to three, you come in. I'll jump in at two. Okay?" She nodded her head in agreement.

Marcus started the count, "One, and two." He picked up his controller, and reappeared on the screen. "Three." Rosie reappeared next to him. This time she felt much better. Once again, dust, bloodstains cuts and scratches covered their bodies, painfully reminding them of where they were up to in the game.

Bending down Marcus picked the rock light up off the floor and called out, "Illuminate." The rock flared up brightly in the darkness. He passed it over to Rosie who walked around the room which measured about ten metres by ten metres and was octagonal in shape. All sides of the room were equal in length. One wall had a carved wooden door through which they had entered. On the opposite side hung a large octagonal door made from what looked like very thick steel plate. Keeping it secure were two enormous locks hooked through two hefty lugs one at the top, the other at the bottom. The white walls of the octagonal room reflected light off the perfectly positioned and beautifully cut marble blocks. The room didn't appear to have a ceiling. The walls went higher and higher, disappearing into the darkness where the light of the rock couldn't penetrate.

Rosie pointed to the octagonal doors, "Well, we're not going to get out that way, are we?"

A deep voice boomed out of the darkness, "And why would you like to go that way, my dear?"

If Marcus was scared this time, Rosie was simply petrified and couldn't move a muscle. Marcus summoned up all his courage to whisper timidly, "Who are you?"

"I am the gatekeeper, and I mean you no harm."

Rosie held the light up as high as she could but still could not see anything.

"Sit down and I will reveal myself to you."

The twins sat down with their backs up against the wall.

"I am a creature of the dark and light is not a friend, nor is it an enemy. Please dim your light down, so I can show myself to you."

Marcus knew how to make the light glow but wasn't sure how to make it go down and he certainly wasn't going to let it go out.

"Try dim," Rosie suggested.

Marcus focused on the word in his mind and slowly the light grew dimmer. He managed to stop it before it went out completely.

"That was very good. You are learning the skills you will need for your journey," said the voice from the darkness.

CHAPTER 12

THE GATEKEEPER

In the centre of the octagonal room, dust started slowly rising and spiralling up from the floor. Gathering speed the spiralling dust grew higher and higher until it towered above the twins. An eerie purple light started to glow from the middle. Then with a loud, CRACKLE, purple sparks flew in all directions. The dust turned into a cloud of smoke, and standing in the middle of the smoke haze, stood the gatekeeper. When the smoke cleared, the twins could make out the shape and height of the creature. He was enormous, over three metres tall, but extremely thin. His skin was pale and very crinkled. A long white beard, evenly braided into thin strands half covered the heavily wrinkled face. The neatly brushed long white hair, parted in the middle, cascaded down the back of the giant. His slightly bent, hooked nose sat between the most outstanding features on his face—his eyes. Enormous eyes like an owl's on a human face, big purple eyes that ... Hang on a minute, Rosie thought quietly to herself, I've seen those eyes before.

"So have I," whispered Marcus.

The twins glanced at each other, "That's not the first time we've been able to read each others thoughts," said Rosie.

"I know," he said.

The gatekeeper reached out to the twins with both hands. Each hand had six long and willowy fingers and a short strong thumb; the fingernails were cracked and dirty. The arms, thin but muscular. He wore a long purple robe that glistened in the dimmed blue light of the rock. A thick black belt with three pouches tied the robe together neatly. They could see the yellow, purple and brown crystals showing out the top of each pouch. Sticking out under the long robe, soft sparkling purple slippers covered the gatekeeper's feet.

Behind the white beard was a gentle and kind mouth that smiled at them, and when he smiled, you could see his teeth were as white and perfect as the marble stone of the room in which they were standing. Extending his long arms, he offered to help them to their feet, "Come, and stand up children."

Marcus spoke first, "Who are you, and what do you do?"

"Welcome, welcome. My name is Delostyek," he said in a tired and gravelly voice. "I am the gatekeeper, and I allow travellers to come and go through the gate," he said, pointing his long fingers to the steel door behind him.

"But it's locked," said the ever observant Rosie.

"I know, and it will remain so until the key is returned to me," said the gatekeeper.

Marcus looked across at the huge locks, thinking, the key must be enormous.

"Lord Theda stole the key from me nearly one hundred years ago. I am still waiting for it to come back. Even I cannot open the gate without it. Those who desire and seek to travel from this door cannot open it, only a gatekeeper."

Rosie asked politely, "What is on the other side of the door?"

The gatekeeper looked sadly at the door and turned back to face the twins. He had such a dejected look on his face, and when he replied, the twins easily detected the sadness in his voice, "That, my dear, is a gateway to all the other worlds in the universe."

"What's it like through there?"

"Yes, Yes," said Delostyek who seemed lost in another world and didn't listen to the question. Thinking about the past brought a brief smile to the gatekeeper's face, "Hundreds of travellers from all over the universe would pass through here every day, living beings of all shapes and sizes. We had a thriving market, trading gold, silver and many other minerals with every world in the known universe. For thousands of years our society was generous and law abiding. One day, a traveller we had not seen before, passed through these doors. After that day, many strange things began to happen. That's when things started to go bad. The traveller disguised himself as a mineral trader. Over a period of ten years, he brought hundreds of helpers in from the outside and traded just like everyone else. Then many traders we had dealt with for centuries left our world, never to return. Their businesses ended up under his control and eventually he grew more powerful. During this period, many tonnes of minerals went missing and our security forces could not piece together enough evidence to bring charges against him. However, some of his associates murdered the family of another trader. The security forces traced it back to him, and he escaped to the Dark Kingdom on the other side of our world. It is a cold, dark, barren and lonely place. The only light that exists is the light reflected from the two moons.

Delostyek stopped talking for a moment and absently gazed down at the twins. "Our world has one sun and two very large moons. This means one third of our world is in constant darkness. Every one hundred years we have an eclipse, which extends the darkness over another one third of the planet. This darkness lasts for six days. During this time, the dark army runs through our land destroying and stealing everything in its path. They are a thieving, murderous and hideous race of creatures that worship the darkness and give total obedience to the new Lord Theda." Suddenly the resentment showed in his face, tears welled up in his eyes and there was a real and bitter anger in his voice, "That's the creature that … " Delostyek stopped in mid sentence. "That is enough for today. You must go back the way you came." Before the twins had a chance to say anything, the gatekeeper vanished in a flash of purple light and smoke. "You must come here again before you continue on your journey," he said

Marcus started to call out, "Hey come ba..." but Rosie elbowed him in the stomach. "Hey what'd you do that for?"

Rosie turned to him, "Can't you see he was upset about something. We'll have to find out next time."

"Whatever. You always seem to understand those sorts of things."

"That's because I listen," said Rosie smirking.

Marcus glared angrily at her, "Come on, I've had enough for today." He looked around the room, "Now. How do we get out of here?" not really expecting an answer. He made the rock light grow brighter.

"You just don't listen, do you Marcus? That's your problem. You don't listen and you barge into things without thinking," she growled at him. "The gatekeeper said to go back the way we came. Now come on, let's give it a try."

Rosie snatched the light out of her brother's hand, and then pushed him across the room, over to the small door they had originally come through. Marcus pulled the door open, only to be greeted by a thick, impenetrable wall of dust.

Turning to Rosie, he said sarcastically, "Brilliant suggestion. What are we going to do now?"

Confused, her shoulders slumped forward. "I don't know," when a tingling sensation surged through their bodies. Thousands of tiny purple lights shimmered and swirled around them. The cuts and scratches on their arms and legs and the pain simply vanished.

"That's amazing," Rosie whispered.

"That's not just amazing," Marcus, corrected her. "That's awesome."

Their clothes were completely clean. Turning in the direction of the gatekeeper, who remained hidden in the darkness, she said, "Thank you."

"You're welcome, my dear," replied the gatekeeper. She turned back to the door and was astonished to see the tiny swirling purple lights move en masse through the doorway. The twins stuck their heads into the stairwell to see the swirling lights surge like a huge wave up the stairwell, cleansing it all the way to the top. When the lights reached the top, a deafening grinding noise filled the stairwell.

Rosie yelled over the noise, "What's happening now?"

"Look," Marcus yelled back, as they stepped into the stairwell. "The stones are forming back into a staircase again." Covering their ears to block out the deafening noise, they watched as the large stone steps slide out of the wall as the staircase repositioned itself right to the top. Everything was clean, immaculately spotless, not a speck of dust to be found. The marble wall, now beautifully cleaned and polished, was such that Rosie could clearly see her reflection in the white stone. The lights formed themselves into a glowing purple handrail that spiralled around the stairwell from where she was standing right up to the top of the stairs.

Marcus stuck his head through the door into the octagonal room and said, "Thank you."

"You're welcome, my boy. Travel safely and come and talk to me again," said the invisible gatekeeper. "By the way, the forest will not harm you when you leave."

"That's great to know," said Marcus turning around to face Rosie. Marcus took the light from her and said, "We won't need this anymore. OUT." The twins started climbing the steep staircase.

Halfway up the staircase Rosie stopped and sat down. "I need a rest, just for a couple of minutes."

Even though reasonably fit, Marcus was happy for the break, and sat down next to his sister.

After about five minutes, Marcus stood and helped his weary sister to her feet. "Come on let's get back to the clearing," he said, looking forward to hopping into bed.

"All right," she said.

The rest of the journey was uneventful; they climbed through the fallen roof of the gatekeeper's house. They walked cautiously through the long forest tunnel, which had reformed and made their way back to the clearing where they had started playing the game.

The clock on the study wall clicked over to one minute past four when Rosie and Marcus found themselves sitting back in the chairs in front of the screen.

She sat for a few seconds shaking her head in disbelief, yawned and said, "That was truly amazing but I'm really tired. I'm going to bed."

"Yep," Marcus agreed.

Rosie climbed out of the chair and trudged up to her room. He sat for a couple of minutes longer before pulling out the cables before going to bed himself. As soon their heads hit the pillow, they were both sound asleep.

Just as the twins dozed off, the ten Imitators gathered again in the forest clearing.

Their leader Electra asked, "What happened with the children?"

Imagen answered, "They no longer need us to play the game. The strength of their thoughts brought them straight back into the game."

"Good," said Electra. "Everything is still going according to how the Master planned it. Did anything else happen?"

"Yes. They have met the gatekeeper, Delostyek, but he only told them half of the story. He couldn't continue and withdrew from them, but he did ask them to come back."

"That was to be expected, for he is a very emotional creature," said Electra. "It is going to slow us up for a small amount of time."

"There is one more thing," said Imagen.

"What is that?"

"The gatekeeper used the purple crystal to heal the children and cleanse the staircase."

"Interesting! Apart from the Master, he hasn't spoken or done anything for anyone for nearly a hundred years, yet he did that for the children. The Master will be pleased." Electra turned to Copia. "What did you learn about the girl?"

"She is intelligent and is more prepared to listen than the boy. She does have courage, but is easily frightened. She thinks before she acts whereas and he acts on instinct, although he has made the right choices so far."

"Good. I will now report this to the Master. Remember Imagen and Copia, you are responsible for their safety."

"Yes, we understand," said both Imitators together. The meeting was finished and in a flash, all the creatures vanished.

CHAPTER 13

AN ORDINARY DAY

The phone on the kitchen bench rang at eleven thirty on Sunday morning. Helen Saunders answered it, and recognising her husband's voice said, "How are you?"

"Good thanks. I'm at the airport and I've managed to get a ticket on an earlier flight. Tell the twins we'll go bowling when I get back."

"They'll be happy about that. By the way, did you manage to sort things out?"

"Yes. They've made some serious inroads with the software. We're going to try it out again next weekend."

"Do you have to be there?"

"Yes I do. You know what this means, don't you?"

"Yes."

"Good. I'll tell you more when I get home. See you soon."

"That'll be good. I'll go and wake them up, Bye."

"See you soon. Bye."

After placing the phone back on the recharger, she looked across at the kitchen clock. Thinking it was strange that the twins hadn't emerged from their rooms she went upstairs to check. She went into Marcus' room first and put her hands gently on his shoulders to wake him up. He was in a deep sleep and dreaming about the meeting with the gatekeeper when he felt a hand come down upon his shoulders. "Nooooo," he yelled as he woke up, sitting up in his bed straight away.

"It's okay darling, it's all right. It's me, it's Mum. You must have been having a dream," she reassured him.

"Yes, Yes," he mumbled, still half asleep. "I was, but you surprised me," he said, looking up at his mother.

"Well come on and get up and get dressed. We're picking Dad up from the airport." She ruffled his hair and gave him a kiss on the forehead. She was worried about him and said, "You sure you're okay?"

"I'm fine, really."

His Mum stood up and walked out of the room

If you wake Rosie up like that up like that, Marcus thought, she'll really scream.

This time he was wrong. Rosie was in a deep sleep and it took a fair bit of shaking and cajoling on her mother's behalf to wake her up.

"Come on, sleepyhead. It's time to wake up. We're picking Dad up from the airport so hop up and get dressed." Helen gave her daughter a hug and a kiss, and then walked out of the room, closing the door behind her.

Rosie dragged herself out of bed, and went over to the window and peered out. It was still raining and she could feel the cold coming through the window. At least her father was coming home today.

The twins slipped into the clothes they had had on the night before. Marcus raced downstairs first and was sitting at the table eating breakfast when Rosie walked into the kitchen. "Where's Mum?" she asked.

"She's upstairs getting ready. Cereal?" he asked, pushing the packet across the table.

"Thanks."

"You sound tired."

Rosie gave him a 'What do you think' stare, saying, "Well it was after four o'clock when we went to bed you know. Did Mum say anything?"

"No, but she sounds happy that Dad's coming home early. He's taking us bowling."

All Marcus could think about was beating his father in the games arcade at the bowling alley. However, that wasn't always that easy because somehow his father would let him get close but wouldn't ever let him win. Maybe today, Marcus thought, maybe today.

Rosie brought him back to down to earth, "How are we going to get back onto the game now that Dad's going to be here?"

"I don't know. We'll just have to wait till he goes away again." Marcus sat bolt upright in his chair and looked at Rosie in despair.

She saw the anguish in his face. "What's wrong?"

"I need to re-plug everything back into the computer before he comes home, and make sure it was the same as it was when he left. I'd better do it now while Mum's upstairs."

Marcus raced quickly into his father's room, reconnected all the cables, and switched on the sound system. He checked everything to make sure it was as before. The only thing left to do was replace the controllers. He placed his controller it in its box on the table next to the computer. When he went to touch Rosie's controller a blue flash of light arced across to his hand from the controller giving him a mild electric shock. He pulled his hand back in agony. "Stupid thing," he muttered. When he tried again, the shock hit him again, this time with twice the force. He heard a distinctive 'CRACK!' as the spark jumped across to his hand. This time it made him jump backwards in agony, "You win! I'm not touching you again," he swore at the controller. Marcus knew Rosie would have to move it and raced back to the kitchen.

When he saw his mother fiddling around in the pantry, Marcus couldn't say anything for fear of giving the game away and tapped Rosie on the shoulder. A small blue spark jumped from his finger across to Rosie.

Rosie winked and whispered, "I know," as she walked out of the kitchen and down the hall. Their mother was still looking for something in the pantry when she arrived back. All done, she thought and touched Marcus on the arm. Immediately he understood.

The afternoon was perfect. Their father's plane arrived on time and they went ten-pin bowling. Everyone had a great time. When their parents went to buy some refreshments, the twins had time for a quick chat.

Marcus asked, "How did you know what I wanted you to do with the controller this morning?"

"I just did. When you touched me on the shoulder, I felt a little electric shock and what you were thinking just came into my mind. It has sort of happened before but never that clearly," answered Rosie.

Marcus saw his parents returning from the kiosk and said quickly, "Yes I've had that feeling before as well. Now I'm one hundred percent certain. When you touched me on the arm, I knew exactly what you meant. We'll have to think about how to make use of that."

She agreed.

He changed the subject, "Anyway, Dad's in a good mood for a change and I even beat him on Daytona."

Rosie smiled, "Yes. He must have had a good meeting with those games people. Shush, here they come."

Carrying ice creams and milkshakes, their parents sat down beside the twins.

"You two deserve a surprise," said their father and pulled out two beautifully wrapped presents from his coat pocket. Rosie received hers first. Her father had wrapped it in white perfumed paper covered in beautiful hand-painted flowers in the most amazing colours imaginable. The flowers seemed to come alive in her hands. Just for a moment, she thought she recognized the aroma. Thanking her father, she unwrapped the present, laying the paper down on the seat beside her. In her hands was a plain flat jewellery box. Rosie opened it slowly expecting something nice. Her mouth dropped open in surprise. This went beyond her wildest expectations. A fine silver chain glistened in the light. The pendant at the end of the chain was the most magnificent piece of jewellery she had ever seen. Rosie examined it closely before picking it up. Six tiny dark blue sapphires formed a triangle in the centre of the perfectly circular silver pendant. Silver stitching weaved it way around the edge of the pendant. Engraved just inside the edge, were strange markings, which looked like ancient symbols she had seen in her history books. She looked up at her father, tears in her eyes, "Oh Dad, it's beautiful." She placed it carefully back in the box and wrapped her arms around her father's neck.

For a few seconds he hugged her then gently pushed her away, saying, "It'll look a lot better around your neck." Her father picked up the necklace, positioning it lovingly around her neck. Helen Saunders knew how much this necklace meant to her husband. She explained to the twins that the pendant had belonged to their Aunty who'd died shortly after arriving here. This was the first time the twins had heard this story about their family.

Rose was shocked. When she realised the true value of the pendant and how much it meant to her father she asked, "Why are you giving it to me?"

Poter placed his hands on his daughter's shoulders and smiled as he looked at her, "She received it from your grandfather when she was the same age as you. We feel you are ready to wear it. Anyway, I wanted you to have it. That's all you need to know for the moment."

Helen said, "It suits you Rosie. It's very beautiful, and you're a lucky girl to be wearing it," she said holding back the tears.

Rosie felt proud to be wearing something that was so important to her father. Her small round face simply glowed with happiness.

Marcus couldn't believe this. Although his father was generous at times, this was a big surprise. His father turned to him and gave him his gift.

Wondering what it could be, he, unlike his sister, quickly ripped open the blue wrapping to reveal a small square box. Inside the box was an XP15 Sports watch.

"Wow. This is awesome. Thanks Dad," he said gratefully. He had always wanted one of these and hugged his dad, all be it briefly. His mother and sister both winked at him.

"Hey, that looks fantastic," said Rosie. "The other kids will be really jealous when you go to school tomorrow."

"Now," his father spoke firmly yet quietly to him. "Your watch has a few built in extras. You'll need to read the instructions carefully," handing Marcus the booklet. "And by the way it's fully waterproof."

"I will," said Marcus, slipping the instruction booklet into his back pocket.

"Come on, let's get going," said their mother. "Time to go home and get dinner started."

Their father put his arm around her waist and gave her a hug. "How about we eat out tonight?"

By the time they arrived home, it was well after nine o'clock and the twins didn't even change into their pyjamas. They both collapsed into bed. Within minutes, they were asleep. In a distant land, someone bade them goodnight, a purple mist covered their sleeping bodies and then faded away.

CHAPTER 14

UNEXPECTED ASSISTANCE

The next morning their mother called out to the twins from the top of the staircase, "Rosie, Marcus, wake up."

Rosie sat up in bed and pulled back the curtains allowing the sunlight to pour into the room. She gleefully jumped out of bed and dressed herself in her uniform. Marcus was still in a deep sleep with the doona pulled up over his head, when Rosie ran in and jumped on his bed, "Wake up!" she shouted.

"Get lost," growled Marcus.

Their father called out from the bottom of the stairs, "Come on you two, hurry up, I'm taking you to school today and I'm leaving in forty-five minutes. We haven't any time to waste this morning."

While Rosie ran downstairs, Marcus dragged himself slowly out of bed, had a shower, dressed and eventually descended the stairs to the kitchen.

His breakfast was ready and waiting on the kitchen table.

"Hurry up Marcus we leave in fifteen minutes," his father called out from the laundry. He ate slowly.

"Get a move on Marcus," said his mother. He trudged back up to his room, packed his bags and returned to the kitchen as slowly as possible. Rosie and her father were waiting in the kitchen when he finally returned.

Marcus knew his father loved punctuality and wasn't surprised when he found him, waiting in the kitchen tapping on his watch. "About time."

Rosie was really looking forward to showing off her new necklace at school. Marcus, on the other hand, wasn't feeling the same way. Sitting in the back seat, he stared out the window without paying attention to anything. He was worried about Billy and Fred, the school bullies. They were a particularly nasty pair and had frightened many of the other kids on more than one occasion. Fortunately, he had been able to avoid them on Friday, but today was another day. He hoped to do the same today but had a feeling Billy and Fred would be waiting. The best thing to do would be to hang around with Hamish. That should keep them away. Hope he's at school today. All these thoughts buzzed around inside his head making him feel even more anxious and worried. His face mirrored his thoughts as he stared blankly out the car window.

Seeing the concern, his father asked, "What's the matter Marcus? You look worried about something."

"Oh, it's nothing Dad," Marcus lied. "Nothing really."

Rosie piped up from the back seat, "It's Billy and Fred. They pick on the other kids all the time and no one does anything about it."

His father was annoyed and asked, "How long has this been going on for Marcus? "A couple of months," mumbled Marcus.

"Right then. I'm not angry with you, but you'll have to speak to someone at the school or I'll do it this afternoon. The best way to stop bullies is to face up to them, not by yourself, but with someone else you trust."

When they pulled up at the school, Marcus waved at Hamish, who was waiting for him at the front gates. His father, still concerned, twisted around in the front seat and said, "Now Marcus is there something I can do?"

Marcus was still worried, but at least his father knew about it, and that helped a great deal, "I'll speak to the head teacher about it today."

"Good. You do that, and if you don't get any support, you let me know."

The twins climbed out of the car and walked over to their friends. Rosie joined her group of friends, showing off her necklace. There were exclamations of surprise and lots of giggling as they walked away.

Hamish in his usual manner punched Marcus softly on the arm. "How're you going?"

"Great. Hey, look what I got yesterday."

Hamish's eyes nearly fell out of his head, "Wow. That's a XP15 sports watch. It does all sorts of things. What'd you do to deserve that?"

Hamish reached over to touch the watch but pulled his hand back in surprise. "That just gave me an electric shock. How did you make it do that?"

"I didn't do anything," said Marcus, looking down at his watch just as the tiny purple flashing lights faded away.

Without thinking Marcus blurted out, "I've seen those before."

Marcus' heart sank when he heard Billy's voice behind him, "Seen what before?"

Fred said, "Hey look, Billy. The little freak's got himself a new watch"

Billy threatened Marcus, "Give it to me. I want to look at it."

Marcus stood his ground. "It's mine and you're not going to touch it." He tried to sound brave, but was actually feeling very scared and worried. Questions flashed through his head, Where are the teachers when you need them? Where are your friends when you need them? Marcus felt frightened and alone.

Billy rushed to grab Marcus' watch, but Hamish jumped in between them.

Hamish had had enough of these two. They had picked on his friends a number of times in the last week. "You'll have to deal with me to get to him," said Hamish, confident he could take on Billy. Hamish was taller and probably stronger than Billy, but Billy was quicker and threw a punch. It surprised Hamish. He managed to move his head sideways but it wasn't enough. The punch crunched into the side of his head, causing him to collapse to the ground. Billy knelt on Hamish's shoulders pinning him to the ground and raised his hand to throw another punch. Digging deep, Marcus found courage he never thought he had and grabbed Billy's wrist to stop him hitting Hamish.

Fred, who up until now had been watching, made the first mistake of the day. He grabbed Marcus on his arm, right next to his watch. Fred stopped and stood as though frozen in time, when he saw a tall creature appear behind Marcus. The colour drained from Fred's face, his mouth dropped open in surprise and his eyes stared in disbelief. He tried to run but he couldn't move a muscle. The creature towered over him, and for the first time in his life, Fred was scared. A burst of purple sparks burst out from the watch and arced across to Fred's arm giving him a fierce electrical shock. Fred pulled his hands away, screaming in agony.

"Do that again and it will be twice as bad," shouted Marcus angrily, unaware of what had occurred behind him. Fred ran off. He wasn't going to hang around. The electric shock really hurt and now his arm ached with the pain. But it was what he had seen that really frightened him.

Billy couldn't believe his eyes when Fred ran off and left him on his own. Not only that, the fight had caught the eye of the teacher patrolling the playground. He came striding purposefully towards them. Marcus pushed Billy off Hamish. Both boys leapt to their feet and stood facing each other. Hamish, his face glowing red with anger, wanted to punch Billy's lights out. Marcus was so scared he found he couldn't talk. He tried desperately to send his thoughts to Hamish. Don't do it Hamish, please don't, otherwise you'll be in just as much trouble. Hamish, on the other hand was smart and he knew by hitting Billy he would find himself suspended for a week, so he held back.

Billy, on the other hand wasn't smart. He still wanted the watch. Lunging towards Marcus, he tried to grab it. "Give it here," he demanded. A spurt of purple light shot out of the watch and hit Billy squarely in the palm of his right hand. Only Marcus saw it.

Billy screamed out at the top of his voice and collapsed to the ground writhing in agony. "Help me! My hand hurts. Help! My hand is on fire." In a matter of seconds, the fight was over.

Hamish turned to Marcus and with a great sigh of relief said, "Thanks."

Marcus shook his head and said, "No way. I should be thanking you."

Finally, the teacher arrived on the scene, "What's going on here boys?" He had seen the fight himself but wanted the boys themselves to tell him what happened. "Right-e-o you three. It's the principal's office for you lot," ordered Mr Evans, as he kept the two parties separated. "Come with me."

"Hamish Harris and Marcus Saunders," announced Mr. Evans as he closed the principal's door behind them.

"Well boys," said the principal. "This is disappointing. Fighting in the schoolyard is not acceptable. I would however, like to hear your side of the story. Who's going to tell me what happened?"

The boys traded looks of uncertainty. Hamish started to talk first and told the principal exactly what happened, but he couldn't explain what had happened to Billy and Fred. Hamish finished off with, "and Marcus came in to try and stop it, Sir."

"That's admirable boys, but it still doesn't excuse the fact you were both fighting. We have notified your parents and they will meet with us after school. Fortunately, you two were not the aggressors in this situation and therefore no further punishment will occur. Now then, I don't want to see you in here again."

Both boys breathed a sigh of relief.

"Mr. Evans, please take these boys back to their classroom. Thank you."

Hamish and Marcus walked past Billy. He was waiting for his mother to pick him up. Billy saw them, but didn't look up.

When they arrived at their classroom, they took their seats at the front of the room.

Mr. Evans said, "Miss Spencer, could I have a word with you please?"

The two teachers walked out of the room, closing the door behind them. The entire class saw them talking and tried guessing what it was about. Other kids called out, "Good on you Hamish. They both had it coming."

"Well done, Marcus," said someone else.

"Great work," called out another.

Marcus looked across at his sister and she smiled at him, Good on you.

Marcus grinned sheepishly and said softly, "Thanks."

The classroom door opened and Miss Spencer came back into the room, "Quiet please everyone, and back to your work." As she walked past the boys she bent down and spoke quietly to them, "We're working on page 112 of *How Science Works,* and by the way, good job boys. It's about time someone stood up to those two. Now, get to work."

"Thank you Miss," said Marcus.

The boys looked at each other now feeling quite proud of themselves.

CHAPTER 15

HEROES

Marcus and Hamish were happy when the lunch bell finally rang. They sat together eating.

"I think nearly everyone in the school has congratulated us," said Marcus.

Hamish agreed but was more interested to know what had happened to Billy and Fred, "What did you do to them?"

"I didn't do anything," said Marcus.

"You must have done something. They were both crying like babies."

Thankfully, Rosie and her friend Isobel sat down next to the boys interrupting the conversation. Marcus welcomed the distraction. For now, at least, he didn't have to explain anything to Hamish but he did want to talk with Rosie.

Isobel had a slight frame and long legs and was slightly shorter than Hamish. Her short black hair, cut in a bob, framed a slightly round face with blue eyes and a fair complexion. Most of the boys thought she was pretty, but more importantly to Marcus she was smart and was the current school cross-country champion.

She sat down next to Marcus, and Rosie next to Hamish.

Isobel broke the awkward silence, "Well, everyone is talking about you two. Apparently, Billy is now on home detention and they are still trying to find Fred. What did you do to him Marcus? It really scared him off."

Marcus responded firmly, "I didn't do anything. It was Hamish who was hit by Billy not me."

"We know silly," said Isobel. "We want to know what happened to Billy and Fred and how you did it. It was so good to see those two idiots humiliated at last."

Marcus looked worried, "We'll still have to watch them. Once they get over this they will want to get back at us."

Hamish agreed. "You're right about that. They'll try to get back at us, just you watch." The boys were in complete agreement. Rosie and her brother looked at each other and both knew they had to talk privately. Rosie turned and spoke to the other two, "Excuse me a minute. I just want to talk to Marcus for a moment."

The twins left the other two sitting together and walked about ten metres away. Rosie asked her brother, "Okay, what really happened?"

Marcus couldn't wait to tell his sister, "When Fred touched the watch it zapped him with a beam of those purple lights we saw in the gatekeeper's staircase. The same happened with Billy. I could feel this tingling sensation and it was much, much stronger. My watch gave both of them an electric shock. I could feel it and see it but I'm pretty sure nobody else saw it."

"Good," said Rosie. "Can I have a look at the watch please?" Marcus undid the strap, and handed the watch to her. As soon as she touched it, a tiny wisp of purple light appeared out of the watch, spiralled up her arm, crossed her chest, and vanished into her necklace.

"See what I mean Sis."

"That's the same light we saw in the gatekeeper's stair case," said Rosie starting to worry.

"I already know that," Marcus replied sarcastically.

Rosie gave him a, don't start on me look.

"Sorry. What's going on Rosie? This is all a bit weird. Do you think we need to talk to someone about this?"

"No. Not yet." She handed the watch back to Marcus, asked, "Have you read the instruction manual for this?"

"No. I've been busy doing other things."

"It might be a good time to have a look. Seriously."

"Yeah you're right. I'll do it tonight."

"Good. Now Listen. We can't mention this to Mum and Dad, all right?" She thought for a moment, "When Dad's away next time well try and organise for Hamish and Isobel to come over and we'll show them what we've found out so far. Hamish is supposed to be really good at these things."

"Yeah. He certainly is."

"Well, thanks," she said, smiling happily back at her brother.

The school bell rang out loudly, signalling the end of lunch. It was time to go back into class. The twins walked back over to their friends. The two boys went off to get a drink of water while the girls made their way back to class.

After school, Marcus sat outside the principal's office while his parents discussed the morning's events with Mr. Evans and the school principal, Mr. Pollock. Hamish's mother had already had her meeting and taken her son home. Marcus kept on going over and over the fight in his mind. The fear he had felt this morning haunted him for a moment and a cold shiver went right through him. He shuddered involuntarily and thought of how badly it could have turned out if Hamish hadn't been with him.

The principal's door opened and Marcus's father came out of the room first, followed by his mother.
    Standing up, head bowed, he walked over to his parents. He saw his father smile and wink at him, then change back to a more serious expression. His mother looked furious, and he thought she was just about to give him a tongue-lashing. He had expected it, but it didn't come.

Earlier in the afternoon, Rosie went home with Isobel and he sat in the back seat in silence. His parents said nothing to him on the way home. Helen waited until he sat down at the kitchen table before saying a single word. His father stood behind his mother in such a way she couldn't see his face. He winked and shrugged his shoulders. Marcus started to smile but thinking that would be a mistake, quickly tried to look serious.

"Marcus," she said gently, her face breaking into a smile. "Mr Evans explained the whole incident to us. When I first heard about this, I was very angry Marcus, firstly at you, and then at those other silly boys. We will not tolerate fighting. Do you understand?"

"Yes Mum," he said softly.

"However, in this case we are both very proud of you and how you stood up to those two bullies. More importantly was the way you handled yourself. You stayed with Hamish when he was in trouble." She walked around the table and gave him an affectionate hug and kiss, "I'm proud of you."

"Muuum," he said, struggling free from his mother's embrace, feeling a little embarrassed.

She ruffled his hair. "Go on. I'll call you when dinner's ready."

Hopping down from the table, he walked up to his bedroom and flopped across his bed, feeling very relieved.

"That was close," he said aloud, "If they had ..."

A deep, soft voice standing behind him, asked, "What?"

Marcus nearly jumped out of his skin and rolled over to look up at his father, "I didn't hear you come in."

"You shouldn't talk out loud to yourself. You give yourself away too easily. Now tell me what really happened today."

He told his father everything, except for the bit about the purple flash and the electric shock to the two bullies.

"I see," said his father. "Are you sure you're telling me everything?"

Looking up at his father, he felt his stomach churning. He could remember the two purple flashes hitting the bullies and wanted to talk to his father about it. However, he had promised Rosie not to say a word. Rather than say anything and give it away, he just nodded his head in the affirmative.

His father asked him again, "You're sure?"

This time Marcus counted to three before he spoke again. "Yes, that's all of it."

Sitting down on the bed next him his father said, "I'm proud of you Marcus. Standing up to bullies takes real courage," pointing to Marcus's heart, "right from in there. You can't always run away, Marcus. Sometimes you have to make a stand and today you and Hamish did just that."

"But Hamish was the one standing up for me. If it wasn't for him, Billy and Fred would have had the watch."

"Yes, that may be true, Marcus. Hamish did come to your assistance, but you stuck with him when he was hurt and lying on the ground. That's what matters. Anyway I don't think those two will bother you again."

Marcus was quiet for a couple of seconds because he wasn't quite so sure, "How do you know that?"

"Well for a start, the principal said that they had found Fred hiding in his uncle's back shed. Fred is adamant he was electrocuted by a huge purple monster he saw standing behind you. Billy said you electrocuted him with your finger."

His father started laughing, "I know it sounds ridiculous, but that's what they said. I even asked Mr. Evans, did you see anything like that and he said, 'no what a load of rubbish.'"

Marcus sighed, "Oh did he?"

"Marcus, bullies are usually cowards who threaten people smaller than themselves to get their own way or to get something they want. All it takes is someone to stand up to them at the right time and they'll run away. It's not easy. I know," his father said.

"But I didn't feel brave, I was really scared," said Marcus, his eyes firmly focused on the floor.

"Marcus, being brave is about helping others in difficult situations, even when you are scared and that, my boy is what you did today." His father paused for a moment. Then in a strange, off-handed-manner asked, "By the way, how was the watch today?"

Marcus was a bit surprised, "It ... sorry. What do you mean?"

His father reached across and tapped the watch on the glass cover. Each time he did purple sparks arced across to his finger. Marcus tried not to look too interested, but he couldn't hide the surprise on his face.

"This watch," said his father, "does things no other watch has ever done before. Remember what I said yesterday. Read the instruction book. Now is there anything else you want to ask?"

Marcus, wondering what was going on, swallowed before answering, "No."

"Okay then," said his father. "Never be afraid to ask for help."

Marcus found himself in a difficult situation, on one hand, he was busting to tell his father everything, but on the other, he had promised Rosie not to say a word.

A voice from the kitchen called out, "Dinner's ready."

"Come on, let's eat," said his father, ruffling his son's black hair as they left the room together.

CHAPTER 16

THE EXPERIMENT CONTINUES

The week passed quickly and without incident. Billy was at home on detention and Fred, it was rumoured, was too afraid to return to school.

"I'm looking forward to coming over tonight," said Hamish. "What's the surprise?"

Marcus turned towards his friend. "You'll have to wait. If I told you, you wouldn't believe me."

"Okay whatever but it better be good."

"Oh, it will be," said Marcus. "It will be," then changed the subject. "You know who comes back on Monday, don't you?"

"You mean Tuesday, it's a long weekend. Anyway, that's not something I've been thinking about," said Hamish. "I don't think Fred will be back. Reckons he saw a gigantic purple monster behind you in the schoolyard. Everyone thinks he's a nutter."

The rumours were floating around and Marcus was aware of all of them. "Yeah, I've heard that."

"Imagine, a big nasty purple monster right here," as Hamish screwed his face up, raised his arms in the air, and growled, "GRRRRRRR."

"Stop it," said Marcus seriously. "You never know what you might see."

"You can't be serious, Marcus."

Marcus laughed and then said softly, "if only you knew, if only you knew."

The final bell of the day rang out across the school. Rosie and Isobel walked towards the car park together.

Rosie said to Isobel, "See you tonight."

"Yes, see you later, Rosie," she shouted as she raced off.

It was now Friday afternoon, and Isobel and Hamish were coming over to stay for the long weekend. Rosie had overheard her parents talking a couple of nights ago. Their father announced he had to fly up to the Northern office for important meetings, and probably wouldn't be home until late on Sunday.

Marcus raced to the car, arriving first, and climbed in the front seat. Rosie sat in the back behind her mother.

Helen asked the twins, "What happened today?"

"Not much," said Marcus.

Rosie was much more informative, talking about science, modern maths and how she'd finally received a better mark than Isobel and Hamish in a speech she'd given today.

"Well good for you, Rosie. All that hard work has finally paid off. I wish you'd try harder like your sister, Marcus. By the way, what time are the others coming over?"

"Isobel has cross-country training and Hamish's playing tennis. She said her mother was dropping her off around six thirty," said Rosie.

"Right, then, when we get home, I want you to clean up your rooms and take out the rubbish out. Okay?"

"Yes, Mum," they answered together.

As the twins arrived home from school, Peter Saunders walked into the meeting room, where Zig and Chloe were waiting for him. It was late on Friday afternoon.

"Where's Andrew?" he asked.

"Don't know. He left about an hour ago," said Zig.

"That's disappointing," Peter said to the others. "Andrew used to be right behind this project." Something wasn't right. Peter stood there thinking, racking his brain, trying to think if there was anything he'd missed. He looked across at Zig, who shrugged his shoulders and shook his head.

"How about we give you an update on the wormhole technology?" Zig asked.

"Yes. Sorry about that. Lost in my own thoughts, I'm afraid. Please Chloe go ahead."

"Well, since last weekend we have worked around the clock on this." Chloe described in minute detail all the technical changes they had made to the software. Peter knew she'd put a lot of effort into this and didn't interrupt her. Finally, she finished and Zig looked across at Peter, "We're just about to run another test."

"Good, that's why I'm here," said Peter. "Let's see what you've found out."

The secure room was set up as before. Two plasma screens sat on a table in the middle of the room, one marked Exit and the other Entry. Peter looked around the room and saw the cracks in the armoured glass window, a reminder of the previous experiment.

Zig and Chloe sat in the control room, the armoured glass window right in front of them, computer terminals off to either side.

Peter stood behind them, arms folded, waiting impatiently, and asked, "How long to go?"

"Not long," replied Chloe. "Based on previous experiments, we've adjusted the settings and we really expect this to work. The previous settings on the initial energy burst were too high. This caused pressure waves in the energy cycle and then the wormhole collapsed and consumed itself."

"And everything in the room," Peter added.

Chloe smiled at that, but continued flicking on the bank of switches of the control panel situated on her right. "Right, now we're ready." She pushed the start button and flicked both plasma screen switches on. All three of them watched the screens in the secure room through the central glass panel.

After a couple of seconds, both screens went snowy. Five seconds later on the screen labelled 'Entry,' there was a bright flash of light. This turned into a whirlpool of light, blue around the outside with a centre of intense bright white light.

Zig, nervous at what lay ahead, asked Chloe, "How are the energy levels?"

"It's stable, Zig! It's stable. There are no fluctuations. It works! It works!" exclaimed Chloe, punching Zig on the arm.

Zig responded with a tired smile, relaxed and leaned back in his chair, "Now let's see if we can pass something through it."

Peter stood behind them not saying a word, proud of the work of both of them, "What happens now, Zig?"

"Now is the moment of truth," said Zig, as he opened the draw under the desk, pulled out a pair of heavily insulated gloves and lifted an umbrella off his desk. "What I am going to do now is push this umbrella through our wormhole. Well, try to, anyway. Is it still stable?"

"Yes it's stable, but please be careful," said Chloe, worried about what Zig was going to do next.

He'd been in a few dangerous circumstances before, but this was different. It was about as scary as it could get. If the wormhole collapsed like it did in the previous experiment, it would suck him in. He'd be crushed into the size of a pinhead within nanoseconds. "At least I won't feel it, if it goes wrong," he said, half-heartedly. Time would tell.

Opening the door, he stepped inside the secure room. His first instinct told him to leave the door open but he was worried about Peter and Chloe, particularly if something went wrong so closed the door behind him.

Zig could feel every beat of his heart as it thumped away inside his chest. His breathing became more rapid. Nervous perspiration ran down his forehead and dripped off his nose; he felt it trickle uncomfortably down his back as he slowly approached the table. Although it was only three steps from the door, he still took his time. After what seemed like an eternity, he found himself looking directly into the vortex of light.

"Still stable," Chloe called out.

Zig raised the umbrella and plunged it deep into the swirling whirlpool of light. The tip appeared in the exit screen. He couldn't believe it. "It works, it bloody works." He reached across, grabbed the tip of the umbrella, and pulled it all the way out. "Yes!" he yelled, holding the umbrella above his head.

"Power fluctuation, Zig! Shutting down! Get Out!" Chloe yelled out, as her hands quickly switched off the equipment.

Zig reacted quickly and raced out of the room, slamming the heavy door closed behind him.

In the meantime, Andrew had managed to sneak back into his office, unseen. Locking the door, he walked briskly over to his desk. Sitting down behind his desk, he monitored the progress of the latest wormhole test. He smiled confidently. Nobody knew he was here. It won't be long now, he thought, smiling at the prospect of escaping from this place, "So they think they're smart," he said, speaking loudly to himself. Over the last couple of months, he'd created several highly secure and, undetectable links into both Zig and Chloe's computers. During this period every experiment conducted by Zig and Chloe had been meticulously copied and stored away. Andrew could still take control of their computers from his office, but only for a few moments before the security system cut him off. One chance, one moment in time, he had to pick his opportunity, but more importantly, he had to be patient. He typed all the new co-ordinates into the keyboard and set them as the default settings. Looking around his office, he thought of how much he would have achieved, but for one silly mistake all those years ago. Still annoyed with himself he thumped his closed fist on the table. He breathed in deeply, growled to himself and leaned back in his chair.

Zig, Chloe and Peter sat down in the control room. It was obvious to Peter they were pretty chuffed with what they'd achieved. Chloe was thinking of the work ahead, putting all of this down on paper. Zig was dreaming he was walking up to the rostrum to accept the National Prize for Scientific Discovery and Achievement.

Chloe brought him back to reality, "We had a power fluctuation, Zig. We need to examine the data again and calculate new settings. Peter, this is going to take us a couple of hours to evaluate before we conduct the next trial."

Chloe yawned, without realising how tired she was.

Peter asked, "How long since you have both had a good rest?"

"It's been a good day and a bit now," she said.

"Right. Go and catch a couple of hours of sleep before you start again. There are couches in the spare office and it's very quiet in there."

Zig opened his mouth to argue but Peter didn't give him the chance to say a word, "Just do as you're told, otherwise I'll call security to lock down the lab. Peter smiled, "I'll call you in four hours, or so."

"All right. You're the boss. Come on, Chloe. It can't harm us to grab a couple of hours," and they walked off together.

Sitting down on the couch, Chloe wanted to talk about what went wrong but Zig stopped her from saying anything, "We're tired and that's what probably caused us to make an error in our calculations. We'll check it in a couple of hours and then we should be able to fix it. You take the couch in the other room and I'll stay on this one. Go on and get some sleep."

She stood up, stretched and walked slowly into the other room. Kicking off her shoes, she lay down on the couch. In a matter of a couple of minutes, she was sound asleep. Zig wasn't far behind her and when Peter checked in on them five minutes later, they were both dead to the world. Peter turned off the desk light and closed the door behind him.

CHAPTER 17

DISBELIEVING FRIENDS

The phone at the Saunders house rang at just after ten o'clock on Friday night.

"I'll get it," shouted Rosie, who was in the kitchen organising some food for the others. Answering politely, she recognized the voice on the other end of the line. Rosie talked to her father for a few minutes and said, "This is the second weekend in a row that you've been away. What are you doing up there?"

"We're working on some pretty amazing stuff. That's all I can tell you now. Anyway, what are you up to tonight?"

"Isobel and Hamish are over for the weekend. We're watching movies and I'm just getting some food. Do you want to speak to Mum?"

"Yes, please," he said. "Where is she?"

"Upstairs, I'll get her for you." Peter waited to hear the familiar yell as Rosie called her mother. She didn't disappoint him "MUUUUM! Dad's on the phone," she yelled. "Bye Dad. Love you."

"Bye," and there was silence for about fifteen seconds.

Rosie hung up the phone when she heard her mother's voice. Peter and Helen chatted for a while. He told her about the experiment.

"That's fantastic news. It's been such a long time," she said. Helen shared her husband's excitement, feeling both relieved and thrilled about the news.

They talked a little longer before saying goodbye to each other. Helen hung up the phone and walked downstairs to check on the twins and their friends. She stuck her head around the corner of the T.V room. "Goodnight, kids. Don't stay up too late," she said.

"We won't," replied Rosie.

Isobel pushed the button on the controller to pause the DVD player and said, "Good night, Mrs. Saunders."

"Goodnight guys." She then spoke directly to the twins. "Now remember, not too late."

"Mum," said Marcus. "We heard you."

Helen turned away and smiled as she headed off to bed. She was secretly wishing Peter was home tonight but understood the nature of the work he was doing. Helen was looking forward to the matter being resolved.

Marcus waited about twenty minutes before going upstairs to make sure his mother was actually in bed. He peeked through the gap in the door only to find her reading a book. He went back downstairs and told the others she was still awake.

The four of them watched a movie for another quarter of an hour before Marcus decided to check on his mother again. Racing up the stairs something caught his attention. He stopped suddenly and thought, what was that? He quickly took a couple of steps back down the stairs and peered up the hallway towards his fathers' study. He'd thought he had seen a light under the door but when he checked, there was only darkness. Thinking he must have been imagining things, he continued up to check on his mother. This time the bedside light was out and her soft breathing told him she was asleep. Pulling the door gently, he closed it and went downstairs.

Earlier that evening, Marcus had checked out the computer, and to his astonishment, found it as he'd left it the previous weekend. His first thought was that his father had left it on again but Peter had simply been too busy to work on it during the week. Rosie, Isobel and Hamish were sitting on the lounge chair waiting for him to return.

Isobel was intrigued with the secrecy and asked, "What's this all about?"

"We've discovered this new game on Dad's computer. It's totally awesome and different to anything we've ever played before. We've played it a couple of times and heaps of strange things have been happening that we just can't explain. We needed to talk to someone and well ... we could only trust you two."

Rosie took over from her brother, "You're both really good at games and we thought you could help us to figure it out."

"Cool. Let's go and have a look," said Hamish.

Rosie warned her friends, "You have to be quiet."

"All right," whispered Isobel, teasing her friend. "We get the message."

"It's not funny, Isobel," said Rosie, frowning at her friend. "I'm serious."

"All right, we'll keep quiet, won't we Hamish."

Hamish, eager to see what the twins were talking about, simply grunted.

All four walked quietly up the hallway to Peter's study. Rosie heard a creak as she passed the staircase. She turned her head towards the noise, but saw nothing.

Marcus whispered, "What's the matter?"

Peering into the semi-darkness of the staircase, she couldn't see anything, "I thought I heard something. That's all. It's nothing." She followed the others into her father's study. Hamish hadn't been in here before. It was full of equipment he had never seen before and the huge plasma screen on the wall left him staring in awe. It stretched right across one wall. Rosie organised the chairs while Marcus plugged in four headsets and switched on the game. On the wall next to the screen, the clock read Friday 14th June, 10.54pm.

Everyone sat down and the screen filled, as it had the previous weekend, with the beautiful picture of a large, heavily grassed clearing in the middle of a forest.

"That's incredible," said Isobel. "It looks so real."

Rosie looked at the others and said firmly, "Listen guys, there are a couple of things you need to know. Don't touch the controllers until we tell you to, and don't touch someone else's controller, no matter what happens. Do you understand?" she said firmly. "And finally, when you get into trouble you must drop the controller straight away."

Hamish didn't believe a word of it, "What are you going on about. It can't be that bad."

Marcus saw the look on Hamish's face and said, "She's deadly serious. This really is different. If you hurt yourself in the game you'll feel it in this room."

Isobel didn't believe it either, "Yeah. Right. We know your Dad's good at creating games but you're stretching the truth a bit now, aren't you?"

The twins glanced at each other and Marcus said, "Okay then, we'll show you."

Marcus handed them a set of headphones each, "Here, put these on." The sound of the forest flooded their senses through the headphones. Isobel and Hamish couldn't believe it. They thought they were actually standing in the middle of the forest clearing itself.

Hamish saw the controllers sitting on the desk and reached over to pick up one of them whilst the others weren't looking, "PZZZZZZZT." A blue spark arced across and zapped Hamish's right hand.

"OUCH!" he squealed. "That hurt!"

"Shush," Marcus whispered angrily. "You'll wake up Mum and that'll be the end of it. You have to listen, because if you don't, you're going to regret it. Now sit there and don't touch anything."

"Whatever. Keep it under control," said Hamish. This time, he did as Marcus asked him, sat down, and kept quiet.

Marcus reached across Hamish and picked up his own controller. His sister picked up hers and immediately both their images appeared on the screen.

Hamish and Isobel turned, staring at each other in total shock, "That's amazing. They look exactly like you," said Isobel.

"I know," said Rosie.

Hamish was excited, "I've never seen anything like it before. Can we have a go?"

Rosie said, "Isobel you have number three and Hamish you have number four, and remember if you get into trouble, drop it straight away and you'll be safe."

Isobel picked up a controller, while Hamish grabbed the last controller. The cable became taut and snagged itself under the corner of a heavy book. Hamish gave the controller a strong tug, pulling the cable free. Unseen by anyone in the room, a small coloured wire in the base of the controller tore loose, creating a bad connection.

When their friends picked up the controllers, their images appeared on the screen.

Hamish was stunned, "Look at that. It's wearing what I've got on." His image wasn't as clear and appeared to be fuzzy around the edges.

"See. Told you so," smirked Rosie.

Hamish fiddled with the controls to make his image move but nothing happened.

Isobel did the same. "It's not working," she complained.

"You have to think about what you want to do," Rosie instructed them. "Just try something."

Isobel looked around and then down the hill, "I'd like to run down there." Her image took off downhill with a sudden burst of speed that surprised her. Initially it was fun until Isobel realised she couldn't control her speed and started to panic. "Help!" she cried out.

"Just think about slowing down," suggested Rosie. Luckily, Isobel's image reached the bottom of the hill without falling over and finally slowed down, eventually coming to a stop. Her image walked back up the hill again but Isobel, sitting in the chair, found herself breathing rapidly and heavily from the exertion.

"I see what you mean," panted Isobel. "I just thought about staying upright and it worked."

"Well done. Do you believe us now," said Marcus.

Hamish sat there amazed at what he'd seen so far and said, "What do you guys want to do now?"

Rosie and Marcus continued their private conversation. Rosie wanted to see the gatekeeper again and Marcus agreed. Rosie looked across at her brother. Perhaps we should try reading Isobel's and Hamish's minds.

Marcus smiled back and shook his head, I've already tried and it didn't seem to work. I think the gatekeeper is best, don't you?

Yes, I do, she nodded. Don't mention anything about Imagen and Copia, not yet anyway.

Okay but they'll find out later anyway.

Maybe, but I just have a feeling it's best kept between us now.

Marcus and Rosie nodded in agreement.

Marcus finally responded to Hamish's question. "We're going to go and see the gatekeeper."

His friend asked, "Who's the gatekeeper?"

"You'll see. Come on."

CHAPTER 18

HELPLESS

Deep within the computer, the thought reading processors their father had installed to run the game recognised the twins, overriding the need for the Imitators. It transformed the twins and then, amazingly, Isobel straight into the game. Hamish on the other hand, disappeared off the screen.

Isobel watched in awe, as the room disappeared in front of her. She was even more surprised when she discovered the forest now surrounded her. Isobel walked over to the nearest tree. Reaching out, tentatively at first, she touched its trunk feeling the rough texture of the bark with the ends of her fingers.

Isobel shaking with excitement said, "This is so real."

Meanwhile, Rosie walked off the path, bent down and picked a couple of handfuls of wildflowers, then returned to her friend. "Have a smell of these," she said, handing them to Isobel.

Isobel sniffed the flowers and breathed in the perfume, "That's beautiful."

"I know and there's so much more to see here."

Rosie noticed Hamish wasn't with them. She walked over, tapped Marcus on the shoulder, and told him, "Hamish's gone."

In the study, Hamish watched the other three relax in their chairs. Their heads fell forward slowly as if they were asleep. Just as he was about to complain about being left behind he heard a door bang upstairs, followed a few seconds later by footsteps. He held his breath as he listened to someone talking upstairs. Sitting perfectly still, he waited for a few seconds before asking Marcus, just loud enough to be heard, "What's going on? You three have fallen asleep but I can see you up on the screen?"

"We're not asleep, Hamish. We're in the game but for some reason you're not."

Marcus said to the two girls, "Stay here. I'm going back to see if I can help him."

"All right," said Rosie. "Don't be too long."

"Okay," then dropped his controller. Within the blink of an eye he was back in the room, sitting next to Hamish. Reaching across, he poked his friend on the arm.

Hamish, concentrating on the screen saw Marcus disappear and then nearly jumped out of his chair when something poked him in the arm, "Who's that?" Twisting around quickly to see who it was, he found Marcus sitting next to him, apparently awake again and laughing.

"Great. Thanks. You gave me a real fright."

Marcus laughed. "I know. Anyway, we need to work out what's happened. Let's have a look at your controller."

Hamish held it out for Marcus to take.

"No. I can't touch it. Just hold it up so I can see."

Hamish held the controller up for Marcus to have a close look. Marcus could see the multi-colours of the internal wiring showing where the cable went into the back of the controller.

Marcus pointed to the problem and said, "Great. You must have damaged the cable."

"No I didn't," said Hamish, giving the controller a shake.

Marcus pointed to the coloured wires, "See that. The controller's damaged."

Hamish groaned, "Great. Isn't there another one."

"No." Marcus wasn't sure what else he could do. He suggested to Hamish that he try tipping the controller on its side. Hamish didn't really have an option. Tilting it from side to side, he found holding it at a certain angle made his image reappear on the screen.

Hamish said, "This is a bit of a pain."

"Well you only have yourself to blame, Hamish. So get used to it. At least you can see your image on the screen and hear what's going on. Now let's go," and picked up his controller, returning to the game. He explained to Rosie and Isobel what had happened.

Marcus checked with his friend, "You ready to go?"

Hamish grumbled, "Yeah. Suppose so."

"Good. Let's go," Marcus followed Rosie and Isobel down the path.

They'd walked twenty metres or so when they found Hamish's image wasn't keeping up with them.

Marcus rolled his eyes. Hamish was really testing his patience, "What's up now?"

"I just can't seem to get it to work. I'm stuck here and can't move."

"You just have to relax and really concentrate. Just imagine yourself walking." The real Hamish closed his eyes and concentrated hard, trying to make his image walk. At first, he struggled to move his feet.

Rosie encouraged him, "Come on. You can do it."

Slowly Hamish's image moved forward, starting with small steps, finally breaking into a slow walk.

"This is not easy," said Hamish.

Even though Hamish had brought this upon himself, Marcus relented a little and said, "What do you think. Your controller isn't working properly. You'll just have to do the best you can."

With practise, Hamish found it a lot easier to walk, but the computer refused to transport him into the game like the others. The loose connection within the controller prevented it. The only way was for Reflekta, another Imitator, to imitate him allowing him to continue in the game.

After walking steadily for just under an hour, they reached the fork in the path. Hamish's image shuffled along slowly behind the others. He was walking as quickly as he could but the others had to stop and wait for him to catch up on several occasions. When they reached the tunnel leading into the gatekeeper's garden, the twins found nothing had changed. For Rosie and Marcus, the painful memories came flooding back. They shuddered as they remembered the attack and the terror they felt as the tunnel closed in on them. It gave both of them the creeps.

Isobel saw the concerned looks and asked, "What's the problem?"

"This is not what it seems," said Rosie, pointing to the tunnel through the forest.

"I'm beginning to understand that," said Isobel, starting to worry.

Marcus said, "It's probably best if you two," talking to Rosie and Isobel, "go through together and I'll stay with Hamish's image."

"The tunnel's pretty dark, Rosie," observed Isobel.

"Are you frightened?" asked Rosie.

"No, Well yes. Just a little."

"Good. Because you should be. This is really scary," Rosie replied, as they moved closer to the tunnel entrance.

Isobel felt goose bumps rising up on the back of her neck as she sensed a deep sadness emanating from the tunnel. Hamish felt the same sensation.

Marcus asked his friend, "You all right?"

"No. I feel something bad is going to happen."

Marcus reassured him, "When we left the gatekeeper last time he said the forest wouldn't hurt us."

"That was last time, Marcus," said Rosie.

"I know. That's why I'm being careful." Turning back to Hamish, "You'll be all right. You must not look back. Just trust me. Rosie and I were here last week and we managed to make it through."

"He's right, Hamish. This time we know what's going to happen," said Rosie.

Isobel felt so uncomfortable that she asked, "Go on. What did happen last time?"

Rosie and Marcus traded thoughts. *It's only fair Marcus. You have to tell them.*

The others listened as Marcus told them what had happened on their last visit. He asked, "Do you still want to go through? I can't make you but if you want to meet the gatekeeper you have to go through this tunnel."

Isobel walked over to Hamish's image. They whispered to each other for a few seconds then Isobel turned to the others, "Yes. We're ready to go."

"Good, but this will not be easy. Let's go. NOW!" he shouted.

The girls took off ahead of the boys and were easily ten metres in front by the time Hamish's image started to move in a quick walk. The forest ignored Rosie and Isobel as they raced through. Rosie was relieved and Isobel wondered what all the fuss was about.

Marcus saw that Isobel and Rosie had made it without any problems and encouraged his friend, "Come on Hamish, you need to go faster. Come on. Just a little quicker."

Hamish's image struggled to keep up with Marcus as he walked on ahead. The branches sprung to life, rapidly growing longer and larger, without any warning. At first, the branches snatched at his arm, trying to slow him down. "Something's wrong," Hamish shouted anxiously to Marcus.

He heard Hamish call out just before the tunnel started screaming.

Marcus knew they were in trouble, "Oh no," he exclaimed, with a look of complete despair. "You need to get a move on, Hamish."

"I want to go back," said Hamish, his voice full of panic.

Marcus yelled, "No. Don't look back."

Hamish didn't listen and his image turned to look behind him, only to see the branches had now grown so quickly across the path, the way back was now completely blocked. He now only had one way to go. That small moment of hesitation cost Hamish and his image dearly.

Marcus shouted, "Run faster!" and tried to go back to help his friend's image when a huge branch appeared out of nowhere, grabbing Marcus around the waist and powerfully flinging him out into the gatekeeper's courtyard. After landing heavily, he rolled over, only to see more branches reaching out, trying to capture his friend's image. The fearful frenzied screams continued to grow louder and louder as two long slender branches snaked over the image's shoulder, grew rapidly down across his chest, and then hooked around his waist, tightly. Hamish's image stopped dead in its tracks as hundreds of branches rapidly wrapped and entwined themselves savagely around his hands and arms. The screaming from the tunnel reached a crescendo as it dragged Hamish's image back into the dense, tightly packed wall of foliage. Hamish screamed, "Help! Help! I can't breathe." The terrible screaming from the tunnel stopped when Hamish's image disappeared from sight.

Marcus who now lay flat on his stomach in the courtyard, yelled out to Hamish in desperation, "Let go of the controller."

Rosie cried out to her brother to do something.

Marcus dropped his controller and returned to the room. Hamish was curled up like a ball in the chair, gasping and struggling for breath. Marcus grabbed his friend's arms, trying to shake the controller out of Hamish's hands, but it wouldn't budge. "Drop the controller, Hamish," Marcus commanded desperately.

"I can't," he cried helplessly, as tears streamed down his face. Hamish had never felt so hopeless before. Something invisible had wrapped itself tightly around his hands and, try as he might, he couldn't open them to let go of the controller. He was finding it more difficult to breathe as each moment passed and only just managed to call out, in a very weak, strained voice, "My hands are tied together."

Marcus was desperate and said, "No, they're not, Hamish. Just let go."

"I can't," he sobbed. Hamish looked desperately at his friend, his face screwed up in agony. "I can't let go."

There was only one thing left for Marcus to do. Grabbing Hamish's controller with both hands he pulled hard. An enormous blue spark spurted out of the controller hitting him squarely in the chest. The force of the blow lifted Marcus out of his chair. He managed to hold onto the controller yanking it free from Hamish's grip. Marcus heard the controller clatter to the floor next to him as he slowly crawled back to his chair.

Totally unharmed, sitting up as though nothing had happened, Hamish said, "What's going on?"

"You were trapped in the tunnel and it was squeezing you to death. You're now out of the game Hamish until we figure out what to do."

"You're joking. Doesn't this thing go back to the beginning so we can start again?"

Marcus was not impressed and told Hamish very clearly, "No, it does not. Don't you listen? You are now out of the game! You've got to believe me when I tell you this sort of stuff. Do you understand me?"

Hamish could see how worked up Marcus had become, "Yes," he said, feebly, feeling rather upset with himself.

Marcus realised he'd been a little harsh on his friend and, calming down a little, rested his hand firmly on his friend's shoulder. "Sorry about that but you could have been killed. There is a chance that the gatekeeper might be able to help," he said gently.

Hamish sat up in his chair, "That's good. Who is he?"

"Well, we were just about to meet him when you were caught by the tunnel. It was trying to kill you, Hamish. Touch the controller if you don't believe me."

"No thank you. I'm not that stupid."

"Good," said Marcus. "Now sit back and watch." Picking his controller up off the floor, he went straight back into the game.

CHAPTER 19

NO SECOND CHANCE

Hamish was feeling very sorry for himself. He couldn't sit still. Up on the large screen, he watched the others walk towards the domed building in the courtyard wishing he could be there with them. Hamish eyed off the controller on the floor. He knew they couldn't see him and thought it was worth a go. Nobody will know. All he wanted to do was touch it, just once, to see if Marcus was telling the truth. He just couldn't help himself. Reaching down he was about to pick up the controller when, at the last minute, he decided to be a little more cautious and touched the controller with the tip of his finger. Hamish wished he'd left it alone. A powerful invisible force wrapped itself very tightly around his hands again. Cuts and scratches immediately reappeared on his hands and spread rapidly up his arm. Hamish groaned as the torturous pain raced through his body. Desperately he tried to pull his finger away from the controller. The controller was stuck to the end of his finger and he tried but couldn't flick it off. Unbearable pain surged through his body. He tried again to flick the controller off but it wouldn't budge. Hamish started to panic as he felt the tightness around his chest squeeze harder. It was hard to breathe and he knew he had to try something soon. Placing the controller awkwardly between his feet, Hamish pushed with all his strength. The controller went flying across the room as Hamish yelped in pain as he tore a great chunk of skin off the end of his finger. The deep crushing pain and the scratches disappeared instantly. He collapsed back in his chair, greatly relieved it was over. He swore to himself that from now on he would listen to Marcus, and sat back to watch the others up on the screen.

Marcus could hardly believe it. The entrance to the gatekeeper's staircase no longer lay in ruins, "It's been rebuilt," he said.

"It's beautiful," said Rosie. "When we were here last weekend, Isobel, it was lying on the ground totally destroyed."

Isobel strolled over to the structure and ran her hands over the intricately carved marble columns, feeling the cool, smooth stone under her fingers.

Marcus turned to Rosie and Isobel, "After what happened with Hamish, we have to be very careful, because one mistake could be the end of it. Remember, Isobel, if you get into trouble, you must drop your controller. Okay, have you got that ?"

Isobel, annoyed by the patronising way Marcus spoke to her, answered back harshly, "Yes Marcus. I know that."

The two girls exchanged looks and Rosie had words with her brother, "Don't be so bossy."

Marcus, more concerned about the others, said to them, "Sorry. I just don't want you two to get hurt like Hamish. Okay?"

"Well that's fine, but we're all in this together. We saw what happened to Hamish too," she said, less angrily than before.

Marcus searched around for the rock he'd used as a light last time he was here. Eventually he found it hidden in the long grass and walked back to the others, held the rock in his right hand and called out, "Illuminate." Blue sparks fizzed out everywhere just before the rock burst into a bright blue light.

Isobel was astonished. "That's incredible," she said, sitting down on one of the marble stones at the base of the building. "This is like a dream. I don't know what's real and what's not."

Rosie sat down next to her friend, "I know the feeling. That's exactly how I felt the first time. This is part of Dad's game. We need to be very careful how we play it."

Isobel shook her head in disbelief before answering, "I can see that."

Meanwhile Marcus waited impatiently on the top step of the staircase, "Do you two want to go down these stairs in the darkness by yourselves or not?"

"Don't be so impatient, Marcus," replied Rosie.

"I'm not."

"Yes you are," said Rosie.

Marcus knew he wasn't going to win this argument and decided to keep his mouth shut. All he wanted to do was see the gatekeeper. "All right I'm sorry. I just want to find out what's going on."

"So do we," replied Rosie, "but can't you just wait until Isobel is ready."

"I suppose so," he said sitting down next to the others, passing the rock light to Isobel.

When she felt the warmth radiating from the rock, she whispered, "Thank you." She pointed towards the staircase with her free hand asked, "Anyway, what is down there?"

"The gatekeeper," said Rosie.

"Who's that?"

"He's someone we met last time. He told us to come back and see him again. Marcus jumped up enthusiastically. "Let's go down and you'll see for yourself," and started walking down the staircase, hoping the others would follow.

"We'd better go with him," said Rosie, making sure he heard. "Before he starts to get bossy again."

Isobel begrudgingly followed them down the stairs.

They reached the bottom of the staircase in no time at all. Isobel was amazed at how deep it was. When she looked up all that was visible was a tiny spot of light right at the top of the stairwell.

"A lot easier than last time," said Marcus.

"Ummm," Rosie replied.

When they reached the bottom, Rosie opened the door into the octagonal room and walked straight into the darkness. Isobel followed, still carrying the light and Marcus came in last.

As Marcus closed the door behind him, dust rose from the floor and spiralled up into the air. Gathering speed rapidly, it towered above all of them. An eerie purple light started to glow from the middle and then, CRACKLE, purple sparks flew in all directions. Isobel's jaw dropped in fright. The gatekeeper stood before them. He welcomed them in his gravelly voice. He was particularly courteous toward Isobel. "Hello my dear, my name is Delostyek. I am the gatekeeper. Do not be frightened. You are amongst friends."

Isobel couldn't believe her eyes and with her mouth wide open stared impolitely at the creature towering above her.

"My dear, it is rude to stare, particularly when you are a guest in one's house."

"I'm so ... so sorry. I didn't mean to stare. I was just a little surprised," said Isobel, as she backed away and moved in behind Rosie.

Marcus hadn't forgotten about Hamish and asked the gatekeeper, "Our other friend is, I mean, was stuck in the tunnel above. Is there anything you can do to get him out?"

"Of course, my boy. Watch. Would you please open the door?"

Marcus ran straight over and opened it.

"Thank you my boy," the gatekeeper said, as he pulled a purple crystal from his belt and pointed it at the doorway. A jet of tiny purple lights burst out from the end of the crystal, sparkling as they hovered in mid-air before shaping themselves into an arrow. The arrow shot out through the door and rocketed up the stairwell.

The arrow reached the top, turned ninety degrees, and headed straight towards the closed tunnel at high speed. With tremendous power, the arrow plummeted into the tangled web of branches and exploded, blasting bits and pieces of vegetation in all directions. The purple light then wrapped itself like a blanket around an unrecognisable body lying in the undergrowth, carried it out and laid it down gently in the middle of the courtyard. The lights disappeared down the stairs and returned to the gatekeeper's crystal.

"You may now ask your friend to rejoin the game," the gatekeeper said. "Remember this: I cannot do that for him again. Warn him that …"

Marcus didn't wait for the gatekeeper to finish and called out, "Hamish, pick up the controller."

Hamish didn't listen either and bent down, grabbing the controller off the floor. The body lying on the ground turned into his image. Hamish groaned as the severe pain returned. Bloodstains reappeared on his clothing from the cuts and scratches he'd received in the vicious attack. Slowly Hamish's image rose gingerly to his feet and walked in obvious discomfort towards the staircase.

Delostyek said, "Your friend was at the very edge of death's door. He must be very careful from now on. Tell him to climb down the staircase. It is lit for him as it was for you when you departed last time."

Hamish's image still couldn't walk properly, and every step he took was extremely painful. He wondered if he would ever make it to the bottom of the staircase. A faint purple light glowed around his image as he climbed down the stairs and vanished when he reached the bottom. The other three were pleased to see his image arrive in the octagonal room.

CHAPTER 20

THE GATEKEEPERS GRIEF

Rosie greeted him at the door, "How are you feeling?"

"How do you think I'm feeling? I'm sore all over and every time I breathe, it hurts. I don't ever want to go through that again." Then he noticed the gatekeeper, and for a moment, forgot about the pain and stood staring. "You look exactly like the creature Fred said he saw last week in the school yard."

"I'm afraid that is impossible. I am unable to leave this place," the gatekeeper said and winked in such a way that Marcus was the only one to see it.

Marcus had often wondered about that day in the schoolyard but never quite believed it was true. He couldn't hide these thoughts from Rosie.

Rosie asked, what was that?

Oh, nothing. Sorry—just thinking.

Rubbish, she answered back.

The twins stood staring at each other, without saying a word. Isobel was on to them straight away, "Stop it, both of you. I want to know what's going on."

The gatekeeper interrupted, directing his comments at Marcus and the two girls, "That's enough of this nonsense."

Rosie apologised to the gatekeeper.

"That's all right, my dear."

Rosie wondered why the forest tunnel attacked Hamish this time and not them and asked the gatekeeper for an explanation.

"It recognised you from last time," he said.

"Yes, but Isobel wasn't here last time."

"That is true, but she was with you." Then he spoke to Marcus, "You thought it was safe didn't you?"

"Yes... well sort of."

"Because Hamish was left by himself the forest didn't recognise him and attacked." He looked down his long nose at the twins, "I trust this is a lesson for you. In this game never take anything for granted and always stay close to your friends."

Hamish, however, was far more interested in the octagonal room than listening to the others. He walked around the wall, running his hands over the cool, smooth marble, ending up next to the large octagonal door. Hamish's image lifted one of the enormous locks, and finding it quite heavy let it fall. It crashed down heavily, the noise echoing around the room. He went to lift it again and said, "What are they for?"

"Leave them alone," snapped the gatekeeper, noticeably annoyed with Hamish. "And sit down."

Hamish didn't like the rebuke and grumbled to himself as his image walked painfully across the room. It was difficult for him to sit down easily and he complained bitterly about the pain.

The gatekeeper asked Marcus politely, "My boy, could you please adjust your light?"

Without saying it Marcus thought, 'dim' and the light became duller until it provided just enough light so they could still see each other's faces.

Hamish, feeling quite tender and sore wanted to know what the gatekeeper did, and asked the question.

"I am the gatekeeper and I allow travellers to come and go through the gate," he said, pointing his long arms to the steel door behind him.

"But it's locked," said Hamish.

"That is very observant of you. It will remain so until the key is returned to me," said the gatekeeper. "Now please keep quiet," and continued. "The key was stolen many decades ago and has yet to be returned. The gate can only be opened with the key, by me."

Isobel asked very politely this time, "What's on the other side of the door?"

"That, my dear, is a gateway to all the other worlds in the universe. Now please do not interrupt while I tell you the story."

Rosie noticed the gatekeeper was becoming irritable with the interruptions and whispered to the others to be quiet.

The gatekeeper told Isobel and Hamish everything the twins had heard previously on their last visit. Although they'd heard the story before the twins sat quietly, listening to every word the gatekeeper had to say.

Resentment showed in his face, and his voice became angry, as the tears welled up in his eyes, "That's the evil creature who murdered my family... right here." Delostyek stopped. Huge tears ran down his cheeks as he remembered that dark, dark night.

The gatekeeper sniffled a couple of times and then continued, "Many in our world were sick and tired of having friends and family go missing without a trace, and seeing that nothing was being done to stop it. Many believed that some within our security forces were purposefully ignoring this state of affairs. That was until Dalastar and his wife Phoebe, from the City of Light, decided to stand up to the corruption in the city. Both were from rich trading families who returned here to set up business just after the arrival of Lord Theda. Both of the family business's were untouched by the crime and corruption caused by Lord Theda. They tried to make the leadership take stronger and more effective action against the Dark Kingdom but alas, the Commissioners wouldn't listen. Apart from Dalastar and his friends, nobody anticipated the attack on the City of Light."

"Excuse me," said Hamish's image. "What's so important about the City Of Light?"

"The City of Light, my boy was the capital of trade in the universe. All transactions for minerals sold or purchased went through the City of Light. This was a city of great wealth with magnificent buildings, restaurants and theatres. It was the centre of learning, for business, finance, all the sciences, but most importantly, for geology. Many of the finest gemstones, minerals and crystals were stored here. At the centre of the City was the greatest collection of the rarest crystals ever seen in our world. Travellers from all over the universe came here to study them. However, more importantly, this is where the energy crystals under the city released energy into our world, keeping everything in natural balance. The City of Light was, and still is, essential, to the long term survival of our world."

Delostyek paused for a few seconds before continuing with his story, "Please understand that the City of Light had never, ever fallen into the darkness caused by the eclipse nor had it been attacked. The surprise attack on the City of Light, led by Lord Theda, caught everyone, except Dalastar and his friends, by surprise."

"The assault came late in the day. Out of nowhere, dark arrows of death rained down on the city. Many hundreds died in the streets in the first assault. There are few survivors when this weapon is used. Nothing remains. Those that did survive the first attack escaped from the city thinking they would be safe in the garden above us. It was a horrible trick. The archers in the dark army ambushed the survivors from the city. Less than two hundred escaped through these doors. Lord Theda himself organised the slaughter as the survivors entered the gatekeeper's garden."

Tears flowed down Rosie's face, "That's terrible."

"Yes. It was," agreed the gatekeeper.

A heavy silence filled the room before the gatekeeper started again, "When someone is hit by an arrow of death, the ground beneath them swallows up the body and they remain buried there forever. Many hundreds died there that day, souls from all over the universe. Each tree in the forest above represents a soul killed that day. That is why the forest grows so quickly. It seeks revenge, on behalf of the lost souls, on the one that caused their deaths. But their judgment has been clouded by the anger they feel and they attack anyone who enters the garden."

The gatekeeper paused again as he stood up and walked over to the locked steel door. "They were trying to go through here," he said sadly, resting a hand on the door. "They were so close, only one hundred and fifty escaped that day. There was nothing more I could do."

The gatekeeper struggled to finish his story, "Eventually Lord Theda arrived here in this room," he stammered, tears pouring down his face. He started talking slightly faster than before, "He burst in and demanded I unlock this door. I was here with my wife and child. We were determined not to let him past but he was too quick for me and threw two death arrows, which stopped in mid air just a hair's breadth away from my family. He yelled at me, demanding that I open the door, 'Open the door gatekeeper! Do it now. Otherwise on one command from me they will be dead'

My wife called out to me, 'Don't do it Delostyek! This murderer must remain here.' They were the last words my wife said to me," cried the gatekeeper.

Lord Theda waved his hand and the arrow continued on its journey of death. Not even a sigh of pain, she just vanished as though she never existed. Her soul is up there," he said, pointing to the garden upstairs, "along with all the others."

The gatekeeper stood quietly with his big eyes closed. He was remembering that terrible moment from the past and shuddered at the horror of it. He didn't want to relive it. Slowly he lifted his head and continued speaking, "He roared at me, 'Open the door gatekeeper. My patience is at an end. Do it now!' My wife was gone, my child was crying in fear. What could I do?" It was all too much for the gatekeeper and he broke down, tears flooding down his face.

Rosie stood up, walked over to Delostyek, held his hand, and said softly, "What happened then?" The gatekeeper smiled at this kind gesture from Rosie. They all sat in silence giving the gatekeeper time to compose his thoughts.

Delostyek lifted his head up and started to speak, "I opened the door and gave him the key, expecting him to spare my child's life. As he entered the doorway to the universe, he turned to me and said, 'You old fool' and with a swish of his hand the other arrow delivered my child to be with his mother. And then Lord Theda vanished." The gatekeeper was now completely inconsolable, as tears, like rivers of water, flowed down his face.

Everyone felt sad for the gatekeeper, finding it difficult to imagine what he'd been through. Rosie said she would stay with the gatekeeper and told the others to return to the study.

CHAPTER 21

SUCKED IN

Hamish was quite happy to put the controller down, and be relieved of the pain he'd put up with. He would not forget the encounter with the tunnel in the gatekeeper's garden for a long time to come.

Hamish stretched out in the chair, yawned and said to Marcus, "I'm really tired."

"So am I. This game is really demanding isn't it?"

"You can say that again. You have to feel sorry for the gatekeeper, Marcus. What a story. "

"This Lord Theda is probably the one we'll have to face when we get towards the end of the game," said Marcus.

Hamish jumped up out of the chair, stood up, stretched, and said, "Guess so. Anyway I'm going to bed."

"You're not going anywhere," growled Isobel. "We haven't heard the full story yet."

"I'm really tired," Hamish complained.

"No way, Hamish," she said. "We have to go on and we have to go on together. We…, I mean, you, owe it to the gatekeeper. After all he is the one who got you back in the game."

"Come on Hamish. Just another fifteen minutes, then we'll call it a night," Marcus said, encouraging his friend to stay.

"Oh, all right," he grumbled. "I'm interested, but it did get a little scary tonight you know."

They all sat down and together picked up their controllers.

Isobel, Marcus and Hamish's image returned to the octagonal room to find Rosie sitting with Delostyek on the floor, still holding his hand.

"Sorry about that, but I have only told that story once before," the gatekeeper said.

Rosie looked up at him, "Are you sure you're ready to continue?"

"Yes, my dear. I am all right now. Thank you."

The others sat down on the floor again and he continued.

"Dalastar and his friends came through the door just as Lord Theda disappeared. I explained to them everything that had happened. Dalastar said, 'If only we had prevented Lord Theda from taking the leadership of this city into his control. All those who had been killed would still be alive. We must shut this door to the outside world to stop him from ever returning here. Delostyek, never give up hope and despair not, for we will return one day with the key. Stay and guard this place until then.'

Stepping into the doorway, they waved goodbye and left. Ever since that day this door has been locked and our world has not had any travellers, until you came."

Everyone sat silently on the floor. Rosie glanced across at her brother and he nodded his head.

"Thank you for listening to my story," said the gatekeeper.

"That's okay," replied Rosie. "Is there anything else we can do for you?"

"No, no thank you my dear. You have already done enough. I think, however, it is time for you to go. Thank you for being so patient and kind to me. Turning to Hamish he stated, "The tunnel through the forest will no longer hurt you. It now understands you are here to help."

The gatekeeper then spoke directly to Marcus, "You will need to come back to me one more time. There is something else that I need to teach you before you continue on your journey."

Marcus, keen to learn more, was just about to ask, when he felt Rosie glaring at him.

Rosie stared at her brother and shook her head as she projected her thoughts to him. Don't even think about it. That's enough for today.

Marcus gave a slight nod of his head. They all said their farewells and walked out to the staircase.

"Out," said Marcus to the rock light.

Purple lights guided them up the stairway on their way out. When they reached the top, they approached the forest tunnel cautiously, with the exception of Rosie, who walked right in and said, "He said it was safe. You have to trust him."

The others followed Rosie carefully, through the thick branches. This time the forest stayed still and quiet. Rosie felt it first, followed by the others, as they entered the tunnel. The air was heavy with an invisible yet oppressive sadness that weighed down heavily on them. It haunted them and they were all glad to exit the tunnel at the other end.

Hamish, stiff and sore from his encounter with the vines and tress of the tunnel, asked Marcus, "Why can't we just let go of the controllers and drop out of the game?"

"One of the rules is we have to come back to a safe place," answered Marcus. "For us it is the clearing, otherwise we would come back to exactly where we left off. You wouldn't want to return to something like the tunnel again when it attacked you would you?"

Hamish thought for a moment then said, "No. I suppose you're right," and left it at that.

Finally, they reached the clearing.

Marcus looked upwards, "It's only about half as bright as it was when we arrived," he said.

"Probably what they call evening here. Anyway, I am too tired to worry about it now. Let's go," said Rosie with a distinct tone of authority in her voice. They all returned to the computer room. Hamish placed his controller on the desk. The others dropped theirs to the floor. Picking their controllers up by the cords, they placed their controllers back in the correct boxes on the desk. They leaned back in their chairs.

"That feels much better," said Hamish, who was delighted to be back. "No more aches and pains. I'm going to bed right now."

Marcus, exhausted himself, glanced at his watch, "It's just after three o'clock."

The other three stretched out in their chairs as Hamish stood up.

Hamish noticed it first. Up on the screen a swirling circle of light, looking remarkably like a whirlpool, burst into existence, replacing the forest scenery. Spinning slowly at first he watched as its speed increased. The circumference had a blue tinge to it, while the centre was a brilliant white. A breath of wind kissed his cheek and inquisitive as ever, he reached out and touched the screen.

His hand disappeared right into the screen. It was as though he'd put his hand into a curtain of water, where the liquid flowed around it completely. Hamish spun around to face the others, "What's happen...?"

The swirling whirlpool of light sucked Hamish out of the room. The others sat there gobsmacked. Everything started to go mad. A strong gust of wind invaded the room causing some loose paper to flutter around the study. In no time at all it had grown into a raging gale force wind, swirling menacingly around the small room. Papers, pens and books flew past the children. The speed of the ferocious wind continued to increase, pulling paintings and bookshelves off the wall. The suction pulled the drawers from the desk. Marcus saw the purple folder lying in the top drawer and grabbed it to stop the wind from sucking it away. He only just managed to stuff it down the front of his shirt. The three children gripped the desk in front of them, holding on as tightly as they could.

Isobel yelled out over the horrendous noise, "Come on, let's get out of…" as strong invisible hands lifted all three of them, up out of their chairs to join the other debris flying around the room. In a bright flash of light, the swirling maelstrom on the screen sucked everything into it. As quickly as it started, it stopped, finishing with a violent, thunderous rumble. The beautiful and peaceful forest scenery returned to the screen in stark contrast to the destruction of just a few moments before.

CHAPTER 22

EXPERIMENTAL DISASTER

The desk clock had just clicked over to three o'clock in the morning when Chloe and Zig sat down to run the experiment again. Peter had woken them at around eleven o'clock. Since then the three of them had spent the time reviewing the data from the last experiment. They made the necessary changes and were ready to try again. On the entry screen, the swirling, sunken whirlpool effect appeared in a brilliant flash of light.

On the exit screen, a bluish white swirling vortex burst outwards as it had done in the previous experiment.

Zig asked, "How is the energy level Chloe?"

"It's stable. There are no power fluctuations. It works! It works Zig!" exclaimed Chloe punching him in the left arm.

"That's the second time today, Chloe," he smiled, and walked over to try the experiment again. His hand was turning the handle of the door to the secure room when Chloe cried out in shock, "We've lost control!"

Zig raced back to the others, "What's going on?"

Chloe, surprised with what she saw on the screen said, "It's stable but it's being controlled from Andrew's computer."

Zig couldn't believe it, "No. That's impossible!"

Fearing the worst, Peter commanded, "Shut it down NOW."

Peter and Zig had turned away to check the computer equipment when Chloe caught a glimpse of a reddish-green flash, about the size of a large man, which came out of the exit screen. In less than a second, it disappeared into the entry screen.

Thinking aloud, she said, "I've seen that flash before. But where?" Then she remembered, "That can't be," and turned to face Peter and Zig, "I've seen that before."

Peter said, "Seen what before?"

"That reddish-green flash."

Peter's heart missed a beat, "Which flash?"

"Didn't you see it?"

"No."

Chloe explained what she'd seen. "I'll show you," and reached across to push the replay button on the security camera. Peter and Zig watched the replay while Chloe pointed out what she'd seen.

Peter, swore under his breath, then placed his hands firmly on Chloe's shoulders, "Where? Where did you see it before? This is very important."

"I saw it in Andrew's eyes. It was only a glimpse... last week in the office when he stormed out of the meeting. At the time, it gave me the creeps and made my skin crawl. I thought it was because he was angry. I am sorry, Peter. I should have mentioned it before."

Peter started walking back and forth across the room, completely oblivious to the other two, who watched on in silence. Finally he stopped and spoke to Chloe, "That's all right. You weren't to know."

Peter said to Zig, "That explains the sunglasses. Damn. How did I miss that?"

Chloe looked up at Peter then across at Zig. "What's happening here?"

"Look, Chloe, it's a long story." Peter's mobile phone rang, interrupting the conversation. "Yes, what is it?" he asked angrily. "Right, we're coming now. Chloe you stay here and make sure you switch this system off. Zig you come with me."

Zig and Peter raced up the corridor to Andrew's office. When they arrived, they found the security guard standing at the door.

Peter asked him, "Have you been in?"

"No, I thought I'd wait until you arrived."

"Good," said Peter, pushing open the heavy door. Thick, black smoke billowed out through the door, into the hallway. They all turned up their noses at the smell of burnt plastic. The smoky darkness of the room sent shivers up Peter's spine as he reached for the light switch and flicked it on. "Nothing," he called out to the others, and then asked the security guard, "Do you have a torch?"

"Yes, Sir," he said, handing it to Peter. When most of the smoke had dissipated, Zig followed Peter into the room. The beam of torch light cut a path through the wisps of remaining smoke and darkness. Apart from the furniture, the room was empty.

"Psst. Over there on the wall Peter," Zig pointed, and the light followed in the direction of his outstretched arm. "Looks like whatever happened in here tripped the circuit breakers."

"Looks like it," Peter agreed. "See if you can turn them on again."

Zig walked over and flicked on all the circuit breakers. The room filled with light. Switching off the torch, Peter put it down on Andrew's desk.

"Everything's back on again," said Zig, looking around the office, "except the computers."

Peter spoke with the security guard who then raced out of the room to attend to Peter's instructions.

Peter looked around at what was left of the computer equipment in the room, and said, "It's nothing more than a heap of worthless junk. Damn. Whatever hit this system has certainly destroyed any information it may have contained."

Chloe walked into the room just as Peter's mobile phone rang again.

"It's Helen," he said, wondering, why she would call this late.

Turning his head away to speak to his wife, the others heard him say, "What's the matter?" He was half expecting bad news with a call at three o'clock in the morning, but he didn't expect to hear what his wife was describing. He listened for a little while then screamed at the top of his voice, "NO."

Helen Saunders had woken up to a loud thunderous rumble that shook the house and everything in it. At first, thinking it was a thunderstorm; she'd hopped out of bed, pulled on her dressing gown and peered out through the curtains. All she could see was the dark, cloudless sky filled with stars. Checking the children's bedrooms, she discovered they weren't there. Helen raced downstairs, calling out, "Rosie? Marcus? Where are you?" Only silence. Now she was starting to worry. "Rosie. Marcus," she called out again, walking from one room to another. She searched the house thoroughly and found nothing. Her husband's study was the only place she hadn't checked. Opening the door cautiously, her despair deepened when she looked around at the remains of what had been her husband's study. Everything had disappeared. Books, rubbish bins, shelving, keyboards, chairs, paintings, everything except the plasma screen, the clock on the wall and all of Peter's computer equipment which had just recently been installed and bolted to the floor.

Helen was desperate, trembling with fear and sobbing uncontrollably with tears streaming down her face. She struggled hard to stay calm as she dialled her husband's number. As he asked "what's the matter?" She gave her worried reply, "The kids are gone, all four of them and so has everything in your study. What am I going to do? What's happened to them?"

She heard her husband scream out, "NO" then agonising seconds of silence as she waited for him to speak. When he did, his voice had a controlled yet apprehensive tone to it, "I don't know. But I'm sure this'll work out somehow"

"How did this happen? Why now? I thought ..."

Peter let his wife talk wishing he could be there with her.

"It hurts to know we can't help them," she said.

"We will be able to help and you know that too. We have to be patient. Okay?"

"No. It is not okay! This wasn't supposed to happen," she fired back angrily at him.

"They'll be fine, you have to believe that. Look, we have a lot to do here to try to find them before I leave. I'll be on the first plane home in the morning."

"I'm really worried about them too."

"They're smart kids. I'm sure they'll be all right. We just have to believe that. Anyway, Zig and Chloe are just about to start working on what happened. I'll call you back soon."

"I'll be waiting. Love you," she said, desperately anxious about the kids.

"Love you too. Bye."

He turned towards the others, "Did you hear that? My children's lives are at stake. We have to go through the data now."

"Thirty minutes and I'll have it ready for you," said Chloe, before running out of the room. Peter pulled a small plastic bag from his pocket and showed it to Zig, "I found this on Andrew's desk." The bag contained a mixture of small sparking red and green coloured crystals.

"Seen these before?"

Zig nodded and sighed in dread, "That's not good."

"No it's not. In addition, Andrew may be there with them too. If that's the case, that's bad, very bad. I'll have to tell Helen. See if you can help Chloe, and contact the others."

"I understand," Zig replied and walked off leaving Peter alone.

Peter called his wife. They spoke to for just over half an hour.

Half an hour had passed when Chloe and Zig walked into the meeting room. Chloe cleared the books and papers from the table with one sweep of her arm. Laying the data out on the table, she sat down to wait for Peter who walked in a minute or so later and asked Zig, "How did you go?"

"They are not responding."

"Keep trying."

"I will."

"Damn," said Peter. "What the hell was a wormhole doing in my study, Zig?"

Zig shrugged his shoulders, "I'm not one hundred percent sure, but best guess is this. You have an optical fibre secure link into the computers here —just like Andrew, by the way. It would appear a pulse of energy from the wormhole we produced has travelled down the line energising the doorway, sorry, the screen at your place, turning it into a wormhole entrance.

Peter stared angrily at Zig as soon as he mentioned the doorway. Chloe missed the connection and took over the explanation, swallowing hard before speaking, "I don't know if you know it or not, but your kids were playing your new game tonight on your computer and they finished just as we started up the experiment."

Peter rested his head in his hands with this news. He'd hoped this wasn't the case but Chloe had confirmed his worst fears. Chloe pulled out a chart from her folder to show the others, "Andrew took control at 3.00.45 and at 3.00.55 the security locked him out so that's when he travelled down the wormhole. A pulse of energy occurred at 3.01

and one life form travelled at 3.01.10 and then another three life forms about fifteen seconds later. Peter this is going to sound quite extraordinary, but Andrew, your kids and their friends appear to have been transported to another world."

Peter sat quietly, as Chloe continued. "I don't know exactly where they are. The rest of the data is either corrupted or destroyed. I have to rebuild it."

He was angry with himself and swore under his breath. Looking up he asked Chloe, "How long to get this wormhole fired up again? We have to get them back!"

"About three days," she replied quietly, knowing what Peter's response would be.

"What the hell do you mean, three days?" Peter nearly lost his temper but stopped short of giving them a blast, knowing that it wasn't really their fault. He stood up and paced across the room for a couple of minutes, breathing deeply in and out, trying to control his thoughts. He said to Chloe, "Sorry Chloe. It's not your fault. Please continue."

"Andrew changed the defaults, and then he set the server to delete everything, even all the backups. All the data is gone. It will take about three days to type the code back in."

Peter stood up, "Chloe. You have forty-eight hours to make it happen. It doesn't matter what you have to do. Just make it happen! Do I make myself clear?"

"Yes."

"And Chloe."

"Yes Peter."

"I don't want any mistakes."

"With respect Peter. Neither do I." Chloe paused to think, and then said bluntly, "You knew didn't you. You're not telling me something. What is going on?"

When Peter flicked a glance in Zigs' direction, Zig shrugged his shoulders, and said, "Peter, it can't hurt to tell her. We'll need all the help we can get on this one." He paused and said, "She deserves to know."

"Deserve to know what," she fired back quickly.

Until now, Peter had been able to hide the past. Now it was time to share it with someone else he could trust, "Get comfortable, Chloe. This is going to take a while."

CHAPTER 23

DUMPED AND DELIVERED

High on the barren slopes of the dark mountains, located three days walk from the City of Light, it was pitch black and bitterly cold. Patches of snow dotted the desolate landscape. For a moment, the darkness retreated when a brilliant flash of light illuminated the bleak mountaintop. A wormhole burst into existence, opening at precisely the location Andrew had chosen. Andrew tumbled down the wormhole and shot out the end. In all his meticulous planning, he'd made one small mistake in his calculations. The gravity here was slightly different, and the wormhole didn't stop in one location, as he'd expected it to. It kept travelling forward at a considerable speed. Misjudging its pace, he landed awkwardly on the uneven and rocky ground and tumbled over, hitting his head hard on the ground. There was a loud crack of bone on rock. All he could remember hearing was a loud crash nearby, where something large and heavy hit the ground not far from him, then several pairs of hands tried to pick him up. He heard a couple of voices call out, "Lord ..." as he slipped into unconsciousness.

The wormhole continued its southward journey down the mountainside. It travelled quickly, following the hills and valleys characteristic of this part of the world. Continuing down the mountain it reached the vast grasslands covering the undulating plains at the foot of the dark mountains.

Hamish's journey through the wormhole was terrifying. A moment ago, he'd been standing in front of the plasma screen with his friends. Hamish had no sense of any forward movement. The journey down the tunnel was rough and bumpy. It tossed him wildly from side to side where he bounced off the walls of the tunnel of bright light. The tunnel ended abruptly and Hamish found himself falling. He screamed out in terror. Bracing himself for a hard landing, he curled up into a ball, using his arms to protect his head. He did so just in time hitting the ground heavily, tumbling over and over in a field covered with long thick green grass, which helped to absorb the impact of his fall. Eventually he came to a stop and lay there, perfectly still, breathing heavily. After a couple of minutes, he sat up slowly and sighed loudly in relief. Apart from a few bumps and bruises, he felt fine. Hamish took his time getting to his feet, and turned around three hundred and sixty degrees to try to get his bearings. The thick grass came up to his chest, and even in the starry light of the early morning appeared to extend as far as he could see. It swayed in the gentle breeze, moving like waves on the ocean, rolling on and on into the distance.

He screamed out, "Where am I?"

"Who are you to make such a horrible noise?" A voice answered back from immediately behind him.

Hamish got the fright of his life and not expecting a response, jumped forward. Spinning around quickly he only just caught a fleeting glimpse of the tiny creature.

The creature behind Hamish spoke to him again, "What are you?"

Twisting around as quickly as he could, Hamish found he was again too slow to see the creature properly, "Why don't you stand still so I can talk to you?"

"We don't want to."

"Are you scared of me?"

"We're not scared of anything."

Hamish, tired and sore, had had enough, and demanded, "Stand still and talk to me."

One by one, four tiny creatures appeared before him. They were about a metre tall and had the most beautiful features. Their symmetrical faces had dainty little noses not too big or too small but perfectly in proportion with the rest of their face. Their evenly positioned lavender coloured eyes and mouths were near faultless. The dimples on their wonderfully rounded chins added an extra dimension to their appearance. Their light brown hair was long and tied neatly in ponytails. Under their multi-coloured tunics, tied around the middle with an intricately made hand-woven brown leather cord, their bodies were trim and well toned. They were all identical.

One of them asked, "What are you?" The voice had a high pitch and a slight coarseness about it.

"My name is Hamish."

"What's a Hamish?" it asked, scratching its head at the same time.

"No, that's my name"

"What's a name?"

The creatures scratched their heads every time they asked a question. What a funny thing to do, Hamish thought, smiling at the strange behaviour.

Hamish could see that this wasn't getting him anywhere, "I am a Hamish," he said, feeling somewhat frustrated with them.

"Oh," they all replied.

Hamish asked, "What are you?"

"We're Ebrags, or that's what others call us." Hamish thought he was finally making some progress.

"Well that's what others call me. They call me a Hamish. Why do they call you Ebrags?"

"The others say that all we do is talk a lot about ourselves"

Hamish found it hard not to laugh because at the end of every sentence, the Ebrags stuck their tongue out just a little bit but at an angle that aimed down towards their chin. In a way, it was cute, but this conversation wasn't going anywhere.

"Who are the others and where do they live?"

"The others rarely bother us for they live a long way away. Many days travel from here, in the City of Light."

So, that's where I am. I must be back in the game, he thought. At least I know that much, and asked, "Which way is The City of Light from here?"

"We know which way it is," said one of the Ebrags.

"Look. I'm tired, hungry and a long way from home. Is there some place I can stay for the night?"

They talked among themselves for a few moments, "Follow us and we will take you to our palace."

"Thank you," said a very tired and relieved young man.

The walk to the palace of the Ebrags took just over half an hour. Hamish imagined many great buildings with high walls, lots of balconies, beautiful gardens, paved roads and hot running water. Oh, for a nice bed to sleep in, was all he was thinking.

They reached the top of a small hill overlooking their palace.

"This is our magnificent palace," said one of the Ebrags. The smiles on their little faces showed how proud they were of what lay before them. Tiredness and a deepening sense of loneliness finally overwhelmed Hamish and he collapsed to the ground, exhausted.

Within a couple of seconds, more of the creatures had gathered around Hamish's exhausted body.

One of the Ebrags said, "What will we do with him?"

"You will carry him to the visitors' room," said the Ebrag leader, who had arrived in the blink of an eye. "Let the stranger sleep and then we will find out who he is and what he wants to do."

"He is a Hamish. He said so," said the Ebrag who had met him first. "He asked the way to the City of Light."

"What does he want there I wonder?" asked their leader, who scratched his head like the others, "Take him now and we will talk to him when he rises from his slumber."

CHAPTER 24

THE LACWEVELDS

After leaving Hamish, the wormhole, still containing Rosie, Isobel and Marcus, continued to travel southwards. Reaching the edge of the vast grasslands, it swept over the majestic pine forests and dropped down close to the surface of the Great Southern Lake. The great lake stretched out in all directions. A densely wooded forest covered the steep slopes on the lake's northern shore. On the eastern and western shores, steep vertical cliffs ran the full length of the lake. Scattered along the shoreline were hundreds of pebbly beaches of various shapes and sizes. Behind some of the larger beaches were flat, treeless areas, covered with a mixture of exotic wildflowers and long thick grass.

Two very big, thickset men sat in a wooden boat on the lake. After a hard day's work in the mines, Pieter and Slvad loved to go fishing and were now the best in their community. The Lacwevelds' lived in and mined the caves surrounding this side of The Great Lake. The two of them had been out on the lake fishing for a number of hours and the boat was practically full of fish from the evening's catch.

"Tonight catch good," said Pieter to his friend.

"Yes," Slvad replied. "Time home."

Pieter caught sight of a bright flash of light reflecting off the surface off the surface of the lake and asked, "Hmmm that what?" Both men turned around only to see a massive swirling circle of light approaching rapidly towards them. Their jaws dropped and their eyes opened wide in surprise. They didn't even have time to reach for the oars to row themselves out of harm's way. The bright circle of light passed right over the top of the boat. Pieter and Slvad looked at each other in dread. Above them in the darkness, they heard numerous screams followed by three splashes as the unidentifiable objects fell into the lake.

Isobel and Marcus grunted as they hit the water hard, close to the boat. The miners, hearing the noise moved quickly. As Isobel and Marcus came to the surface, the miners skilfully plucked them from the lake and placed them none too gently on the seat at the back of the boat. One of the miners threw a couple of blankets their way. Marcus wrapped the blankets around both Isobel and himself. He heard one of the miners shout, "There over," pointing to a spot some twenty metres away. The two huge miners put their backs into rowing the boat as quickly as possible towards the spot where something else had fallen into the lake.

Rosie panicked as the freezing cold water closed around her, catching her in its vice like grip. She tried to scream under water but no sound came out. The impact of the fall and the icy cold water had completely forced all the air from her lungs.

She felt herself sinking and sensed a dark foreboding shadow rapidly replacing all her thoughts and memories, when something grabbed her by the arms and hauled her roughly out of the water.

Isobel and Marcus were already huddled together, shivering violently under a couple of rugs in the back of the boat. Rosie sucked in great breathes of fresh, cold air after the miners had dragged her from the freezing cold water of the lake. Her tiny body shook uncontrollably, as one of the men placed her gently next to her brother. Pieter wrapped a warm rug around her shoulders. She couldn't talk and coughed up great mouthfuls of water.

"Lucky you we here," one of the men said to her.

Rosie looked up, tried to smile but couldn't. These two men were huge. They had mammoth hairy arms and hands. Their fingernails were dirty and broken.

In between the coughing and spasms, she whispered to her brother, "They must be nearly as tall as they are wide,"

"They are. But they seem to be kind and fortunately they did save us."

Rosie suffered another about of coughing and shuddered again. She whispered to her brother, "I'm so cold."

"So am I Rosie," he said, teeth chattering while he adjusted her blanket. "Before they fished you out of the water, they said they were going to take us to a warming cave. That's about all they've said so far."

One of their rescuers said, "Come now, home."

Sitting down beside each other, the miners faced the children as they started to row toward the shore. Keen to get the three travellers to warmth and safety, Peter and Slvad hadn't taken any further notice of the wormhole now several hundred meters from the boat. Without warning, it collapsed in on itself, creating a brilliant flash of light that, for a brief moment, illuminated the darkness surrounding them. A great clap of thunder rumbled over the surface of the lake. Everyone turned their heads in the direction of the noise but there was nothing left to see. The wormhole had completed its journey.

Pieter and Slvad rowed as quickly as they could. The boat slid up on the shoreline and the three children felt the bottom of the boat scrape across the pebbly beach. Huge, gentle hands lifted them out of the boat and placed them on the beach. Rosie still shivered violently with the cold and found she couldn't walk and toppled forward. Pieter caught her before she hit the ground and carried her like a baby up the steep, well-worn staircase, leading up to a cave entrance overlooking the lake. She didn't mind at all, and closed her eyes, happy to be safe for the moment.

Soaking wet and shivering, Isobel and Marcus helped each other as they struggled to keep up with the two men on the steep stairs and into the cave. The warmth inside the cave greeted them like an old friend.

"Quick, in warming cave put," said a woman.

The warming cave turned out to be exactly that. Dark ruby coloured crystals lined the ceiling of the tunnel giving off both a dull light and a great deal of heat. The shivering stopped as their bodies warmed up. The hot dry air in the room dried their clothes as well.

"We have a lot to be thankful for," Marcus said to the others.

"I thought I was going to die. I was so scared," said Rosie, who sat there with tears running down her face.

Isobel came over and gave her friend a huge hug, "I know. I've never been so cold before. At least we're safe."

"You're right about that," said Marcus, who was feeling much better.

They had only been in the warming room for a couple of minutes when the door opened and the same woman called to them, "Come now out. Better feel you?"

"We feel a lot better, thank you," answered Marcus for all of them.

"Come now eat. Me follow."

The trio followed the woman further into the tunnel. Marcus stared in awe at the thousands of crystals in a wide assortment of shapes and colours that lined the roof, glittering and sparkling. "Look guys, the blue crystals are providing the light!"

After they'd walked about a hundred meters, the cave widened out into a large cavernous dining room. About fifty of the huge creatures, both men and women sat silently on long stone benches. The tabletops were enormous slabs of pure white marble with beautifully carved legs even more ornate than the columns in the gatekeeper's garden.

Hundreds of eyes stared at them, as the children followed the woman to the far end of the room where they sat down at a table. The two men who had rescued them sat down on the opposite side of the table.

"Come now, eat," said the woman, and placed a large plate of steaming hot fish down in front of them.

The woman also placed a similar sized meal in front of the men, who started eating the fish with their fingers.

"Come now. Eat," said the woman again. "Good is food."

Marcus thought, I don't like fish.

Tough, Rosie thought back. Just eat it and don't be rude.

You sound like Mum.

Rosie glanced briefly at her brother and Isobel, and then, copied the two men opposite, picking up the sweet smelling fish with her fingers to eat. "Mmmm, this smells good," she said.

"Shhhh," said one of the men. "Eating. Talk no."

Rosie nodded her head in acknowledgement. Isobel tried the fish next and finally the reluctant Marcus.

Hey Sis, this is not too bad, he thought, knowing now Rosie would understand.

She whispered, "It's absolutely delicious", reaching for another piece. Soon both plates were empty and when the woman returned she gave them hot towels to wipe their hands. The three children copied the two men opposite so as not to offend their hosts.

"Come now. Sleep," the man opposite said. "Follow."

They walked behind the two men down another tunnel leading off from the dining area.

"Here sleep," one man pointed to three brown, rock slabs, and then turned around and left them. The large bluestone door rolled closed, trapping them in the room. The room was round with a domed roof coming right down to the floor. Marcus ran his hand along the wall feeling the rough surface with his fingers. On closer inspection, he found thousands of tiny crystals in a multitude of colours, glistening in the wall. The room wasn't very big but had two doors, the one they'd come through, and a small door at the rear of the room. Marcus pushed the small door open, finding it led into a little bathroom. There was a basin and a very basic toilet. He returned to the main bedroom with the others, "Toilet and washroom in there, but where do we sleep?"

The only form of light in the room came from two light blue crystals hanging from the roof. In the middle of the room lined up parallel with each other were three brown stone slabs. Each slab was perfectly flat and had blankets neatly folded and stacked at the end.

"Looks like we are supposed to sleep on these," said Rosie standing next to the middle slab.

Isobel examined the stone beds and found thousands of tiny holes in the top of each stone slab, and said, "What do all these holes do?"

Rosie, who just wanted to go to bed, said, "Who knows and who cares? I'll sleep anywhere." Climbing up on to the stone slab, she lay down and pulled a blanket up over her tired body, placed another blanket under her head as a pillow, curled up and closed her eyes. The others jumped when Rosie called out excitedly, "Hey look at this!" as she pulled the blanket off. "I'm floating." The others could see she was floating a couple of inches above the bed.

"Amazing," said Isobel, astonished at what she saw. She put her hand under Rosie and felt warm air blowing up through the holes in the stone slab, "You're floating on a bed of hot air. That's totally awesome."

Marcus grabbed a blanket from the end of his bed, climbed up onto the slab, and lay down. Just as quickly, he found himself floating the same way, a couple of inches above the slab of rock. "Go on, hop up and try it Isobel," he said.

Isobel copied the others and the last thing they remembered was Marcus saying, "I hope Hamish's all right."

"Yes," said Isobel softly, as they all slipped into a deep sleep.

In the dining room, Pieter, who'd rescued the children earlier, said to his friend, Slvad, "Stay you, until me return, Fetch master I."

Slvad responded, "When back?"

"Morning. Child not sleeping give food. All time watch keep."

Pieter walked over to his wife Magda. Rosie's description of these people was almost right. They were about one and a half metres tall and nearly about a metre wide. Massive hands were at the end of strong muscular hairy arms; sculptured by to the physical tasks they performed each day. Their dark hair was long and straggly but clean. The Lacwevelds' faces were quite round. The most striking features were their very pronounced chins and protruding foreheads. All the men had thick black beards, and a big flat nose below two large protruding eyes that exuded kindness. Both sexes wore hand sewn animal skin shirts and dresses, and thick leather boots tied with leather laces. Their legs were short but immensely powerful, more like those of a weightlifter than a miner.

"Magda, master those three find I. Ahead dark times."

"Carefully travel," she said, reaching out and squeezing his arm. The others in the dining hall watched them. A show of affection was rare for the Lacwevelds, but they all knew about the troubles that lay ahead, so there was a certain amount of understanding. Pieter nodded his head, grabbed his thick jacket and walked out of the room to begin his long journey through the night.

Arriving back at his boat Pieter looked up at the planet's two moons. They half covered the sun creating a blackness that had started to spread out over the countryside. Soon the terror of the dark period would begin and he had a vision that this would be worse than last time.

"Ahead times dark. Gone be children," he said to his brother Padreig.

He and his family, and many others, had mined this mountain for hundreds of years. Although they were miners and lived simply, they were happy with their lives and didn't seek the comforts of those in the City of Light. Not that they weren't wealthy. Others paid them handsomely for the finest crystals and jewels in the universe. That was up until the trading gate near the City of Light closed nearly one hundred years ago. They all held onto the promise that one day the Gate would open again. Whilst excited by the promise of the return of the master, the coming eclipse brought fear and terror to his community. The appearance of strangers was an important event. He had to find the Protectors of the City of Light and tell them what he had found. Pieter wasn't afraid of the journey to the other side of the lake. Once on the other side of the lake he faced a solid walk to reach the watchtower, where he would send a message to the Protectors of the City of Light. They would advise him on the best course of action. Fortunately, he had his brother Padreig with him.

"Row hurry! Other side quickly reach."

They both put their backs into rowing as quickly as possible.

The ten Imitators appeared and gathered again in the forest clearing.

"The human children are here," their leader Electra declared, "in our world."

Imagen and Copia stared at each in utter astonishment, and then back at their leader, "This cannot be, we just left them in the clearing," said Imagen.

Mirra and Reflekta agreed with the others.

"Silence!" commanded Electra. "We were warned this may happen. Remember our duty now is to find and protect them. Go now. We must not fail." The meeting ended and they vanished.

CHAPTER 25

THE EBRAGS EXODUS

It was now seven o'clock on Saturday morning and Peter was asleep, twisted up on the couch in the office. He woke to find someone standing over him.

"Time to go Peter," said Zig tapping his watch, "The plane leaves in an hour."

"Thanks for that," Peter didn't want to get up. He was tired, stiff, sore, and wanted to stay here and sleep, but he needed to fly home and be with Helen.

"It's been an interesting night," said Zig.

"Yes. One I'd wished never happened. I hope those kids are okay."

"I'm sure they will be all right. We just have to trust the others to find them."

"Hmmm, I hope so. I really do hope so," Peter said, as he stood up and stretched.

When the plane touched down at the airport at 9.30 am, Helen, her heart pounding, raced up to her husband. She looked a little dishevelled from being up most of the night worrying about the children. Tears streamed down her face as Peter hugged her tightly.

"Helen, they'll be fine. There's nothing we can do to help just at the moment, you know that. We'll be working overtime over the next two days to get them back."

"But they could be in serious ..." she sobbed.

Peter reached over and gently placed a finger on her mouth and spoke softly to her, "We have to trust them and trust their judgment. They're smart kids and Hamish and Isobel are with them. The others will be looking for them. We'll get them back."

"We should have been more careful."

"Helen, I certainly didn't know there was going to be a wormhole in my study to whisk them away. Trust them. We have to believe in them. They should be fine."

Helen wasn't so sure about that.

"Hi, Helen," said Zig. "How are you holding up?"

"Oh hi Zig. Sorry, but I'm worried. I'm very worried."

"That's understandable ... but Peter is right. They will be all right," changing the subject. "We've had an interesting night ourselves. Has he told you what happened?"

"No."

Zig started to explain as they walked to the car. He was still talking about the previous night as the car pulled up at the house.

Helen switched off the engine, saying, "Sounds like the whole thing was well planned."

Since arriving in town, she had established a successful jewellery business without any help from her husband. Peter's business had grown steadily as well but she still wished that he would spend more time at home. However, she did understood what was driving him to succeed.

While Zig unpacked the car, Hamish woke up in another world. After sleeping well, apart from being a little stiff and sore, he felt much better. Hopping out of bed, he discovered to his shock and horror that someone or something had dressed him in the same multi-coloured tunic the Ebrags wore. Sometime during the night, someone had also left a jug of water and a bowl of nuts and berries on the table next to the bed. Hungry, he scoffed everything down and followed it with a long cool drink.

Walking over to the door of the grass hut, Hamish stuck his head out and watched the Ebrags scurry about the town.

So I wasn't dreaming, he thought.

From what the Ebrags had been saying on the way back to their palace ... village ... he'd had great visions of a large city full of magnificent buildings. There were perfect rows of beautifully constructed grass huts set out symmetrically on the side of a hill. Hamish couldn't help but notice they were all identical.

"It's so gloomy outside," Hamish said, looking up. There wasn't a cloud in the sky. What he saw made him think about what the gatekeeper had said. The eclipse was coming. The two moons now half covered the sun. It was hard to get anyone's attention, as they were so busy scurrying around. Hamish had a great idea, and called out, "Oh great and mighty leader. I would like to speak to your highness," hoping to speak to someone in authority.

Hamish jumped as he felt a tap on his shoulder, "I wish you people wouldn't do that. It is quite rude. Hmmm, I guess you guys don't know that, do you?"

The Ebrag leader scratched his head, "What is it you wish to talk to me about?"

Hamish smiled at this because it was an amusing habit. The only way you could distinguish the leader from the others was by the large gold ceremonial medallion he wore around his neck.

Hamish said, "I need to go to the City of Light."

"We are going in that direction now. Do you wish to come?"

"Yes. How far is it?"

"The darkness approaches and we must move from here. We are preparing to leave now. It will take nearly two days to get there." The serious expression on the leader's face worried Hamish. "This is a dangerous time. You must stay with us, the darkness is not a place you want to be, and there is a creature that we fear," he said, with genuine apprehension in his voice. Hamish wanting to know all about the danger asked, "What's that?"

"The Scragitch. It's a ferocious, blood-thirsty animal. It hunts us down and kills us if we stray away from each other. There is nothing left when it has finished. That is why we scurry around in numbers to try to watch out for each other. When my people are out of danger, we will take you to the City of Light."

"I will come with you, but may I have my clothes back, please?"

The leader clicked his fingers, and Hamish's clothes appeared magically in front of him, washed, cleaned and neatly folded. Even his old running shoes were spotless.

"Thanks," he said, as he walked off to the hut to change. Hamish hurried, as all the Ebrags gathered in the village centre, ready to start marching out as soon as their leader gave the sign to leave.

The exodus was about to commence.

CHAPTER 26

ACCEPTING THE TRUTH

Marcus woke up with a start and couldn't believe it was so late in the morning. It took a few moments for him to realise where he was. He twisted around and looked across at his sister. She was already sitting up, stretching out her arms, yawning loudly, "That was really comfortable. I slept really well."

"It sure was," said Marcus, breaking into a yawn himself. "Isobel's still asleep, I see"

"Well, it was really early when we got here." She swung her legs over the edge of the bed and asked her brother, "Anyway what did happen last night?"

"I'm not sure, but it'll have something to do with Dad's game, I expect."

"That thing we travelled through to get here, what was it?"

"Not sure, but I remember reading something about it in a magazine." He thought for a couple of seconds, trying to think of the name.

Rosie glared at her brother, "What on earth are you talking about?"

"Rosie, it was a story about someone who reckons they once travelled down a tunnel of light, like we did. They're called wormholes and apparently you can use them to travel through the universe."

Rosie sighed impatiently, "That's totally ridiculous. You really do say some weird things you know."

"Well at least I'm trying to explain what's going on," he shot back angrily. "What's your explanation?"

"No need to get angry. I'm only saying this is all a little hard to believe." Rosie sighed, and looked directly at her brother, "I'm sorry. It is just that I thought I was going to drown this morning. If it wasn't for those creat... um, people, we would all have died. It was frightening." She shivered involuntarily as she remembered how the freezing cold water closed in around her. "What are we going to do?"

Isobel yawned loudly, interrupting the conversation. As the twins turned towards her, the bluestone door rolled open behind them. Isobel threw her legs over the side of the bed, "Good morn..." she started to say, then — she screamed, "Look out!" as she quickly pulled her legs back up onto the bed. The twins spun around to see what was going on behind them. Three huge black panthers were standing at the door with Pieter, who looked particularly tired, and Magda, who was standing behind them.

Rosie breathed a sigh of relief when she recognised the creatures, "It's okay Isobel, we know them."

With the look of astonishment on her face, Isobel asked, "How? When?"

"Last week, when we first played the game," said Rosie as she jumped down off the bed.

Isobel was miffed. "Thanks for telling me," she glared harshly at Rosie.

"I forgot."

"Yeah right," she said angry that her friend was hiding things from her.

Marcus greeted the Imitators.

"Hello Marcus," said Imagen, "and you too Rosie."

"And who is this?" asked Marcus, pointing to the third Imitator.

"My name is Mirra. I was Isobel's imitator when she started playing the game last night."

"How did you get here, Imagen?" asked Rosie.

"Pieter brought us here. He has travelled many hours to find us," he said.

Rosie looked directly across at Pieter and Magda and said, "Thank you for rescuing us last night."

"Lucky you. Last night fishing late. Light tunnel come boat near. Splash water you."

Magda more worried about feeding them said, "Come now. Eat," indicating they were to follow her to the dining room. The three Imitators followed along behind. Rosie explained to Isobel where the Imitators fitted into the picture, as they all walked along.

Everyone ate in silence, which seemed to be the custom here. Magda served up poached fish, cooked mushrooms, and then poured steaming hot milk into big mugs. Slvad and Pieter ate with their hands as they had the previous night. Once again, when they'd finished eating, Magda brought them warm, wet towels to wipe their hands.

Both Marcus and Isobel were anxious to ask more questions but they sat quietly not wanting to offend their hosts.

Pieter stood up from the table and said, "Come now Slvad. Work we do. Day good child. Day good, Protector."

Magda came over to clean up the table, saying, "Stay now here you. Clean up I."

Isobel stood up to help but Imagen whispered, just enough for her to hear, "Sit down or you will offend her."

She sat down again, "Sorry, I was only trying to help."

"I understand that. These people like to look after themselves and you are their special guests. You are the first travellers this world has seen for nearly a hundred years. Pieter and most of the other elders believe you are a sign that Dalastar will soon return and open the gateway to the universe."

Marcus was a little puzzled, "How can we be a sign?"

"Let's start with what we know. You are now part of the game you started to play last week. We believe a powerful burst of energy unexpectedly formed in your world, which then carried you into ours."

Marcus smirked at Rosie, "See, told you so."

Rosie's response was quick and snappy, "All right then, Marcus. So what are you going to do to get us home again?"

Isobel nudged Rosie with her elbow, "Shut up you two. I want to listen to what Imagen has to say."

Imagen continued, "As you know, when you landed in the lake, Pieter and Magda saw this as a sign. Remember what the gatekeeper said, it was a hundred years ago when he locked the gateway. Well, when you three plummeted into the lake, out of nowhere, Pieter originally thought Dalastar had returned. After cleaning you up and giving you somewhere to sleep, Pieter, and his brother set out to find us. They travelled for many hours last night to reach the watchtower. Fortunately we were there trying to find you. From what Pieter told us you three were lucky to survive."

"We were," said Rosie, shuddering again with the thought.

Marcus worried about his friend, said, "Do you know what happened to Hamish?"

"No, but Reflekta is looking for him now."

"Who's Reflekta?"

"Reflekta was originally Hamish's image. He was not pleased when the tunnel squashed him. Hamish was a difficult creature to imitate."

Marcus knew what had caused that, and in a serious tone said, "Yes, he had a loose connection."

This comment broke the tension and Rosie and Isobel laughed heartily.

"Very funny, Marcus," said Rosie, with a huge smile on her face.

"What?" Marcus asked, then realised what he'd said, smiled, and laughed as well.

Rosie turned her mind back to more serious matters, asked Imagen, "Who are these people?"

"And why do they speak so badly?" asked Marcus, forgetting his manners.

Imagen growled at Marcus, "Do not judge them by the way they speak. They are brave and thoughtful and their actions always speak louder than their words."

Marcus, red faced and embarrassed, said, "Sorry. I didn't mean that."

"Good and don't forget it," said Imagen firmly and then turned to Rosie and answered her question.

"These people are known as the Lacwevelds. They are crystal miners and dwell in the caves they work in. When the gateway was open, these mines produced the most exquisite crystals and jewels. Buyers from all over the cosmos bought them, transporting and selling them all over the universe. More importantly, this mine produced crystals which were used to make weapons, both to defend ourselves and attack the enemy, when the need arose." He paused a little before going on, "The dark army has one weapon and one weapon only. Everyone knows them as the arrows of death. Once they strike a living creature, that creature is no longer. There are no remains. You simply vanish into the ground, where your soul remains buried forever."

"That's what the gatekeeper said," Rosie whispered to Isobel.

Imagen continued, "The death arrow is not like an ordinary arrow. Once fired, a death arrow obeys the thoughts of the archer who shoots it. A death arrow can stop within a whisker of you, hovering in mid-air, holding you prisoner while the evil one controlling it tortures you, before killing you."

As Marcus sat listening, he felt a lot less courageous than he had before. Isobel and Rosie were worried about what they were getting themselves in to too.

Rosie said, "So what are we supposed to do, Imagen? And how do we get home?"

"Copia and I need to prepare you for the journey ahead. We will guide and protect you here in this world. We can only attack the soldiers from the dark army. We are not powerful enough to attack Lord Theda himself. We were to be the Protectors of the City of Light, but the Council of Commissioners constantly turned down Dalastar's requests to protect the city. When the dark army attacked one hundred years ago, many of our citizens and visitors died, only ten of us survived. Therefore, we, like you, must be careful how we proceed from here. You must train hard to learn some of the basic skills you will need to survive. Our task is to teach you these."

Isobel sensed danger in these words and asked, "Train hard for what?"

"To fight the army of the Dark Kingdom and help protect the City of Light."

Isobel and Rosie's hearts sunk with despair. The expression on their faces described their worst fears. Both girls shook their heads in disbelief, and then Rosie said, "What on earth are you talking about?"

"We can't do that. We have no idea what we're doing," the tone in her voice expressed the terror she felt.

Imagen laid it out plainly to them. He finished with, "You have no choice; you cannot fight this. You two decided to play the game so you have to finish the game."

CHAPTER 27

OF KEY IMPORTANCE

Marcus listened attentively to what Imagen had to say about the dangers that lay ahead. "Hang on a second. I've got an idea," and raced off, leaving Rosie and Isobel quite puzzled. Two minutes later, he returned, throwing a purple plastic folder onto the table. "This is Dad's notebook about the game. I tried reading it last weekend but his handwriting was too hard to understand."

Rosie was furious, "You didn't tell me about this. I can read his writing better than you can. Why didn't you tell me about this before?"

"I didn't think it was important at the time," said Marcus sheepishly.

His sister glared at him and grunted a response but no one understood what she said. Rosie removed the notebook carefully from the plastic envelope. She could see the water had damaged the document when Marcus landed in the lake. The ink had run in long lines down the page, and the writing on the first page was completely unreadable. With a great deal of patience, she turned the first page, then the second. The first six pages were ruined. Rosie took her time, slowly peeling back each page. Each page stuck to the next. The others watched on in quiet anticipation. Rosie knew she had to be patient; otherwise, the paper could easily tear, and wreck any chance they had of being able to read whatever information the book contained. She turned another page, and then spoke for the first time in a few minutes, "Look, this page is only damaged around the edge."

Isobel asked excitedly, "What does it say, Rosie?"

"You were right. This is hard to read." Rosie ran her finger along each sentence, trying to decipher her father's writing. "It says here, there are crystals that help protect the wearer. Whoever takes on Lord Theda needs them. It doesn't say where, when, how, or why someone is supposed to find them. Then there's something here about a key."

Imagen had been waiting for this opportunity and said to Marcus, "I need you to empty out your pockets."

Marcus, a little surprised, said, "What for? What's this about?"

"Please do as I ask," said Imagen.

Isobel and Rosie looked puzzled as Marcus reached into his pockets and pulled out an assortment of bits and pieces, and then opened up the palm of his hand. Rosie saw it first and knew instantly what Imagen was talking about, and said, "That's impossible."

The tiny purple key glistened in the light. Rosie stared at her brother for a few moments then across at Imagen. "That's the key to the gateway, isn't it?"

Imagen nodded, "Yes."

"It can't be, it's so tiny," said Rosie.

"You need to keep your mind open to all possibilities, because nothing in this world is as it seems."

Marcus stared at the tiny key lying flat in the palm of his hand, "I never ever thought this was the key. I thought it was too small," as he remembered how big the locks were. He lifted his eyes and looked straight at Imagen, "So all we have to do is deliver this to the gatekeeper. Isn't it?"

"That is correct."

All of a sudden, Marcus was anxious to get going and said, "What are we waiting for? Let's go now."

"No. There are now many dangers between here and the gatekeeper. Firstly, you need to choose your weapons. Please follow me," said Imagen, heading off before they could ask any more questions. However, he'd underestimated Rosie's intuition. As the others stood to follow him, Rosie still seated, said, "Hang on a second. If that's the key the gatekeeper lost a hundred years ago, how did Marcus find it in the boot of our car?"

The three Imitators talked quietly between themselves. Imagen spoke on their behalf, "We do not have an answer for that. Perhaps it is your destiny, and fate has placed it in your possession."

Rosie didn't believe a word of it and said, "No way. The only way for that key to be in the car was..."

Marcus's face changed from surprise to disbelief after reading Rosie's thoughts. "No way Rosie! That would make them over a hundred years old. That's impossible," he blurted out aloud.

Isobel knew the two of them were talking or thinking about something and not including her, "Who is over a hundred?"

Rosie stood up and stomped angrily over to her brother, whispering to him, "Keep quiet and don't say another word, Marcus!"

Isobel asked again, only more forcefully this time, "Who's over a hundred?"

"Mum and Dad," said Marcus. "Rosie thinks they could be Dalastar and Phoebe. Don't you Rosie?"

Isobel just as surprised as Marcus said, "That's impossible. They're the same age as my parents. Anybody could have placed it in the car."

Rosie wouldn't have a word of it, and told them, "It's the only explanation that makes sense. How else did the key get in our car?"

"Sorry Rosie," said her friend. "It's the only explanation you want to believe."

Imagen interrupted, "This is a pointless argument. What is important is that it is now Marcus's duty to return the key to the gatekeeper. Now it is time to follow me, and no more arguing."

Imagen walked towards the entrance to two tunnels in the wall on the other side of the dining room, as Rosie, Isobel and Marcus, looked at each other in stunned silence.

Turning around, Imagen said to the children, "Come on, otherwise we'll run out of time."

It was just after one o'clock when everyone followed Imagen down the tunnel on the right.

They had to watch where they were going as huge rough chunks of hard rock jutted out at various angles making the tunnel narrow and difficult to travel through. It veered off to the left or right, and at times the steepness of the descent varied, but it always continued downwards.

Isobel could scarcely believe it, "How did they find this in the first place?"

"They were mining crystals and jewels and came across it many hundreds of years ago. It leads down to a large cavern in which the crystal miners store their weapons," said Imagen.

Isobel noticed small drops of water forming on the roof. The drips soon turned into little streams of water, and it didn't take long before they were soaking wet. Marcus didn't mind too much, but the two girls hated every minute of it, as they squelched along uncomfortably in waterlogged clothing and shoes. They half slid, half walked down a steep section of the tunnel.

"We must be under the lake," Marcus said confidently to the others.

This intrigued Rosie and she asked, "You haven't been here before. How do you know that?"

"I don't know. I just do," shrugging his shoulders and shivered at the thought. He realised that he didn't really know why, but somehow he knew. Strange, he thought.

Isobel was just as surprised, but didn't want to dwell on it any longer, "Come on you two, let's just keep going."

Light blue crystals spaced regularly along the roof of the tunnel provided a dim blue light. They came to a steep section of the tunnel and slid down the slope on their backsides. When they reached the bottom Marcus noticed how much darker it had become. The distance between the crystals had increased and the light dimmed noticeably. Stopping suddenly, he bent down and picked up a small rock about the size of a tennis ball.

Behind him, Isobel, who was concentrating on the wall, which glistened in the darkness, bumped into Marcus. She cried out, "What'd you stop for?"

"I just thought we could use a little extra light. Illuminate," said Marcus, to the rock. A few sparks came out of the rock and it glowed dimly at first, and then went out.

Imagen said, "Relax, Marcus, and concentrate."

Marcus closed his eyes again and thought about the bright light. He visualised it glowing in his hand. The rock burst into the same bright blue light he'd made in the gatekeeper's staircase, flooding the tunnel with light.

"Yes!" shouted Marcus triumphantly, holding it above his head.

Pleased with himself, he spun around and smiled at his sister.

"I'm impressed," she said.

"There you go Sis, we really are in this game, don't know how, but we are. We do need to take this seriously."

"You don't have to remind me. I'm here too, you know," said Rosie, a little annoyed with her brother.

"And so am I," Isobel reminded both of them. "Come on, getting angry at each other isn't going to help. Let's go."

It was easier now that they could see. The tunnel levelled out and the water stopped dripping from the roof. Turning at ninety degrees, they walked several paces before finding that the tunnel ended abruptly. Rather than a wall of stone, it ended with a dark black hole. Even with the rock light glowing brightly, they could not see into it.

CHAPTER 28

FIRESTONES AND WHITE ARROWS

Marcus moved closer to the dark hole and tried to shine the light in. As he did, the brightness of the rock light rapidly diminished.

Marcus called out, "Illuminate," but nothing happened.

"You can't do that until the crystals are chosen, Marcus," said Imagen. You must make your choice in the darkness. The crystals will reveal all."

Marcus tried to carry the light into the dark hole but it went right out, leaving everyone standing in total darkness. The light glowed dimly again when he backed out into the tunnel.

Imagen growled at Marcus. "Why don't you listen when I tell you something," worried that the boy's curiosity would get him into trouble. He then instructed Marcus, "Leave the light with your sister. You enter first and walk around the armoury. You will know what crystals to choose."

Marcus passed the light to Rosie and walked boldly into the dark room, turning around he found he couldn't even see the others. He stopped, closed his eyes then opened them slowly. At first Marcus thought his eyes were adjusting to the lack of light, but soon he realised that a soft glow came from a circle of blue crystals, set into the floor, providing just enough light so he didn't trip over the objects scattered all over the floor. Swords, spears, bows and arrows, shields and an assortment of other weapons lay covered in a thick layer of dust. A large misshapen rock, much taller than Marcus, protruded through the floor in the middle of the room. He could just make out the crystals of various sizes and colours jutting out of the rock at different heights and angles, glowing softly with different intensities, as he walked around.

Reaching out, he tried to feel for the wall of the dark room with his right hand, to help give him some sense of direction. There was nothing there. He shuffled slowly but surely to his right until he could feel the roughness of the rock wall with his fingers. Cautiously, with his fingers touching the wall, he continued around the room. Marcus was beginning to wonder if anything was going to happen when two crystals glowed brightly in front of him. He continued walking around the misshapen rock and the light glowing from the two crystals dimmed. He went right around the rock but nothing else lit up for him.

Marcus went back to the two crystals, one white and the other blue. They glowed brightly as he stopped in front of them. He reached across and found that these crystals were easy to pull out of the rock.

When he returned to the others, he examined them carefully and discovered they were about forty millimetres long, with absolutely no flaws.

Isobel and the twins sensed the importance of the moment in silence.

Imagen said, "Rosie, it's your turn."

Rosie passed the rock light to Isobel. Not as bold as her brother she reluctantly stepped into the darkness. She took her time walking around the misshapen rock. A few crystals glowed softly then faded out as she continued. She had almost walked around the room when two purple crystals glowed intensely as she came towards them.

She called out to Imagen, "Two of them are glowing. Which one do I choose?"

"Just try one at a time and see what happens," said Imagen.

Rosie reached for the closest crystal. As she touched it, a flash of purple light struck her on the back of her hand. She felt as though someone had stabbed her with a needle and instantly pulled her hand away, "OUCH!" she cried in pain. "One zapped me."

"Try the other one, Rosie," said Imagen patiently.

Afraid about being zapped again, she reached out cautiously for the other crystal. When she touched it a fine mist of very tiny purple lights rose up, swirled around her arm and vanished into the sapphire pendent. Although the crystal was warm to her touch and lifted her spirits, Rosie wasn't so confident so she quickly grabbed the crystal and returned to the others.

"Isobel, it's now your turn," said Imagen.

Handing the rock light to Marcus, she stepped timidly into the dark room.

"I really don't want to do this," she said.

"Just take your time, Isobel. This is very important," said Imagen.

Important it might be, but all she really wanted was to go home. She walked cautiously towards the pile of weapons and started to circle around the room.

A number of crystals glowed as she walked around. Like Rosie, she was nearly back to where she started when a crystal glowed brightly in front of her. She moved backwards, and its glow diminished, "I don't want to do this", she said.

"Isobel the choice is already made. You must pick it up because no one else will ever be able to use it," said Imagen.

Isobel did not realise but this crystal was the one that had zapped Rosie.

Warily, Isobel reached down and touched it. A purple mist twisted up around her arm and then disappeared.

"Rosie," she cried out, "It's warm!"

"I know Isobel, mine's the same."

When Isobel stepped back with the others, the crystals in the floor of the dark chamber burst into action, filling the room with an intense blue light. A tunnel appeared on the other side of the armoury.

Marcus looked puzzled, "That wasn't there before. I ran my hand right around that wall."

"That is right, Marcus. It wasn't," said Imagen. "The passage only opens after the crystals are chosen. Come. Follow me, as your crystals will now reveal the weapons you are destined to carry."

The new tunnel led straight into another room. This room was perfectly circular, about five metres in diameter with a domed roof that came right down to meet the floor. A large square rock, about a metre high, sat in the middle of the room, all five sides polished and smooth, except for two small holes on the top surface.

Rosie asked, "What's this all about?"

"You will find out soon enough," said Imagen. "Isobel, you go first this time."

Isobel had no idea what to do and asked, "What am I supposed to do?"

"Place your crystal in one of the holes in the rock."

Isobel could see what Imagen was talking about and carefully dropped her crystal in the hole on the right. It disappeared from sight. The stone block started to glow purple, the same colour as the crystal. Two bright beams of purple light shot up out of each hole then swirled around each other, spinning like a small tornado. Isobel stared, mesmerised by the swirling lights. Without any warning, a soundless explosion of light created thousands of purple sparks that buzzed around her like bees at a honey pot for a few seconds before vanishing from sight. Instinctively, she raised her hands to shield her face and quickly closed her eyes. When she thought it was safe she opened her eyes and discovered, to her amazement, a beautiful bow and a quiver of arrows that she had imagined when she closed her eyes in fear. The flat bow, floating in the purple light, was beautifully carved from hickory, with an exquisitely stitched leather grip.

Reaching in, Isobel removed the bow with her left hand and with her other hand reached for the quiver containing five white arrows. As she walked back to the others, the stone stopped glowing.

In all the excitement, Isobel didn't see her crystal lying on top of the flat stone.

Imagen said, "Isobel, you need to collect your crystal."

Isobel twirled around and there on top of the rock were the remains of her purple crystal.

She went to give Rosie the bow and quiver, "Will you please hold these?"

Imagen spoke out, "No! You cannot pass them to each other. You know what happened with the controllers. Marcus, do you want to touch the weapons?"

"No way," he said emphatically, remembering the incident with the controller.

"Okay I get the point," said Isobel.

"Good," said Imagen. "It's your turn Rosie."

Isobel walked across in front of Rosie to pick up her crystal and without a second thought, she slipped it over her head.

Rosie approached the rock and dropped her crystal into the same hole as Isobel. The stone glowed purple again. Two beams of purple light swirled around as they had earlier. Again, there was a soundless explosion of light with purple sparks flying around her. Once again, a beautiful bow and a quiver of arrows hovered in the purple light before her. The bow, beautifully carved from hickory, had a grip with intricate stitching on the leather. Like

Isobel, she had thought about the bow just before it appeared in front of her.

She reached in, grabbed the bow and arrows, and picked up her purple crystal. Attached to her crystal, too, was a beautiful silver chain.

"Wow!" We've got the same," said Isobel, a little surprised.

"It seems to make sense," replied Rosie. "We both like archery. This is amazing."

Marcus walked confidently over to the stone, unaware that, behind him, Imagen had everyone move well back into the tunnel. Rosie started to say something but Copia, who had been watching silently, told her to be quiet. Marcus put the rock light on the floor and placed his crystals, one in each hole. As soon as they dropped out of sight, two powerful beams of light, one a deep blue and the other pure white, shot upwards out of the stone. They reflected off the ceiling shooting off in different directions. The light beams bounced of the polished walls and floors, and then zeroed in on Marcus. The white beam hit Marcus squarely in the chest. The blue beam struck him right in the middle of his back. The energy from the light of the crystals poured into Marcus. Unseen hands lifted him off the floor. "I can't move my arms or legs!"

"It's okay, Marcus," said Imagen. "Just try to relax. It will not hurt you."

Rosie saw a bluish white mist surround her brother's body as he rose above the floor. She started to move towards him but Isobel grabbed her. "Wait. Imagen wouldn't let him come to any harm."

"I hope you're right," she said as she reluctantly watched the light from the crystals flow into his body. After what seemed like an eternity to Rosie but was no more than a moment, most of the light withdrew back into the stone. The remaining beams swirled around above the stone, spinning and twisting like a mini tornado.

Marcus peered down to see the light mist slowly dissipate. When his feet touched the ground, he found he could move again. Hovering in the swirling lights above the stone in front of him was a plain leather pouch with a long leather strap.

Marcus was bitterly disappointed, "Is that it. That's not what I was expecting, after all that."

"Before you judge what you have, take a look inside," said Imagen.

After removing the bag from the swirling lights, he slung it over his shoulder and then watched as the remaining light finally vanished back into the stone. Lying on top of the stone was a small white crystal attached to a silver chain just as the girls had received. He slipped it over his head and walked over to the others, who had moved back into the domed room.

Rosie's mind was working overtime, going back over everything that had happened today. She turned, and confronted Imagen. Imagen could see from Rosie's face that she was starting to put the pieces together. "You have seen this before, haven't you Imagen?"

"Yes. Dalastar and Phoebe and their friends were the last ones to come here."

"There is more to this whole thing, isn't there?"

"Yes. I will explain when we reach the dining room."

Rosie, realising that she must wait for the explanation, turned back to her brother, "Show us what's in the bag?"

Pulling back the flap of the pouch, he looked inside. "Awesome," he exclaimed when he couldn't believe what he saw,

Isobel and Rosie could see the reflection of blue light in Marcus's eyes, as it shone out from the bag.

"Pick one up and show the others," said Imagen.

Reaching into the bag, Marcus could feel the warmth generated by the stones. His fingers selected one smooth stone and his hand closed around it. Taking his hand out of the pouch, he held it open in front of the others. The small polished stone glowed brightly. Marcus saw it first, "Look at that, there's a small flame inside the stone"

Both the girls stared closely at the stone.

"Look Sis, you can just see it." He turned around and asked Imagen, "What are these?"

"Firestones, Marcus. Only a select few receive these. Firestones are one of the most powerful weapons we have to defeat the dark army. You should consider yourself most fortunate. You will need to use them wisely. I say this because they can cause a lot of damage, as you will see when you try them out later today. Come, our time here is finished."

Isobel walked over, picked up the rock light, and looked around the domed room. "Wonder if I'll ever see this place again?" she said, walking out to catch up with the others.

As the twins, Isobel, and the Imitators walked back up the tunnel to the dining room, Peter Saunders sat in the kitchen thinking about the events of the last twenty-four hours. The most disturbing aspect of it all was that he was still playing catch-up. Andrew had been ahead of him at every turn, and that frustrated him no end. He had just finished speaking with Chloe on the phone and the news wasn't good at all.

"From what Chloe is saying, there is another machine out there that can generate these wormholes."

"Appears that way Peter," said Zig, feeling quite despondent about the discovery.

"And secondly, what's Andrew up to?"

"No idea, Peter. We really need to know exactly where he is, and then we can find the children."

Helen was beside herself with worry and had been pacing around, trying to keep herself busy, but it wasn't working. She looked at the kitchen clock, "It's nearly three o'clock."

"Helen, please sit down," Peter said, as she walked past him in the kitchen for what must have been the fiftieth time.

"Well, I'm worried about them, Peter. How do you expect me to react?"

"And so am I, Helen. Chloe is working on re-establishing the wormhole. Then we'll be able to determine exactly where they are and how we can retrieve them."

"Yes, well, I'm really worried about them," she said to him again, glaring at her husband.

Zigs' phone rang. "Hello this is Zig ... Hi there, Chloe. What have you found out? Right, just a second, I'll write it down."

"Peter, pen and paper please?"

"Right Chloe, what do you have? Okay." Zig wrote down the numbers Chloe was calling out and he repeated them back to her. "Are you sure about this?" Zig was shaking his head in disbelief. "Thanks, Chloe. I'll call you back soon. Bye"

"What was that all about?"

Zig looked at the figures he'd written on the paper and then up at Peter and Helen. "You're not going to believe this," and passed the co-ordinates to Peter and his wife.

Peter looked at Helen, and then at Zig, "No. That's impossible!"

CHAPTER 29

CONTROLLING THE POWER

Once Isobel and the twins returned to the dining room they, spent a couple of minutes drying out in the warming cave. Then they sat down to eat the late lunch Magda had prepared for them. Steam rose from the plates when she removed the covers, revealing an assortment of steamed fish and vegetables.

Not steamed fish again, thought Marcus. "Ouch," he cried out as his sister hit him hard in the ribs with her elbow.

"Stop being ungrateful," she growled at him softly.

I wish I could stop you from doing that, Rosie.

Well, I will when you stop being ungrateful.

Isobel looked over at the twins, "Stop it, you two. If I can see it so can the others."

Rosie tried to put Isobel off, "What on earth are you talking about?"

"You two. The expressions on your faces give it away every time. You're arguing with each other but not talking. It's as though you're reading each other's minds."

"Rubbish," said Marcus. "It's a twin thing."

"And rubbish to you as well. I can see it." She

paused for a moment in thought. "Hang on a tick, can you two read my mind?"

"No," replied Rosie instantly, not telling her friend it wasn't for lack of trying.

"Definitely not," said Marcus, thinking the same.

Magda coughed to interrupt them, "SHHHH. Quiet eat."

Rosie waited until after Magda had cleared the table and walked away, before asking her important question, "What's Lord Theda after, Imagen?"

"Under the City of Light there are extremely rare energy crystals that emit continuous and powerful light waves into our world. They help maintain the natural balance of our environment here, along with the two moons and our sun. These crystals provide all the energy this planet needs to survive and these crystals are what Lord Theda wants. But if Lord Theda manages to steal the crystals our planet will die. The crystals are under the tower in the middle of the City of Light. His race are ferocious consumers of energy, they do not care about this world or any other as long as they can lead the lives they want."

"So how exactly do we fit in?"

"We need you to stop him from getting his hands on the crystals under the tower."

Rosie and Isobel sat back in shock, while Marcus asked, "Why hasn't the dark army already taken the City Of Light?"

"There are two reasons Marcus. The first is that their Leader, Lord Theda has only just returned, and secondly, the dark army would have had to travel in the sunlight, which they despise. It is only now that the darkness is close that they will try to overrun the city to gain access to the crystal caverns below the tower. We expect an attack within the next two days," said Imagen. "You must stop him from getting to those caverns."

"This is unbelievable, Imagen," said Rosie, who was furious with the Imitators, "Just how do you expect us to do this?"

"Come on Sis," said Marcus. "Just try and chill a bit. It's obvious we need to complete the game to get home, and if that means moving on, I'm all for it."

Rosie turned her anger towards her brother again for getting them into this mess.

"And how do you expect us to do that?"

"By doing exactly what the Imitators tell us to do, Sis."

"He's right you know," added Isobel. "And you know that. We'll just have to work it out."

Rosie felt deflated. Her brother was probably right but she had a terrible feeling something was going to go wrong.

"Don't think that way Sis," said Marcus, "We'll work it out."

"I'm glad you think that way," she looked sadly back at him.

Imagen sensed the uncertainty in the two girls, "Come, let's go outside and I will show you."

"About time," said Marcus, who jumped up out of the seat. He'd been waiting patiently, which was unusual for him. All he wanted to do was try out the firestones. He had a strange feeling about them because since he'd selected his crystals he'd had an inner feeling of quiet confidence everything would work out positively. However, even with his newfound confidence, he still felt a little nervous about it, as they all walked back along the tunnel to the mine entrance.

The view from the cave entrance was breathtaking. "Wow!" exclaimed Rosie. They stood on a large flat area, which extended a couple of hundred metres to the left of the cave entrance before sloping gradually upwards to a heavily treed forest. The steep, winding stairs led down to the lake on the other side. In front of them was a dangerous cliff that dropped vertically down to the lake below. It was the largest lake she had ever seen and continued beyond the horizon to the North and the East.

"It's so beautiful, Rosie," said Isobel.

Rosie stood admiring the view and answered softly to her friend, "Yes. It is."

Marcus looked up at the sky and said, "There isn't a cloud yet it's very gloomy now," and then, after a brief pause, "And there's the reason why." Marcus pointed his finger up towards the sun. "Look, the moons are nearly covering the sun."

The scene before him made him think about what the gatekeeper had told them.

Rosie picked up his thoughts, you really know how to ruin the moment, Marcus, complained his sister.

Marcus shot back straight away, without speaking. Well, it's what the gatekeeper told us. The eclipse is coming.

I know, but sometimes I wish you would keep your thoughts to yourself, mused Rosie.

Without thinking, Marcus spoke his thoughts, "Well I would but if I didn't say it out loud you could just read it couldn't you?"

Isobel had been waiting for this, "Knew it! Didn't I! You can read each other's minds."

Rosie, knowing the game was up, asked, "How long have you known?"

"Since lunch. Now tell me the truth," Isobel enquired of the two of them. "Can you read my thoughts?"

"No," answered the twins truthfully.

"Are you sure?"

"Yes," they said.

Imagen interrupted, "What silly arguments you people have. Come, let's go, time is running out."

Rosie took a couple of seconds to look around once again at the magnificent view. She watched Imagen lead, the others down the steep staircase to the lake. Taking in a deep breath, she followed.

They descended the stairs quietly and walked along the edge of the lake. After about ten minutes, they reached a flat open area. Three large, solid stones, about fifty metres away, sat at the edge of a small clump of trees.

"All right, target practice," said Copia. "Rosie. You go first."

"These are not ordinary arrows. First time around, just shoot one off to get a feel for them," said Copia.

Rosie drew a line in the dirt with her foot, "We'll shoot from here."

Isobel acknowledged with a nod.

Rosie drew out one of the five white arrows from the quiver, setting it in the bow. Drawing back on the bowstring, she aimed just above the stone to take into account the trajectory of the arrow, and let go. Twang, "Cool," she said, then, "That's impossible," as the white arrow continued to climb upwards, flew high over the target and sailed off into the distance. That wasn't the only surprising thing. A trail of white sparks, hung in mid air, showing the path the arrow had taken.

Spinning around in surprise to face the others, she asked, "What's that?"

Copia said, "These arrows are similar to the death arrows, and leave a trail of energy behind them. You will see more in a minute, but now, it's your turn Isobel."

Isobel stood with one foot on the line and took aim at the top of the rock. Twang. The arrow didn't deviate from its path. It hit the rock and a great shower of white sparks and pieces of rock exploded up into the air. A loud CRACK echoed up the valley. When the dust cleared away, everyone could see the great chunk gouged out of the top of the rock. A trail of white sparks hung, glistening in the air for a few seconds showing the trajectory of the arrow.

Isobel, particularly pleased with herself, smiled at her friend, "They go directly where you want them to go."

"Your turn again Rosie, but Isobel is right. You need to tell each arrow where to go," said Copia.

Rosie lined up again and thought about where she wanted the arrow to hit. Twang. The arrow struck, right in the middle of the rock. White sparks and bits of rock fell to the ground as it gouged a sizeable chunk out of the middle of the stone target. The noise of the blast was deafening.

Imagen turned to Marcus, "All right it is your turn now."

"I don't think I can throw that far," said Marcus.

"You need to imagine where you want to hit and the rest will happen, Marcus. Choose one of the stones."

Sticking his hand into the pouch Marcus selected a smooth firestone. Taking aim, he raised his arm to throw. Rosie screamed and Isobel gasped in shock when, without any warning, the firestone burst into a ball of flame about the size of a soccer ball around his hand.

Marcus didn't seem to notice. Throwing it as hard as he could, the fireball zoomed into the ground well short of the target. When it hit the ground, it exploded, hurling dirt and sticks high up into the air.

"Wow!" exclaimed Marcus, "I've always wanted to do that," and immediately reached for another stone.

"Not bad for a first go," laughed Imagen. "You don't need to physically throw it hard to get it to reach the target. Your thoughts control its speed and flight. I just want you to concentrate on where you want it to hit and how fast you want it to hit the target." Marcus tried another four stones without success, each time landing a little closer to the target.

"Marcus, you need to control it with your thoughts, not your muscles," instructed Imagen, wondering if the boy was listening at all.

Marcus looked smugly back at Imagen. "I am listening," he said. Once again, he concentrated on the target. As he took aim, the firestone once again burst into a ball of flame. This time he focused his thoughts, picked a spot and threw.

He watched the ball of fire as it travelled through the air. It smacked right into the middle of the rock target just over half a football field away. The target blew apart, rock and blue flames flying in all directions, the ear-splitting noise of the explosion echoing off the valley walls.

"Yes!" he yelled in excitement.

"What do you think of that, Sis?"

"Oh, that's very impressive," said Rosie. "How about you let us have another turn."

"All right then, go for it," he said, sitting down next to her.

CHAPTER 30

THE SHIELDS

Isobel fired off another three arrows in rapid succession. The result was the same in each case. The arrows smashed right into what was left of the stone targets, each time exploding with a deafening blast.

"One to go," she said and reached over her shoulder only to find another five arrows sitting in her quiver. "That's impossible," she exclaimed, looking across at Rosie. "There are five arrows here and I only had five to start with."

Rosie checked her quiver as well, "Mine's the same."

Isobel was just about to ask the question when Rosie said, "Don't ask."

Marcus didn't wait to be asked and said, "I keep telling you so but you just don't believe it yet, do you? The only explanation is that we are in Dad's game, Rosie, and these things happen. Look at the fireballs; they don't happen in real life, do they?"

"But there has to be a reason we're here Marcus."

"Why?"

"Well there has to be," she growled back at him, getting angry with her stubborn brother.

"Why?"

"Marcus," Rosie demanded, stamping her foot on the ground.

"Look Rosie. We are here. We don't know why we're here but we're here, aren't we?" He paused for a few seconds. "We'll find out soon enough. We have to expect surprises and learn how to deal with them. Remember what Dad says, 'Only worry about things you can do something about.'"

Isobel interrupted them, "The way you two keep arguing is annoying. So stop it! I hate to say this Rosie but... Marcus is right. We are here and we have to accept that. The important thing is that we have to find Hamish and then do whatever we have to do to finish this game."

Isobel left the twins standing there, looking at each other like stunned mullets, before walking off to shoot some more arrows. The destruction of the stones continued with the systematic practising.

The initial excitement was wearing off and the two girls sat down with their backs up against a tree. Meanwhile, Marcus stood at the water's edge looking for some flat pebbles. Selecting a few, he threw them one by one, watching them skip across the top of the very calm surface of the lake, until they disappeared from sight.

"I hope Hamish is all right," he said, worried about his friend, "I wonder what he's doing now?"

"We will find him, Marcus," said Imagen. "A lot of creatures are now looking for him."

"Good."

"Come, we have more to teach you."

The surface of the lake was like a mirror and it reflected the gloomy sky above and the silence.

Isobel noticed it first, "It's peaceful here," she said quietly. "Actually, it's too quiet. There isn't any noise."

"That is because all the creatures of the forest have already left to escape from the coming darkness," Imagen informed them. "Now you need to know how to defend yourself using the crystals around your neck. The crystals offer you protection against the enemy's fearsome weapon—the death arrow. They work when the energy stored within each crystal is released, forming a shield that will protect you. However, you will need to concentrate for this to work properly. This is not going to be easy for you. You will need to picture what sort of protection you require. Isobel you can go first," instructed Imagen.

Isobel stood up and faced Imagen. "Isobel, imagine Marcus throwing a fire ball at you. You have seen what they can do. How would you protect yourself? Just think about what you want and call out, 'Shield.'"

Isobel's first thought, was of something big and strong, strong enough to stop her from being hurt. She closed her eyes and concentrated. The crystal around her neck burst into a sparkling ball of tiny purple lights, and she heard a soft fizzle as a solid purple rectangular shield appeared in front of her. The emblem on the shield depicted two picks crossing each other.

"Open your eyes, Isobel," said Mirra.

"Wow," was all she could say at first. "That's a bit big and heavy isn't it?"

"Don't worry. This is not as easy as you think, and that was your first go," Mirra said.

Isobel asked, "Can I shoot arrows through it from this side?" Without waiting for an answer, she turned around quickly to pick up her bow. This was all it took for her to lose concentration causing the shield to disappear, transforming back into a crystal. Disappointed, Isobel sat down feeling quite exhausted from her effort. "You have to concentrate really hard to make it work," Isobel told Rosie as she came across to sit next to her.

"Yes," said Imagen, "Creating something big and heavy takes a lot more energy. Next time try something a lot lighter, it will be just as strong."

Marcus jumped up to take his turn. He'd had time to think about the type of shield he wanted. "SHIELD," he called out and the crystal responded straight away. A fine misty cloud of thousands of tiny white lights fizzed through the air forming a small white ball before growing into a white shield floating in mid air in front of him. Adorning the front of the shield was a fire-breathing panther standing on its hind legs, ready to fight. It glistened fiercely in the dull afternoon light.

The Imitators recognised the emblem, which they'd been hoping to see, and remained silent. We now have a chance, Copia thought. Reading her mind, the other Imitators agreed.

Yes, replied Imagen in thought. He is the one. Only he who carries the white shield with the mark of the panther can defeat the Master of the Dark Kingdom. However, time is running out, and he still has a lot to learn.

Marcus was quite chuffed with himself as he put his arm through the straps at the back of the shield. It was light and easy to manoeuvre. Strange, he thought. He felt as though he'd done this before, but knew that couldn't be possible. Rosie came over and congratulated him, "This time I am really impressed."

What he asked her to do next really frightened her, "Rosie, I want you to fire an arrow at me. I need to check this out," he said as he waved the shield about.

"No way," said Rosie, not at all sure about any of this. "You could get hurt."

"I need to know if this is going to work," he said excitedly.

She turned to Imagen, who said to her, "You must believe in him, as he does in you."

Lacking confidence, Rosie didn't know what to do.

"Rosie you must," he pleaded. "I need to know what it feels like when an arrow is coming at me."

She walked away for a few moments, thinking, he trusts me to do this.

"Yes I do, Sis," he said.

Turning around she looked at him, only to see him nodding his head.

Rosie picked up her bow and selected an arrow, and walked thirty paces away from her brother.

She turned around to face him, "You ready?"

"Yep. Fire away."

Taking aim, she let go of the bowstring. Twang. Everything seemed to happen in slow motion for her. Rosie watched the arrow leave the bow, white sparks trailing behind it. It seemed to take forever to hit the shield, which Marcus held up in front of him. When the arrow crashed into the shield, a great explosion of sparks fizzed about everywhere, and the brilliance of the blast blinded her temporarily. All she could hear was a triumphant scream from her brother, "YES! It works! It works!"

Marcus was ecstatic. He turned to Isobel, who saw he was grinning from ear to ear. He put the shield out of his mind and it immediately changed back into the crystal.

Rosie was relieved and ran up to him, "Weren't you scared?"

"Just a little. I found I really had to concentrate hard to keep it going. Tell you what though; it does tire you out Sis, even for a short time."

"Your turn now, Rosie, if you wish. It's getting late, and we need to head back to the cave soon," said Copia.

"I'll give it a try," she said as she stood still and concentrated.

"SHIELD," she instructed the crystal. The crystal around her neck disappeared forming a purplish haze as it had for Isobel. To her surprise, the shape of a purple shield appeared before her, slightly smaller than Marcus's shield. The distinctive symbol of the fire-breathing panther stood out clearly.

Rosie struggled, her heart wasn't really in it anymore, and the effort combined with everything else she was thinking about, destroyed her concentration. The shield changed back to its crystal form.

Disappointed, she cried out, "Oh! Sorry about that."

"Don't worry about it, Sis, you did well," said Marcus.

"Not well enough," said Rosie, thoroughly dissatisfied with her effort.

Marcus said, "Don't worry Sis. We'll try again tomorrow. I am sure you'll master it."

"You did well," said Isobel, trying to encourage her friend.

Rosie's disappointment showed and no matter what they said to encourage her, it did not change how she felt. "Thanks, but I know it wasn't good enough."

Marcus looked across the lake and watched a yellow ripple move over the lake's surface, just off the beach. He gazed across the lake again, but saw nothing. I wonder what that was, when Imagen said, "Come, it is time to go."

As they started back to the miners' cave the girls walked off quickly ahead of the others.

"What do you think?" Rosie asked Isobel as they strode along the path.

"I want to take some of those arrows back home with me, they're awesome. But right now I'm really tired. Something to eat, then I'm going to bed."

"No Isobel, not that—the shields. They were all different."

"I know. Mine is ig and heavy and you two have light shields. I've got a bit of work to do I think."

"No, I meant the emblems on the shields? They were different as well. That's got to mean something."

The girls, engrossed in their conversation, didn't see the hole in the path in front of them. Isobel tripped—her foot disappeared into the hole and her ankle rolled over. She screamed loudly in pain and fell awkwardly landing right on her bottom.

CHAPTER 31

WATCHING OUT

When Pieter arrived on the scene, Isobel was on the verge of fainting and mumbled incoherently. He cradled Isobel in his arms and carried her up the stairs, as he had with Rosie the night before. She was asleep when he laid her down on the stone mattress. Her sleeping figure floated comfortably on a cushion of warm air, as Magda pulled a blanket over her.

She said to her husband, "Man out. Leave fix me," and turned back to the child lying on the bed. Magda could see the severe swelling in Isobel's ankle as she gently removed the shoes and socks. Special cooling crystals placed around the ankle helped to reduce the swelling. "Walk not many days girl," Magda said, talking to herself as she fussed busily over the sleeping girl.

Isobel was sleeping soundly when the other two came to bed around an hour later. They climbed up onto their stone beds. Rosie lay down to read her father's notes hoping they would tell her what was going on. Tired, she soon dozed off to sleep. Meanwhile, Marcus pulled out his watch's instruction booklet and studied it. When the book Rosie had been reading landed noisily on to the floor next to her bed, it startled him. He could see she was fast asleep and went back to reading the booklet. Fortunately, the instruction booklet for the watch had been in its plastic packet when he'd landed in the lake. Marcus had read the booklet numerous times before remembering his father's words to him.

'This watch does things no other watch has ever done before. Read the instructions.'

He was annoyed that he couldn't find any information other than the normal operations of the watch. Opening the booklet he unfolded it into a large single sheet. Nothing. The paper was awkward to handle while he was lying down. Feeling even more tired and frustrated, he dropped it and stared at the ceiling as it fell down to the floor. Rolling over he looked down at the booklet on the floor, and nearly fell out of bed in surprise.

There it was, right in front of him—the individual words themselves didn't give the instructions, but groups of words now stood out boldly.

> Turn the glass to quarter past
> Push down to go through it

Marcus annoyed with himself for not seeing that before, reached down and scooped up the booklet to examine it more closely. The letters that made this text were slightly darker than the rest and it was now obvious; the only way to read the booklet was at a distance, so the message stood out. Dropping the booklet to the floor again, he saw the message clearly. "Wow," he said, very quietly. He lay flat on his back wondering what it meant. Lifting his left arm up above his head, he stared at the watch for a minute or so. With his other hand he turned the glass on the face of the watch clockwise towards the quarter past mark. A fine, orange coloured shaft of light, shot out of the side of the watch, then twisted and spiralled down his arm. It disappeared into the crystal hanging around his neck. A fine orange line appeared on the face of the watch from the centre to the edge. Marcus continued to twist the glass until it reached the quarter past mark. He didn't know what to expect and without hesitation pushed down firmly on the glass. Floating on his bed of air, he waited, expecting something amazing to happen.

Nothing did. Disappointed, he rolled over to reach for the instructions lying on the floor with his right hand while holding onto the edge of the bed to maintain his balance.

A cold numbing sensation surged through his left hand and spread quickly up his arm to his chest. He was shocked to see his arm was the same colour and texture as the stone bed top. Terrified, Marcus screamed but nothing came out. He found himself sinking rapidly into the solid stone bed. His head sank below the level of the bed and a strange brown murkiness surrounded him. He could still see the light of the room above him. Panicking, he started to struggle only to find himself sinking further into the bed. He held his breath for as long as possible. His lungs burned and his head felt as if it was ready to explode. Unable to hold his breath any longer he opened his mouth. To his surprise and relief, he gulped down great mouthfuls of air, even though he was floating in something that was like thick brown murky water. Spreading his arms out wide, he swam upwards towards the light. He realised he hadn't fallen as far as he thought and within two upward strokes, broke through the surface of the stone bed.

When his head poked out the top of the bed, he relaxed a little. It took a few minutes and a lot of effort to reposition himself. Eventually he managed to float on his back. Examining his arms, he found they were still the same colour as the stone bed. Carefully lifting one leg at a time, he saw that they too had taken on the same colour and texture. He definitely didn't want to sink back down again, and lay perfectly still on his back as he decided what he should do next. The best option was to roll off the bed and try to land on his feet. With every ounce of energy, he twisted his body, rolled off the edge of the bed and landed feet first on the floor. When he'd broken contact with the bed, there was a small but brilliant flash of orange, followed by a loud pop. The coldness disappeared and Marcus returned to normal.

The noise woke Rosie up, but Isobel remained asleep. Rolling over to see what had woken her, she saw Marcus standing perfectly still in the middle of the room.

Intrigued, she then felt Marcus' uncertainty as she jumped down off the bed and walked quietly around to face her brother. Reaching out, she went to touch him on the shoulder to see if he was all right. "I wouldn't do that, if I were you," he said quietly but firmly.

Rosie jumped backwards, "You gave me a fright."

"Tell me about it."

"What on earth are you talking about? And why are you standing there like a stupid statue?"

"You're not going to believe this, Sis."

"Try me," said Rosie. "I don't think anything would surprise me in this place anymore."

Marcus shook his head, "I think this will. Watch this and don't scream."

"Why would I do that?" Rosie asked as Marcus reached out and touched the edge of the stone bed. The cold numbing feeling coursed through his body. It wasn't unpleasant, just cold and slightly uncomfortable. This time he was prepared, and watched his arms, body and then his legs change to the colour of the stone bed.

Rosie stepped backwards in astonishment. After a couple of seconds, she whispered to him, "How'd you do that?"

Marcus then plunged his arm, up to his shoulder into the stone bed.

She asked, "Can you hear me?

Marcus nodded his head and tried to talk, and found out again he couldn't make a noise. Pulling his arm out of the rock bed, he stepped back, breaking contact with it. With a loud pop and a flash of orange, he once again returned to normal.

Marcus was excited, "I could hear you but I couldn't speak," he said.

Rosie asked him again, "How did you do that?"

"The watch—the instructions had a message in them. I'll show you."

Reaching down he picked up the instruction booklet lying next to his bed. When he touched it, Marcus turned the same colour and texture as the booklet, with black print covering his body.

"Oops," he said and dropped it, returning to normal. "What do you think?"

"That is truly awesome," said Rosie.

Marcus could see she was thinking about something. Realising what it was, he said, "Do you want to try it?"

"Well no... I'm not sure..."

"This might come in really handy later on."

Rosie wasn't convinced but Marcus as usual was keen to try it. Plucking up enough courage, she finally agreed.

They both walked over to the stone door. Carved out of bluestone, it was a very hard piece of rock. Without hesitation, Marcus placed his hand in the centre of the rock, immediately changing colour to the bluish grey of the bluestone. He pushed his hand deep into the rock. It was like putting his hand under a waterfall only now the solid rock had a thin honey like texture to it and flowed slowly around his hand. Rosie grabbed his other hand and a cold numb feeling surged through her, rapidly changing her body and clothing to the same colour as the bluish grey of the door.

Cool, she thought.

It is, isn't it, replied her brother.

She was happy. At least they could read each other's thoughts without having to speak. Do you think we can go right through the door?

Watch this, he thought as they stepped into the rock door, one following the other. The door was only three hundred millimetres thick and in one-step, Marcus went right through, reappearing in the corridor. Rosie, still holding his hand, appeared behind him. A distinctive pop echoed up the corridor as Rosie broke contact with the door. Letting go of Marcus's hand, Rosie touched the door, only to find it solid again, "That's awesome."

"Yes," said Marcus, thinking of all the ways he could use this in the future.

There was a lot of noise coming from the dining room. "I wonder what's going on up there?" said Rosie.

Marcus listened for a minute, "It sounds as though they're having a meeting. Come on. Let's go up and find out."

They walked quickly but quietly up the corridor to the dining room.

Marcus whispered, "We should hide so they don't know we're here."

"I agree," she said. "But where?" When she realised what he was planning, she agreed. "Good idea," and reached out to hold his hand.

Marcus touched the wall, instantly turning the same colour as it, and then walked straight into the rock face with Rosie following.

Making their way along the wall, they found a spot near where Pieter and Slvad were talking with Imagen, Copia and Mirra.

"We must leave tomorrow," said Imagen.

Pieter nodded, "Do what girl?"

"She will not be able to travel with the others," said Mirra.

"No, she will have to stay here with you," said Imagen, quite firmly. "The emblem on her shield showed us that today. Her skills with the bow will be invaluable to you, and that alone is important. Mirra will stay with her. She must be protected."

"Help girl. Cave protect," Pieter replied.

"Yes Pieter. You have done well in the past and the girl will be safe with you. The skills she possesses will help you fight the dark army."

Pieter, showing a great deal of concern said, "Dark Ruler what know?"

"The Ruler of the Dark Kingdom has returned. The other two must reach the City of Light to protect it. Now we have seen their shields, they each must fulfil their destinies," said Imagen.

Pieter and Slvad looked at each other, and then he said, "Decide Elders girl."

"She will not be able to walk and will slow down the others on their journey," said Mirra, cutting him off. "She will be an asset in protecting the cave. We have seen what she can do. You must get the others to agree."

"Try we," said Pieter, "Leave." The Imitators walked away, leaving the miners to join the other elders to discuss the matter.

Pieter opened the discussion and spoke about what the Imitators had witnessed on the beach that afternoon. He let the other Elders talk amongst themselves. There was much discussion and a couple of the Elders were unhappy the children had intruded on their world. Others argued that Isobel's skills would be useful to them. Pieter remained quiet, sitting in his chair listening to the others as the Elders discussed the matter. Eventually, he called everyone to order.

"Quiet. Come now. Decision what?"

Pieter called on the eleven Elders to vote.

"Crystals decide, yes—white, no—red."

Each Elder dropped their blue decision stone onto the special silver plate, which they used when they made important decisions. Pieter placed the plate carefully on the table and covered it with a white cloth.

He looked around the Elders and said, "Come now. Decision make."

They nodded one after the other, indicating each had made a decision.

The white cloth glowed white and red for ten seconds, then stopped.

"Slvad, cloth lift. Decision see."

Slvad lifted the cloth and revealed the decision stones for all to see.

Pieter announced to everyone in the room, "Girl stays," and smiled. Ten stones glowed white, one glowed red. He warned them all, "Prepare tomorrow battle."

They talked in small groups before heading off to their own quarters.

The elder who had voted against Isobel staying

approached Pieter, "Great responsibility. Die girl. Trouble we in."

Pieter looked the other Elder directly in the eye, "I sure. Good mine. Help needed. Die not girl." Pieter was fully aware of his responsibility for the safety of the girl, and was conscious it rested solely on his shoulders.

The older miner grunted an indecipherable word and walked away.

Pieter and Slvad rejoined the Imitators.

"Decision. Stay girl," announced Pieter.

"Very good," said Imagen. "Mirra will stay with her when we leave to ensure she practises the shield. She must play her role in this to fulfil her destiny.

We will tell the others in the morning."

Marcus and Rosie didn't wait any longer. They were cold standing in the rock, and starting to shiver, decided to make their way quickly back to the bedroom. A loud pop followed after they emerged from the door.

Now, safely back in the bedroom, Marcus lifted the dial on the watch face and turned it back to its normal position. The watch let off what sounded like a hiss of air, and the thin orange line on the cover vanished, as though it had never existed. Just to make sure it was safe, he reached out cautiously, touching the edge of his bed. It was solid.

Rosie, who was worried about Isobel, said, "They can't make us leave her behind, can they?"

"I don't want to leave her behind, but she does have a sore ankle. How about we see how she is in the morning. If she can walk, we will take her with us. If she can't, she'll have to stay," he said.

Hearing movement outside the door, he said hurriedly, "We'll talk about it in the morning. Try and get some sleep."

Both of them jumped straight into bed, pulling their blankets up just as the door opened. Magda and Imagen came in. Magda quietly fussed around Isobel's ankle and said to Imagen, "Swollen still, walk not." Magda placed a pink crystal at the head of each bed, saying to Imagen, "Sleep well help." The three pink crystals glowed for a few seconds.

The twins pretended to be asleep anyway, but they were no match for the power of the sleeping crystals. Within a couple of seconds, the twins were sleeping peacefully.

"Good," Imagen said. "They will need it."

CHAPTER 32

FIRE IN THE NIGHT

A half-day's journey away, Hamish sat huddled with the other Ebrags. They had stopped here just on dusk and now it was dark and bitterly cold. After walking all day, his feet ached. He was tired, cold and hungry. On top of this, the Ebrags talked and talked and talked non-stop all day. He had heard it all, how they did this and did that, better than anybody else.

Somehow, the Ebrags had found nuts and berries again for dinner, and then copious amounts of water appeared from nowhere. He was too hungry and thirsty to ask where it came from and just scoffed it down. As Hamish was about to ask the Ebrag leader a question about their plans for tomorrow a chilling howl pierced the night. He felt the tension as all the Ebrags immediately stopped talking and looked fearfully at each other. Although Hamish sat shaking from the cold night air, the howling still sent a fearful chill coursing through him. He looked around at the silent Ebrags; Whatever it is, it must be terrible—to make this lot stop talking, he thought.

With his voice shaking, Hamish asked, "What was that?"

"That, my Hamish is a Scragitch," said the Ebrag leader.

"Whaaat are they?" Hamish stammered.

"They are our enemies. The Scragitch is ruthless—a huge bloodthirsty animal;it never gives up until it gets its prey," explained the Ebrag leader, as another blood-curdling howl broke through the silence of the night. "They normally live in the woods just over that hill," the Ebrag leader said, pointing back over Hamish's shoulder. "Every time we travel to the City of Light, they come after us. There is no way of stopping them." Again the haunting howl came, this time closer than before.

It made Hamish think back to when he and his father had camped out, back home when the noises of the forest had scared him. What was it that his father had said? He jumped up excitedly, "Fire! Do you know how to light a fire?"

The Ebrag leader jumped up just as excited as Hamish and boasted, "Yes, we can light anything. What is it? What is fire?"

Hamish felt thwarted and sat down again, saying, "Well that's it." However, he kept on thinking about it, there had to be a way.

When another spine-tingling howl rang out from the darkness, Hamish jumped to his feet, smiling as he thought of Marcus and the rock light. "I need two very hard stones about this size," he clenched his fists, showing the Ebrag leader, "and lots of little sticks and branches," he said with a great sense of urgency.

The Ebrag leader said to his aides, "Go and get what he wants." Grabbing Hamish by the arm he asked, "What does this fire do?"

"I'll try and show you. It should keep the Scragitch away from us tonight."

Hamish only had to wait a few minutes before the rocks were in his hands and the pile of sticks started to grow higher and higher. Kneeling down on the ground, he scrunched up some dry grass into a ball, and set it on the ground. Picking up the two small hard rocks, he said, "Here goes nothing!," and smashed them together. As he hit the rocks together, Hamish yelled, "IGNITE!" A couple of sparks came from the two rocks but fizzled out before they reached the ball of dry grass.

Hamish tried again and again as the chilling and fearsome howl continued. The unseen beasts were now stalking their prey, waiting for the right moment to pounce.

"Come on, concentrate," he said, trying to encourage himself. Desperate now, he worked on until several tiny sparks fell down, and a fine twisty wisp of smoke started to rise from the small bundle of grass. Very gently, Hamish blew on the grass, happy to see it flare up and burst into flame. The Ebrags, who had never seen fire before, all jumped back in surprise.

Hamish carefully placed small twigs on the tiny flame waiting until they caught alight. Slowly, stick by stick, the fire grew in size until in front of all of them, burnt a raging fire.

"At least I'll be warm tonight," he said softly as he felt the heat of the fire warming his freezing cold body.

The Ebrag leader scratched his head before moving closer to the fire and reached out to touch the flames. Instinctively, Hamish grabbed his arm. "Don't touch... oomph," he grunted, as the Ebrag's guards tackled him to the ground and sat on him.

"Our leader is great. You are not allowed to touch our leader."

"Get off me," he growled. "He'll get burnt."

Just as he said the words, a large ember exploded from the fire and flew down the front of the leader's tunic.

The Ebrag leader immediately started jumping madly up and down, "It hurts!" he cried out.

Hamish screamed out, "Let me up! I can help him!"

"Let him go," wailed their leader.

Hamish felt the weight move off his back, stood up, and grabbed a jug of water, which he poured down the front of the leader's tunic.

The little leader looked up, very wet but relieved, "Thank you."

Hamish explained, "Fire is dangerous, you must be careful. Do you understand?"

"Of course we understand."

"Good" said Hamish as a succession of blood-curdling howls pierced the night. The Ebrags huddled closer together in fear. They muttered amongst themselves.

"There's more than one out there," said Hamish.

"How does this fire help us?" asked the Ebrag leader.

"It will keep the beasts away from us. We will need to build another three fires." Dropping to his knees, Hamish drew a plan in the dirt, "Get the others to put a pile of sticks here, here and here," he pointed, "Then get everyone to sit in this area."

"Do as our Hamish says," commanded their leader.

In typical Ebrag fashion, they all scurried around and, in virtually no time at all, had a collection of twigs, sticks, and branches neatly stacked in three separate piles, exactly according to Hamish's plan.

Picking up a burning stick, Hamish went around each pile, lighting them one at a time. Looking around at the four fires, now burning strongly, Hamish felt proud of himself.

"I will need four helpers to keep the fires going tonight," he said to the Ebrag leader.

"Consider it done," and as the Ebrag leader clicked his fingers, four Ebrags immediately appeared before him.

"The Hamish will tell you what to do."

Hamish spent the next few minutes showing them how to keep the fires going. "Wake me up if you need help," he said, but he knew it wouldn't happen. He knew the Ebrags would be soon better at it than he would. Funnily, that didn't worry Hamish. At least I'm warm, he thought to himself, as he lay down and went off to sleep.

The night passed peacefully except for the occasional howls of the Scragitch; the fires did their job, and kept everyone safe for in the night.

Hamish woke to one of the most beautiful yet strangest sunrises he had ever seen. Standing in awe, he watched as the sky lit up in a spectacular display of vibrant colours. Off to his left he could just see dark clouds gathering in the distance, just above the horizon.

"Wow!" Hamish said to the Ebrag leader, "I've never seen anything like this before."

"It is amazing, isn't it?" replied the Ebrag leader.

However, it was now distinctly darker around them than yesterday, and that would make the rest of the day very interesting. Looking towards the sunrise, Hamish could just make out a line of trees in the distance, "So, that's where they found the firewood last night," he said looking at the edge of the forest, which was only a couple of hundred yards away. As he sat down to another bowl of fruit and nuts, he thought about the twins and Isobel, wondering when he would see them again.

CHAPTER 33

LEFT BEHIND

Isobel woke up to a dull throbbing pain in her ankle, "What a stupid thing to do," she complained. She didn't want to be sitting around all day, "What a pain!"

Rosie, who'd been awake for half an hour reading her fathers' notes, heard her friend and said, "Morning Isobel."

"What's good about it?"

"Geez, you're a grumble bum this morning aren't you?"

"Yeh, well, you're not lying here in bed with a swollen ankle, are you?"

The argument woke Marcus, who said, "What on earth are you two fighting about?"

Isobel ignored him. "What happened last night? All I can remember is falling over."

Marcus summarised the events of the previous evening then looked across at his sister.

Rosie started, "We, I mean I, read some more of Dad's book, well, tried to anyway. I couldn't understand all of it."

Isobel asked impatiently, "Well what happens?"

"There is nothing in it about any of us twisting our ankle."

"That's not very helpful now," said Isobel.

"You're right. We couldn't do much about that. Anyway, it does talk about the symbols on the shields. Apparently, the symbol on your shield means you are supposed to protect the miners' cave, this cave, from the attacks of the dark army. It doesn't say how you're supposed to do that."

"What about the other shields, your shields?"

"Apparently the shields with the fire breathing panthers are given to those who protect the tower in the City of Light. It's obvious Marcus and I have to get there. But, it doesn't tell us how we get there. It mentions creatures who will try to stop us, but not when, how, or where. It's a bit like putting a puzzle together with only half the pieces."

"Well, that's impossible," said Isobel.

"I know. It's really frustrating."

While Rosie talked, Marcus pulled the tiny key out of his pocket and rolled it from hand to hand, "This only means one thing, Isobel. Rosie and I have to return this to the gatekeeper," he said as he held the key up for them to see. "And when we get there, we need to speak to him about what we're supposed to do."

"It would appear that way," said Isobel.

"There's something else you need to know," said Marcus, who then gave Isobel a demonstration of what had taken place the previous evening.

When they told her she wasn't going with them, she sighed deeply accepting her fate. "Well it seems like it's already decided, and anyway my ankle's still sore. I'd only slow you down."

The stone door opened, interrupting their conversation. The three children turned to see who'd entered.

Magda stood in the door, "You," pointing at the twins, "Come now, eat. Leg. I look. Go."

The twins scampered out of the room and headed to the dining room.

Magda walked to Isobel's bed, "Ankle now look. How is?"

Isobel, feeling a little sorry for herself, said, "It's still very sore."

Magda pulled out a purple crystal from the pouch around her waist and held it over the sore ankle. The familiar stream of tiny purple lights exploded out of the crystal, twisting and twirling around Isobel's leg, and disappearing into the swollen ankle. The dull pain gradually diminished and she started to climb out of bed.

"Walk not. Carry we."

"I can try."

"No," Magda said to her sternly and then called out to her husband. "Come now Pieter."

Entering the room, he picked Isobel up and carried her out the door and up the corridor to the dining room to the others.

The twins had just started eating breakfast when Isobel, Pieter, Slvad, and Magda all sat down at the table with them. Marcus glanced across at his sister, you ask Sis, as Imagen walked around to the end of the table. Just as Imagen was about to speak, Rosie asked him, "When do we leave?"

The question surprised Imagen. He thought for a moment before answering. How did she know? Then answered, "We are leaving shortly. You each have your own destiny. Your shield, Isobel, was the first sign. Last night, the Elders held a meeting to decide whether you stayed or not. Their decision crystals said you were to stay and they are never wrong. Therefore Rosie and Marcus, you will continue the journey, and Isobel, you will stay to help the cave miners protect their home."

Imagen waited for the usual questions, but the twins failed to respond in their typical fashion, and surprisingly said, "Okay. Let's go"

They must know, but how? He wondered.

Even Isobel appeared happy with the decision.

Magda reached down under the table and pulled out a couple of warms coats and presenting them to the twins said, "You on journey need."

Rosie held up the thick coats, smiled and thanked Magda, as did Marcus.

"Come on. Let's get changed," said Marcus.

The twins walked quickly out of the dining room and down to their room. Marcus slipped his father's folder in the inside pocket of the thick, warm coat. The clothing was identical to what the miners wore, and fitted them perfectly. Magda and some of the other women in the cave had made the clothing to fit the twins. They changed quickly, stuffing their own clothing into the pockets of their new coats.

"Someone has spent a lot of time making these," said Rosie.

"They're really soft and comfortable. You ready?" he asked.

"Yes," she nodded as they walked back to the others.

By the time they had returned, Magda had a couple of animal skin shoulder bags packed full of food and drink for the journey.

The two girls hugged each other as they said goodbye.

"I'll be okay, Rosie," said a tearful Isobel. "You'd better get going."

"Good luck," said Marcus, and then he walked over to Pieter and Magda. "Thank you for all that you've done for us," he reached out to shake Pieter's hand. Shaking his hand in return, Pieter replied, "Travel safe. Care take. Luck with you. Slvad row lake other side."

"Thank you," said Marcus again.

Rosie did the same, thanking them for their hospitality.

When the twins stepped out of the cave entrance to meet Imagen and Copia, the temperature outside surprised them, as the chilly early morning air bit savagely at the exposed skin on their faces and hands.

Both of them were even more thankful than ever for the warm clothing they were wearing.

The gloomy light of the near total eclipse closed in around them, "Gosh, it's dark now," Marcus said to his sister, "and cold."

Rosie shivered and ignoring Marcus, asked Imagen, "Where are we going exactly?"

"First we travel across the lake with Slvad. Once we get to the other side, there is a steep climb up a cliff face. We then have a long walk to the City of Light."

Marcus glanced at his watch. "At least we're leaving early," he said to his sister.

"Yes. But it's still a long way to go," she said.

CHAPTER 34

THE FIRST ATTACK

After a brisk five-minute walk down to the boat, they meet Slvad and Padraig, who were waiting to take them across the lake.

Slvad said, "Come now, here sit," to the twins, pointing to the back of the boat. The Imitators sat in the bow, Slvad, and Padraig in the middle.

The last time he was on the boat, Marcus had been freezing cold and in complete shock, and this time he decided to have a closer look at it. Beautifully built, the wooden boat had suffered the effects of continued exposure to sunlight and water, giving it a heavily weathered and faded appearance. He asked Slvad, "How old is the boat?"

"Many years. Quiet now," he said.

Meanwhile, Rosie's arm hung over the side of the boat where she dangled her fingers in the icy cold water.

They were about thirty yards from the shore when Slvad asked Imagen to tell them about the Creature of the Lake.

Rosie quickly pulled her hand out of the water and looked up in horror at Imagen, "What creature?"

"Everyone calls her Tallier Fawn. The story goes that those who stare into her yellow eyes shall fall into a watery grave. Quiet now—we don't want to stir up the creature of the lake, she can be very dangerous to those who fall under her stare."

The twins sat quietly, not sure whether to believe what they heard or not. After recent experiences, however, nothing would surprise them. It was quiet, except for the rhythmical splashing of the oars as the two miners powered the boat through the water, and the tiny squeak of the rollicks that followed. The two rowers hardly made a noise as they pulled stroke by stroke, with all their strength. Rosie sat shaking in her seat. Not from the cold, which closed in on all of them, but from the sensation of impending danger she felt, from the creature lurking beneath them.

"I wonder what they meant by the creature of the lake," Rosie whispered softly to her brother.

Marcus replied softly, "I don't know, but I am not going to take the chance to find out."

"No. I agree. I hope we find Hamish."

"Me too. It must be tough to be by yourself in this place."

Then, for no apparent reason, the miners stopped rowing and pulled the oars quickly and skilfully into the boat. Before Rosie could ask the question teetering on the tip of her tongue, Slvad whispered, "Shuuush."

The only noise they could hear was the sound of the water lapping against the side of the boat. Drawn to a yellow glow in the water Rosie looked over the side. Two large yellow eyes stared back up at her. Rosie felt her body go taut, she wanted to scream out, but was so scared that she couldn't even raise a whisper.

A voice, that only Rosie could hear, called out softly, "Rosie, Rosie come to me." Rosie relaxed, and for some strange reason felt compelled to fall into the water. Falling, falling was all she could think of, and she lent further over the side, the yellow eyes beckoning her to come to them. She wanted it to happen and didn't seem to care. She closed her eyes and ... everything became so peaceful and...

Slvad and Padraig had seen the yellow glow approaching from the rear. As they quietly lifted the oars into the boat, Slvad had glanced up, only to see Rosie leaning over the side of the boat. Reaching, he pulled her back roughly, shaking her none too gently until the trance was broken. Once she snapped out of it, he whispered to her, "Quiet. Close eyes now, move not." Marcus heard and did the same.

The creature was now under the boat. They could hear whatever it was sliding along the keel, causing the boat to rock violently from side to side.

Everyone held their breath and sat in absolute silence as the water slapped against the side of the wooden boat. Finally, the scraping stopped and with a splash of its tail, just at the back of the boat, the creature disappeared into the depths of the lake.

Slvad and Padraig sighed with relief, "Close that," said Slvad.

"What was it?" whispered Rosie, who was visibly shaking.

"Gone. Lake Creature. Very bad. Quiet keep."

Marcus put his arm around his sister and pulled her close to him, and asked, "What happened Sis?"

"I don't know. I felt as though I wanted to fall into the water"

"What did you see?"

"Two large yellow eyes. They called out to me. Didn't you hear it?"

"No," said her brother.

"Quiet keep," whispered Slvad angrily.

For the rest of the journey the only noise was the continuous splash of the oars and the monotonous squeak of the rollicks as the two miners rowed across the lake.

Finally, the boat slipped up onto the stony beach and Padraig jumped out, followed by the two Imitators, and pulled the boat further up the bank. The twins were very stiff from sitting still for so long and walked awkwardly on the uneven surface after Slvad had picked them up, then lowered them down onto the ground.

"Come on over here, and keep quiet," Imagen called out softly. "I think we are being watched."

Wishing them safe travel, Padraig pushed the boat out into the water and leapt aboard. Slvad slipped the oars back into the rollicks as Padraig sat down beside him. The two miners waved briefly and rowed off into the gloom of the eclipse, disappearing into the darkness.

Rosie whispered, "What was that creature?" She was feeling a lot better now she was standing on solid ground, but she could still hear the voice of the creature calling out to her.

"That was the Creature of the Lake. Many people have perished because they have fallen under her spell. Slvad's brother disappeared many years ago, when he was fishing. One moment he was there in the boat, and then Slvad heard a splash as his brother fell in the water. By the time he turned around, his brother had vanished. The only sign was the swish of a tail, as you saw tonight."

"I didn't see that, just the yellow eyes and I ... I just wanted to fall into the lake," said Rosie. The thought of it sent a shiver up her spine, "What's going to happen now?"

"Copia is going to check out the path before we climb," said Imagen.

Marcus asked in a whisper, "Won't they see her?"

"No. Remember, we are as dark as the night, and the enemy will not see us. However, they can see you, so you need to be on your guard."

Copia vanished into the darkness without a trace.

"That's amazing," Marcus said excitedly

"No, that's how it is," said Imagen, "You two need to be ready to protect yourselves."

Rosie stood up and walked up and down the small stony beach, "There is only one way out of here, isn't there?"

"Yes. Straight up those stairs.

Rosie was frightened and had another feeling that something was wrong. It was quiet. In fact, it was too quiet. A haunting howl shattered the silence. Rosie scrambled quickly across the pebbled beach and held on tightly to her brother.

She stammered, "What on earth was that?"

"That was a Scragitch," said Imagen.

Rosie asked the question, but already dreaded the answer, "And what are they?"

"They are ferocious creatures who create tremendous terror and panic. All creatures dread their presence, but they themselves fear no one. The darkness is their friend and they hunt mainly at night. It is right to be frightened of them, but do not panic in their presence. They feed off this fear and anxiety; if you remain calm, you will get through this."

"We may need to fight our way through," said Marcus, "That's what this is all about, isn't it?"

"Yes," said Imagen.

Now Rosie was desperate, the fear clearly showing in her voice, "So what are we going to use?"

"Our shields, your arrows, and my fire stones," answered Marcus, quietly excited by the chance to use the weapons he carried.

"What, just the two of us?"

"Yes," said Copia, who appeared behind them. "I cannot see anyone. However, that does not mean they are not there. We still need to be careful."

Another evil howl screamed out from above them.

"You both know the shields will protect you. Your thoughts can control them quicker than your hands; remember that," Imagen told them. "And you each have your weapons, use them wisely. Come it is time to go."

It was quite a steep walk to the top and while they were climbing, they both removed the coats the miners had given them. When they reached the top Marcus said to Imagen, "We need to stop for a rest."

"All right just a short break; we need to get through this forest as quickly as possible."

Rosie sat down in a small clearing, slipped off the shoulder bag and felt around inside. There was an assortment of packages with nuts, fruit, and dried fish inside. Marcus was hungry, and although eating dried fish wasn't his first choice, he wolfed down his portion. They washed down their meagre meal with a couple of gulps of water.

"That feels better," he said, glancing across at his sister.

"Sure does."

After this short break, they pulled on their coats and left the clearing behind. They followed a path leading into the dense undergrowth of the forest. Marcus noticed how dark it had become and looked up towards the sky. Thick black clouds filled the sky. The wind started blowing, whistling noisily through the tops of the trees. The branches creaked and groaned, adding to the terror Rosie, and, to a lesser extent, Marcus, felt. Marcus could only just see the outline of his sister, who was standing next to him.

"Marcus," she called out quietly. "What are we going to do now?"

Rosie hooked onto her brother's arm again, as another fearful howl rang out from the darkness.

Marcus moved quickly forward and tapped Imagen on the shoulder, "What is it Marcus?"

Marcus felt the hairs stand up on the back of his neck and said, "I can feel the presence of someone in the forest."

"So can I," whispered Rosie, surprised at the strange, eerie feeling.

Marcus turned to face her, but didn't get the chance to say anything as she pointed her finger at him, "Your crystal is glowing."

"So is yours, Sis."

"You must be prepared for an attack," whispered Imagen.

"I feel as though I'm living in a nightmare, Marcus," Rosie said tearfully, instinctively grabbing the sapphire necklace her father had given to her. It was strangely warm to her touch.

"Well I'm not happy about it either, but we haven't a choice."

"The creatures of the dark kingdom are close," said Imagen, who was annoyed with himself. The children had detected the presence of the soldiers before he had. The master was right; they were assuming his role.

Over the sound of the howling wind, Marcus heard a distinctive noise off to the right through the undergrowth and caught sight of a tiny flash of green light. Instinctively he yelled out, "SHIELD!" The crystal around his neck disappeared, in a flash his shield appeared in his left hand. The two death arrows smashed into his shield, green and white sparks flying everywhere after the explosive impact, as the wind whipped away the noise of the blast. The force of the explosion lifted him off his feet, throwing him violently backwards where he landed awkwardly and tumbled over.

He lay there slightly winded, but managed to cry out, "Your shield, ROSIE! Make it happen now!"

Rosie stood transfixed by the green trail leading back to the archers hiding in the forest.

Copia stood next to Rosie, yelling, "Your shield! Now!"

Marcus struggled to his feet, and peered anxiously into the forest undergrowth, when he caught sight of another green flash. This time the arrows rocketed directly towards Rosie. Without thinking about his own safety, he leapt off the ground, his arms fully extended, as he dived at full stretch holding his shield with his fingertips. He managed to get his shield in front of Rosie just as the arrows smashed into it. The impact of the collision knocked the shield out of his hands. Sparks scattered everywhere, lighting up the clearing. Rosie screamed as the shock of the blast knocked her off her feet, her ears ringing from the noise. Grabbing his shield Marcus crawled on hands and knees to his sister. In the dim light of his shield, he discovered that Imagen and Copia had disappeared. The twins were alone in the forest.

"Rosie?"

"Yes," she said dazed.

"You have to put your shield up NOW!"

Out of the corner of his eye, he caught sight of another green flash in the distance. "Oh no, not again," he said. This time he calmly manoeuvred his shield with his thoughts alone, and the shield moved in front of them at lightning speed. Two arrows thudded into the shield but this time it stood firm, a shower of green and white sparks scattering harmlessly as the arrows bounced off, broken and useless.

Marcus was waiting for another attack when he heard two muffled screams coming from the direction of the mysterious archers. Without the pressure of arrows flying towards her, Rosie cried out, "SHIELD!" Finally, it appeared in front of her but was very faint in comparison to her brother's.

"It's not from lack of trying," she whispered under her breath and concentrated harder, closing her eyes and imagining a shield as bright and distinctive as her brother's.

When she opened her eyes, her shield was much sharper and brighter than before. Finally, she thought to herself.

Imagen and Copia reappeared out of the darkness as Marcus said to his sister, "That's great."

Imagen, on the other hand was blunt with Rosie, "That needs to be like second nature to you Rosie. If it wasn't for your brother you would have been dead!"

Rosie stood shaking, as the thought finally registered.

Even in the darkness, Marcus saw her face go white and tried to change the subject by asking the Imitators, "Where did you go?" as he put his arm around his sister's shoulders.

"Let me just say, Marcus, that there will be no more attacks from those two," said Imagen.

"Good," said Marcus. He then turned around to his sister, "How are you feeling?"

"I'm okay. I'm sorry for letting you down."

"We were lucky that time, Sis. You have to keep the shield going. It gets easier the more you use it, watch this."

His shield started travelling around him in circles faster and faster then stopped suddenly in front of him. "See, you have to control it with your thoughts. Go on, try it."

"Show-off," she said smiling, and then, in relief, poked her tongue out at him.

Marcus smiled cheekily back at her.

Imagen, knowing the danger around said to the others, "We must keep going before more of the dark creatures arrive. Those two must have been part of an advance scouting party, making sure the miners didn't try to escape this way. Let's go."

Rosie held her shield in her left hand and followed her brother along the path, as it continued into the dark forest. They found it very difficult to walk in almost complete darkness, as the path wound its way around logs, rocks, and trees. The twins tripped or walked into unseen objects time and time again.

Rosie had had enough, and asked Imagen, "Can we use a light to see where we are going? They know we're here, and so do the Scragitchs."

Marcus agreed, "She's right, you know."

Imagen said, "Yes of course, we didn't think of that. We're used to travelling around undetected in the darkness."

Marcus started looking around for a stone but couldn't find one.

Imagen came over to him, "You don't need one."

Marcus was surprised, "What? But I thought that…"

"We only gave you a rock last time so you could focus on something physical and solid," said the

Imitator. "Hold your hand up and think about creating the ball of light."

Marcus, whose confidence was growing, concentrated his thoughts. He imagined holding a rock and instantly a brightly glowing ball of light appeared in his hand. This time he didn't even call out the instructions.

Rosie stood next to him with her mouth wide open in awe. In one way, it was good to be able to see but the light created hundreds of shadows, which added to the eeriness, and didn't help her confidence.

"Here you are Rosie, you hold it," he said.

She put out her hands and felt the warmth radiating out of the small ball of energy. As soon as it dropped into her hands, her shield disappeared.

"You still need a bit of work on that," said Marcus, whose shield stayed loyally at his side.

They continued along the path without incident for another hour and a half before the forest thinned out and finally turned into the massive grasslands characteristic of this part of the world. The terrible howls of the Scragitch continued, still reminding them of the dangers existing in the darkness all around them.

And now, the howls were not far away.

CHAPTER 35

THE PURPLE SHIELD

Padraig and Slvad returned to the cave just before the final darkness closed in around the miners' cave. It was pitch black outside and the miners knew that it wouldn't be long before the initial attack came. Over the last couple of hours, all the miners had been down to the armoury to choose their weapons, and now stood dressed and ready for the battle. They carried an odd assortment of rusted and dirty spears, swords and shields.

Meanwhile Isobel had returned to the bedroom and, sitting on the edge of the stone bed, had been practising with her shield. She had discovered the more relaxed she was, the easier it was to make it appear. After several attempts, she also found she could change the shape and size of the shield. Isobel was about to try again, when she heard someone walking down the corridor. She collapsed the shield as Magda walked in the room.

"Ankle look. Time rest now," said Magda, who placed a pink calming crystal next to Isobel's pillow before examining the ankle. Isobel lay down and unbeknown to her, a fine mist of pink surrounded her head. Within a few seconds, she was sound asleep. Magda would let her sleep, as she would need the rest for the long night ahead.

Pieter met his wife at the bedroom door, "Asleep she?"

"Yes," she answered. "Crystals sleep make."

"Good. Need later girl."

Although the single entrance to the mine made it easy to protect it from attack, the miners had seen the devastating effects last time, when the death arrows penetrated deep into the mine and killed many of their friends. This time they were not taking any chances. They had placed huge stones in a staggered formation in the entrance to the cave to ensure the death arrows couldn't travel directly into the mine.

Two of the miners sat outside as sentries, huddled behind two boulders, "Nothing see," the first sentry whispered.

"Nothing no," said the other.

Although they were well rugged up, the two sentries sat shivering from the cold and their limbs were very stiff from sitting in one position. One of them stood up to stretch his legs. Out of the corner of his eye, he saw a flash of light and started to yell, "Watch ou…" As the arrow slammed into his chest, he vanished in a green flash. The other sentry had just been about to say, "Down ge…" when his companion disappeared in front of his eyes.

"Time go now," he said and tried to move quickly as he crawled back through the maze of stones.

A barrage of death arrows rained down on the entrance to the mines. The arrows exploded against the boulders, blasting great chunks of stone off the huge rocks. The sentry shook off the dust and debris and started moving again. He wasn't as quick as he needed to be, though, and vanished in a green flash as an arrow hit his exposed foot.

Pieter and Magda heard the explosions from the sleeping quarters, and raced back into the dining room.

Slvad met them there, "Two Sentry gone. Vanish. Arrow."

Pieter turned to his wife, "Wake now girl. Shield need."

Magda raced off to wake the sleeping girl, burst into the bedroom, removed the pink calming crystal from Isobel's bed, and shook her gently.

Isobel dreamt she was walking through a thick stand of trees, branches swayed in the gentle breeze, while high up in the foliage birds chirped cheerfully, as she picked handfuls of wildflowers. A huge ugly creature jumped out from behind the nearest tree, grabbing her and shaking her violently. Isobel gave a shriek of surprise before opening her eyes. Even though she recognised Magda, she still pulled away from her. When she recognised who it was she said, "Sorry, you surprised me. I was dreaming."

"Understand this thing. We need you come now help."

"What's happening?"

"Dark army here."

"Oh," she gave a very frightened sigh.

Mirra came into the room, "It will be an interesting time for you."

"What do you want me to do?"

"We need your shield," said Mirra.

Still finding it strange to talk to a panther, Isobel thought, but that's how it is, "All right, show me what you want me to do."

"Follow me," Mirra replied.

Isobel hopped down from the stone bed and hobbled up the tunnel to the dining room. Her ankle was still sore, but it was a lot better than yesterday.

Pieter greeted her, "You help."

Isobel looked at the man who'd carried her up the stairs, "Yes. Of course I will."

Pieter half smiled at her, "Come now. Follow."

She had hobbled a few steps when Slvad picked her up and carried her to the first stone barrier. A couple of miners had carried a comfortable chair here for her, and she sat down, happy to take the weight off her ankle.

Mirra stood in front of her, "Can you remember the cave entrance?"

"Yes," said Isobel, now feeling nervous.

"All right, we need you to picture the entrance and put your shield there, but you have to do it without seeing it. We will take you closer to the entrance once you have made the shield appear. At the moment it's too dangerous."

Isobel heard the explosions resonating loudly down the tunnel from the mine entrance and tried to put the sound out of her mind.

Closing her eyes to concentrate, she drew a mental picture of the entrance in her mind, and then called out. "SHIELD!" The crystal around her neck disappeared, and a small sphere of purplish light, the size of a softball moved rapidly towards the entrance disappearing around the first of the huge stones. Weaving its way around all the stones, the ball of light stopped and hovered in the middle of the cave entrance. In a brilliant flash, a large purple shield filled the entrance to the mine, completely blocking it. On the outside the death arrows striking the shield created a spectacular fireworks display of purple and green each time an arrow struck, lighting up the area around the entrance.

"Isobel you must concentrate on the shield while I go and have a look," Mirra instructed her, before carefully making her way up the tunnel. What he saw came as no surprise to Mirra. A great large purple shield filled the cave entrance, just as the Imitators had seen the day before.

Mirra called out to Pieter, "Bring her up here."

Pieter picked Isobel up and carried her up the tunnel. He lowered her gently to the ground.

"See what you have made Isobel? As long as this shield is here the dark army cannot come in."

The seriousness of the task finally struck home. Isobel took a deep breath, trying to remain calm, and in control. What happens if I fall asleep or get tired? She mused as she worried about letting these people down. Pieter, who correctly guessed how she felt, came over to her and put a hand on her shoulder. "Together work, them stop. Help need. Give we," he said, smiling at her.

"Thank you, that happens to mean a lot to me," she smiled back with a tear in her eye, reaching up to squeeze his hand. These people really do care, she thought. She looked on in amazement as another barrage of arrows hit, cringing a little as the discharge of energy caused a multitude of green and purple sparks to flash outwards, "This is what it must be like standing right next to a fireworks rocket when it explodes," she shouted to Pieter, trying to be heard over the noise.

Pieter didn't know what she was talking about and said, "Come now. Not stay, dangerous." Pieter carried Isobel and Mirra walked behind as they headed back to the dining room.

CHAPTER 36

THE SCRAGITCH

Hamish sat in front of the fire thinking about the other three and wondering what they were doing. The dark clouds he had seen earlier on in the day now completely obliterated the sky and any semblance of natural light vanished. Apart from the light provided by the fires, pitch-black darkness surrounded him. He stared out into the darkness as the sound of a howling Scragitch reached their campsite. The trips into the forest to collect wood for the fires had become less and less frequent. Three of the Ebrags disappeared on their last foray into the forest. Their sickening screams reached the camp, as the Scragitch savagely hunted them down, tearing them apart, limb by limb. Now the Ebrags were not prepared to take any more risks, and Hamish was worried. The Ebrags sat quietly, huddled together in the middle of the camp. They seemed to have already decided their own fate. Standing up he walked over to the Ebrag leader, who was busy discussing something with some of the others. Hamish threw the last bits of wood onto the fires, which burst into flame as soon as they landed on the hot red embers. The brief burst of light even failed to encourage Hamish who knew the Scragitch would probably attack soon.

"Excuse me," he said interrupting the meeting. "What's going on?"

"We need to go soon."

"Yes. Thought that might be the case. Which way are you going to go?"

"That way," said their leader, pointing towards the edge of the forest.

Hamish was puzzled, "But the Scragitch are that way, aren't they?"

"We will out run them," said their leader with confidence, sticking his tongue out in the funny Ebrag way.

Hamish couldn't believe what he was hearing and asked, "How many of you will die?"

The Ebrag leader shrugged his shoulders, "Everyone will take their chance."

"That's a silly thing to do."

"What is a silly?" the leader asked, scratching his head.

"No, what you are doing is silly." Hamish stopped to think how best to explain what he was trying to get across, "Um... It's not the right way of doing it."

"What is the right way?"

"Why don't you stay together? Protect yourselves and fight back."

"We can run quickly."

"But so can they."

"There are more of us than them."

"That's right. If we stay together we might be able to fight them off."

"We have never done that before. Are you sure it will work?"

Hamish looked down at the leader, "The fires worked didn't they?"

"Yes."

Hamish sensed he had convinced them to fight, and spoke quickly, before they had a chance to back out. "Okay. This is what we need," and outlined all the things he wanted them to find for him.

The Ebrag leader called the others together, "The Hamish wants these things. Go now and be quick about it."

"But the Scragitch is out there," one of the aides complained.

Hamish heard the absolute fear in their voices.

"Bring them now," their leader ordered. "But be careful. We want you to come back."

"I will go with them," said Hamish, wanting them to know he was prepared to help.

"No, my Hamish, you will slow them down."

Inwardly he breathed a sigh of relief. He didn't really want to go but wanted to show them his plan could work. Hamish watched as the three Ebrag aides scurried away on their journey, as another chilling howl rang out through the near darkness. This one was so close. He turned back around to talk to the leader, but he had disappeared as well as everyone else. They had all run away at the sound of the last scream.

Hamish found himself standing alone on the edge of the camp. A chill raced up his spine when he heard the heavy breathing behind him. He couldn't move a muscle as a cold, dark feeling of hopelessness descended upon him, smothering him with its weight. For the first time, he felt all was lost.

The hot breath of the creature behind was revolting and stank like rotting flesh. The awful stench, combined with his fear, made him want to be sick. The Scragitch unleashed a chilling howl. Hamish covered his ears as he tumbled to the ground, rolling over onto his back. He shuddered when he saw the creature for the first time. It looked very much like a wolf but it was as big as a horse. The body and legs were wolf-like, but the neck was much longer, like a gazelle, and very muscular. Its head was massive, with an enormous mouth, and two huge, razor sharp, fangs protruding from either side.

The huge animal towered over him, breathing hot, stinking fumes onto his face. Hamish groaned in desperation.

His throat was dry, and with great difficulty, he tried to swallow, realising the situation was hopeless. Everyone he knew, all his friends and his family flashed before his eyes. His ears were still ringing from the fierce, deafening sound of the Scragitch's scream. The Scragitch's face came within millimetres of his own. Hamish looked up in fear; all he could focus on were its huge fangs. Salvia dripped from the ends of is fangs. He shuddered as the hot slimly salvia dropped onto his face. The beast sniffed him. Hamish tried to push himself into the ground to roll away, but couldn't move. The Scragitch let out another bloodcurdling howl close to Hamish's face. The hot, repulsive breath made him choke as another layer of stinking salvia covered his face. He closed his eyes remembering the death of the

Ebrags earlier, hoping for a miracle, but knowing this was the end.

A short distance from Hamish, the Ebrag leader's two aides had whisked their chief away to safety.

He called out loudly to them, "Stop! We cannot leave the Hamish there by himself. He was trying to help us! We must go back," and pulled a short dagger out of his tunic. "You two will help," he commanded them. The two aides were visibly shaking with fear, but they always obeyed their leader.

"We have never attacked a Scragitch before. What will we do?"

He quickly outlined his plan, and then they all scurried back towards the Hamish.

The Ebrags crept up towards the Scragitch and watched as the beast sniffed Hamish's face.

"Now," whispered the Ebrag leader, just as the Scragitch let go a blood-curdling scream. The two Ebrag aides jumped up onto the beast's neck, grabbed its ears, and pulled its head back. The Ebrag leader dived in underneath the Scragitch and completed a difficult jumping handstand while the two aides caught his feet and pulled him up. The momentum of this action helped him swing up underneath the beast, between its front legs, where, with all his strength, he thrust the dagger deep into the beast's chest.

The Scragitch lunged violently backwards in agony. Hamish deafened by the scream, felt the beast move away. He opened one eye then the other and in shock watched two Ebrags riding on the beast's neck. The third Ebrag had deeply embedded a knife into the Scragitch's chest. The beast bucked and kicked violently, flicking its head back, madly trying to throw off its attackers. The deafening screams of anger and pain pierced the night in every direction but the tiny Ebrags held on. The screams of anguish diminished as the Scragitch staggered to a stop then collapsed to the ground, dead. The three Ebrags managed to jump off just before the beast fell down.

"That is how you kill a Scragitch, my Hamish," boasted the Ebrag leader. He and the other two Ebrags stood next to the dead beast, grinning from ear to ear. All of them completely covered in a mixture of blood, saliva, grass and dirt.

"What a... thank you," Hamish was just so relieved to be alive, that he couldn't think of anything else to say. He pinched himself to make sure this wasn't a dream. Hamish and the excited Ebrags were so engrossed in the dead Scragitch, they didn't see another two Scragitchs' galloping towards them. The two remaining Scragitchs, angry about the death of their hunting partner, now sought revenge. Their pace quickened as they headed toward the group.

Out of nowhere, two blue balls of fire, one following the other, whizzed overhead and landed just on the other side of the dead Scragitch, exploding in a cloud of dust, dirt and bluish flames. Hamish and the three Ebrags hit the ground as the first explosion occurred. The two remaining Scragitchs turned and fled into the darkness, howling in a high-pitched howl, sending cold shivers down Hamish's spine.

Hamish lay flat on the ground again, thinking, this is too good to be true, when he heard a familiar voice call his name, "Hamish, Hamish are you okay?" He turned his head towards the voice.

Rosie and Marcus had stopped to rest and to eat when they heard the shrill scream of a Scragitch. This time it was close. The twins looked at each other briefly before racing to the top of the small hill in front of them. They reached the hilltop together and looked down at a campsite about fifty metres away with four dwindling fires burning at each corner. Hundreds of small funny looking creatures were running everywhere, and there, alone in the campsite was a taller figure who turned around.

Rosie was just able to see who it was and cried out, "It's Hamish!"

Marcus gasped in shock, "What's that behind him? It's huge! And look, there are two more of them further back."

"That is a ferocious looking animal ... and it's enormous!" said Rosie, stunned at what was happening.

They saw Hamish fall to the ground as the Scragitch howled.

"Come on Rosie. We have to save him!" Marcus raced downhill through the long grass towards his friend. He saw the Scragitch lean down again and come face to face with Hamish. Marcus thought the worst. The haunting howl they had heard repeatedly over the last couple of hours rang out mercilessly again, "I'm going to be too late!" he cried out as he tried to run faster. "If I can get close enough I'll hit it with a fireball," his hand already reaching into the pouch full of firestones.

Marcus slowed and stopped when he saw the Scragitch reel backwards, screaming in agony.

There were two tiny creatures riding on the neck of the huge animal and they were holding the feet of the one who was upside down. The upside down creature, gripped onto what appeared to be a knife, which was stuck firmly into the chest of the beast. Marcus heard the final growl of the Scragitch as it collapsed to the ground and saw Hamish stagger over to the tiny creatures standing around the dead beast.

Marcus could see another two Scragitchs running toward the group of four and threw one, and then another, firestone over Hamish's head at the advancing beasts. The firestones landed exactly in the right spot; the earth erupted in flames in front of the advancing beasts. It was enough to make the Scragitchs turn and run off, howling, into the night.

"Good shot," he said, congratulating himself. He then called out to his friend, "Hamish! Hamish! Are you okay?"

Marcus ran up to hug his friend but stopped short when he saw the stinking slimy saliva of the Scragitch all over Hamish.

"Hi there," said Hamish. "It's great to see you."

"We were scared we'd never see you again. You'll have to wash before we come anywhere near you. You stink something bad!"

"Thanks, what did you expect? I'll remember that," replied Hamish, who was now grinning from ear to ear.

CHAPTER 37

REUNITED

Rosie walked back down to where they had left the shoulder bag and the ball of light and sat down. Her mind was numb and she was shaking, "I've never seen anything being killed before." Swallowing hard, she sat down resting her head in her hands.

"Rosie come. We should go and be with the others," said Imagen.

Eventually she got to her feet and followed the two Imitators down to the Ebrags' camp.

By the time Rosie and the Imitators reached the campsite, Hamish had washed most of the stench from his face and changed his clothing. He was now wearing the colourful tunic of the Ebrags.

"I owe you two," said Hamish and walked towards Rosie, ready to give her a hug. Hamish jumped back, startled, when he saw Imagen and Copia.

"Rosie, there are two panthers behind you!" he started to panic.

"Don't worry they're with us. They won't hurt you."

"Fine." Hamish wasn't so sure but he did trust Rosie. Realising Isobel wasn't there, he asked the others where she was.

Marcus said, "She's safe. She twisted her ankle yesterday and we had to leave her with the cave miners. We'll explain later."

"I thought that thing was going to kill you," said Rosie.

"So did I," said Hamish. "Thankfully the Ebrags came back and then you turned up."

Rosie said to the Ebrag leader, "Thank you for saving my friend. You were very brave to fight that monster."

"Yes, we were, weren't we? The Hamish is our friend too," said the Ebrag leader, as all three Ebrags stood before them with enormous smiles on their faces.

Rosie chuckled to herself when she saw the little tongues stick out after they finished speaking.

Hamish whispered in her ear, "They scratch their heads when they ask you a question."

"No way."

"Yes."

Rosie decided not to see if this was true, for their heroic actions in saving Hamish was all that mattered. They were cute in a funny sort of way.

Rosie continued chatting away to the Ebrags, and Hamish walked over to talk to Marcus, who was in the process of pulling some food out from his shoulder bag.

Marcus handed his friend some of his clothing, "This should help you keep warm," he said. Hamish quickly pulled them on over the tunic and thanked him. Marcus asked, "Who are these tiny creatures?"

"They call themselves Ebrags," said Hamish and then proceeded to tell Marcus about what had happened from the time he arrived in the Ebrag village to when the twins arrived just moments ago. Hamish paused for a moment as he collected his thoughts. "Marcus I really ... really thought that was the end of everything, and then the Ebrags and you two showed up out of nowhere. I just couldn't believe it!"

There was another long pause before Hamish continued, "Anyway, that's how it turned out for me. So tell me, what happened to you two, and Isobel?"

Marcus wasn't keen to stay here, and neither were the Imitators. He said, "Let's all have something to eat before we head off and I'll tell you once we get going. Are you okay with that?"

"Yes, all right," said his friend, "I can wait."

"Here Rosie, have something to eat," Marcus urged his sister.

She smiled meekly back at him and nibbled away at the small meal Marcus handed to her.

He handed the water container around, "Here, have some of this to wash it down, and then we'll get started."

Rosie, who didn't feel like eating much, was the first to finish. She rolled everything up into the shoulder bag, and slung it over her shoulders. "Let's get away from this place," she said to the others.

The Imitators lead the way, as the party started their journey towards the watchtower. Rosie followed immediately behind the Imitators, with the Ebrags tucked in close beside her. She carried the ball of light, which seemed to give the Ebrags some comfort, while Marcus and Hamish tagged along behind.

For a change, Hamish listened attentively to the others' adventures over the last couple of days, occasionally interrupting with his own questions.

They had been walking parallel to the forest for just over an hour, through the long grass the Ebrags knew so well, when Rosie felt her skin crawl. Danger was lurking. She checked her crystal to find it was glowing. This time, she sensed the danger even more acutely than before. Beads of sweat appeared on her forehead and she shuddered involuntarily.

Marcus felt it as well, and without a second thought, his shield appeared at his side. Rosie had a little more trouble with hers, but eventually it too appeared.

"Awesome!" Hamish exclaimed with surprise, staring at the shields. "When you told me about this I didn't believe you. That's truly amazing!"

"Stay behind me Hamish and you'll be okay. You three thin... thingies ..."

"We are Ebrags," stated their leader with pride.

"Sorry," Marcus apologised. "You need to stay behind my sister's shield."

"Hamish, if you see anything like green light anywhere, tell us."

"Right," said Hamish, who was in a jovial mood now that he was back with his friends.

Marcus turned to his friend, "No Hamish, this is serious. These people fire off death arrows and if they hit you, you are gone forever. Understand?"

"Whatever."

Marcus glared at his friend.

"All right. Fine. I get the point," said Hamish, realising his friend was serious.

No sooner had he made his point with Hamish, Marcus caught a glimpse of a green flash off to his left. Several more flashes of green became visible in the darkness and he started to cry out to his sister. However, Rosie could see the approaching danger, and held her shield out in front of herself and the Ebrags. Three death arrows smashed into it, producing a fireworks display of purple and green sparks, briefly illuminating the darkness. The force of the arrows exploding against her shield nearly knocked her off her feet. Luckily, the Ebrags stopped her from falling backwards. The arrows kept coming down on them, coming in wave after wave. They smashed into the ground with a sickening sound. Thunk. Thunk. Thunk.

Hamish saw it first and firmly grabbed the arm of his friend, "Look at that!" he screamed, tucking up his legs further under the shield. The twins spun around to see why Hamish had called out. When an arrow hit the ground the green grass instantly withered, turned brown, and died, a little puff of icy coldness rising from each small circle. The three friends all stared at each other, wide-eyed, frightened at what they had seen. They didn't need to say a word.

Both shields were busy, protecting them all from the deadly missiles.

Marcus noticed Imagen and Copia had disappeared again and could only guess what they were going to do. He whispered towards his sister, "You okay?"

She growled back at him, "What do you think?"

"All right, sorry," Marcus said, as more arrows rained down upon them.

"Well don't ask stupid questions, Marcus."

"I was only asking." Looking across at her he saw how tightly she held onto her shield and said, "You need to let the shield work by itself."

"I'm trying, Marcus."

Ignoring her he said, "We need to do something to get out of here. Imagen and Copia have gone to take care of the dark creatures."

Rosie turned to find the Imitators had disappeared. She was fresh out of ideas but just wanted to get out of this, and asked, "What do you suggest?"

"We need to fire back and move at the same time. If we make them take cover and create lots of small diversions, we might be able to move further away from the forest; otherwise we'll be stuck here forever."

Hamish tapped his friend on the shoulder, "You mean the same way as we got away from Billy and Fred at the school camp?"

"That's exactly what I mean," smiled Marcus, happy that Hamish had understood.

Marcus remembered when he and Hamish had climbed down a steep rock face to look at some caves near the river on the last school camp. Billy and Fred had seen them go down and waited above. When they came out of the cave, the two bullies pelted them with rocks. The only way to get out was to throw rocks back at them and move while they took cover. Throw and move. They did this for nearly half an hour until they had escaped from Billy and his friend. In this situation, however, they couldn't afford to make a single mistake. He had better make sure they did it carefully.

During a break in the avalanche of arrows, Rosie relaxed her grip on her shield and it fell to the ground. She went to grab it but to her surprise, the shield floated up and hovered at her side. Rosie's confidence grew, and immediately the shield glowed more brightly than before.

"Way to go Sis," said her brother.

With renewed enthusiasm, she grabbed her bow and arrows and winked at him.

"What we're going to do is shoot and move, Hamish and I will move when Rosie fires off the arrows, and you and the Ebrags start running when I throw some fireballs. Agreed?"

Once again, she winked, and nodded her head in acknowledgment.

The Ebrag leader whispered to Rosie, "We can run very fast."

"You might be able to run fast but these arrows will follow you and catch you. You must stay with me."

"Why?" he asked, scratching his head.

She smiled, briefly, at that little habit. Thinking quickly, she knew what she had to say to them, "Because I need brave warriors to help me."

"We're brave," they replied proudly.

"Yes you are, very brave. I would like you to help me"

"Yes," they said in agreement.

Marcus said, "Ready," and he threw three firestones into the forest. Hamish looked on in awe as the tiny stones immediately turned into flaming blue fireballs, "How in the blazes did you do that?"

"I told you before. We chose them in the miners' cave."

"Can I have a go?" and reached into the pouch before Marcus could stop him.

Hamish let out a little yelp, "Ouch! They zapped me."

"That's because they're not yours to use and if you do it again it'll hurt you more. Trust me. Now come on. Let's get ready to move."

Rosie and the three Ebrags moved about ten metres before another deadly assault rained down on them.

"Your turn now," Marcus called out.

Twang! Twang! Twang! Three white arrows in rapid succession flew into the forest. Flashes of white and red in the distance showed the arrows had hit the target. This gave Marcus and Hamish a chance to catch up with the others.

This is how it went on for the next forty minutes, fire, and move, fire, and move. They were just over three hundred metres from the edge of the forest when the death arrows finally stopped. Moments later Imagen and Copia reappeared out of the darkness.

"Well done Marcus and Rosie, your repeated attacks worked well," said Imagen.

"When you attacked, we were able to deal with them one at a time. They will not be bothering you again."

"Thanks for that," said Marcus, happy with this news. He did not want to know the details.

Rosie asked Imagen, "Where to now?"

"Now it is time to go to the watchtower," he replied.

"What's that," she asked Imagen.

"The watchtower is on the outer most edge of the City of Light," said Imagen. "It is where we watch out for the dark army coming out of the eclipse. You will see when we get there."

The Ebrag leader said, "We will show you the way. It is not far now." They scurried off in the direction of the watchtower, everyone else trailing behind him.

Fortunately, the rest of the journey was incident free, and about two hours later, they reached their destination. As they approached the watchtower, the gloomy darkness caused by the eclipse lifted, and they stepped into the normal twilight of the early evening. The heavy burden of gloom and darkness lifted immediately from their shoulders.

"Thank goodness that's over," said Rosie, clearly relieved.

"You can say that again," Hamish agreed.

Marcus's response summed it all up for all of them, "Absolutely!"

All three of them stared in disbelief at the veil of darkness from which they had just emerged. Hanging from the sky, it looked like a black curtain stretching off into the horizon in both directions. Marcus came over and stood beside his sister, who was quietly thinking about her friend.

"Out," Marcus said to the rock light, which immediately went out with a small pop. He put his arms around his sister's shoulders and gave them a squeeze, "You did good."

She muttered to herself, "It's so dark in there and..."

"Yes it is and she'll be fine," said Marcus, knowingly as he guided her to follow the others to find somewhere to rest for the night.

CHAPTER 38

SUFFERING DEFEAT

Just as Rosie, Marcus and Hamish fell asleep in the watchtower, a hooded Commander of the dark army sat down behind a rickety wooden table in a tent the soldiers had erected as a command post. They had set up base camp about fifty metres from the entrance to the miners' cave. The Commander was annoyed with his troops' lack of success and their unexplained failure to capture the crystal mine.

However, no one had expected the Purple Shield of the Miners' Descendents to appear in the entrance either. How was he going to explain this to Lord Theda? As he was contemplating how to handle this, a voice called out from the entrance to the tent.

"Enter," he snapped, angry at being disturbed.

His aide came in, head bowed.

The Commander demanded, "What is it?"

"Two of the scouts we sent to ensure the miners didn't escape, they are dead," said his aide.

The Commander was now equally as surprised as he was furious, "What? How do you know that?"

"There was one survivor who escaped."

"What? Bring him to me. NOW!"

The aide pushed the scout into the tent and had him stand in front of the Commander. The Commander wanted to finish this coward off, but he needed to know more about what had occurred, and demanded, "What happened?"

The soldier stood, head bowed, hands clenched nervously in front of him, "We was waiting at the top of the cliff for de miners, as told to. The others organised three Scragitchs to push 'em deeper into the forest. We fired on 'em and den de white shield appeared and de other ..."

This grabbed the Commander's attention, "Are you sure it was white?"

"Yeh."

"Describe the shield," he demanded.

"It was white. There was a fire breathing panther on it."

The Commander sat down in his chair and swore to himself, "He is not supposed to be here," bringing his hands up to his head, "Was there anything else you saw?"

"There was only two of 'em"

"Well who attacked the others?"

"I dunno," said the scout.

"Why didn't they find you?"

"After the others vanished I hid in the undergrowth."

Any small amount of compassion the commander possessed quickly evaporated. "You miserable coward!" the Commander shouted, standing up and slamming his fist on the table. "Take him outside and deal with him. I will not accept failure. Ensure everyone sees what happens to such cowards. Get him out of my sight!"

The aide took the scout outside, and the Commander saw a sudden flash of green light through the flap of the tent.

Sitting down he began to write a detailed message on a piece of parchment. After he had finished, he called in his aide, handing him the message, "Take this to Lord Theda straight away. Go now."

"Yes Commander." The aide left the Commander in the tent and passed the letter to the messenger.

The Commander knew they would eventually break through the stone barriers. He also acknowledged the resourcefulness of the miners, and their efforts to protect their home. Everyone was susceptible to the death arrows and once they removed the stone barriers, his troops would clean out the mine as ordered. The white shield was another matter all together.

The aide returned to the tent, saying, "The message is on its way, Commander."

"Good. Let's go and examine the mine," and walked out of the tent together.

The Commander surveyed the cave entrance and ordered his aide, "Instruct the archers to aim at the edge of the shield and take out the stone on each side."

The aide gave the order. Hundreds of arrows rained down on the cave entrance. Great splinters of rock were blasted everywhere in a shower of green and purple sparks, but the shield simply changed shape and filled the gaps.

"An impenetrable barrier," said the Commander to his aide, "See where the yellow beast is and bring me an update. I will be in my tent."

"Yes Commander," replied the aide, and ran off barking orders. The Commander stood staring at the shield, quietly thinking about the yellow beast Lord Theda had brought back to them, and the strange little, feeble creatures, that controlled it. He turned and walked off to his tent.

The enormous yellow beast arrived sooner than expected. The Commander pointed at the cave entrance. "I want you to start there," he commanded the strange little men who controlled it.

"All right. We'll start straight away," one of them said, "Come on Neddy. Over there," he called out to his colleague, riding on the back of the enormous yellow beast. He pointed at the cave entrance.

"Fine," Neddy shouted back, over the appalling noise.

Pulling on what looked like reins, Neddy made the ugly and grotesque beast crawl slowly forward with a horrendous noise, as black smoke poured out of its two nostrils. Copious beams of light shone brightly out from its many eyes.

The Commander of the dark army had never seen anything so ungainly or heard anything quite so noisy.

When the beast reached the rock face next to the mine entrance, its abundant, tiny sharp teeth ripped into the hard stone. The noise was deafening. Great clouds of dust blended with the lights, creating an eerie shadowy scene as the beast consumed the solid rock in a powerful eating frenzy.

Inside the cave, Pieter came running down the tunnel, back into the dining room. "Come now quick."

The noise generated from the yellow beast's attack on the rock face reverberated through the tunnel into the dining room.

Isobel could feel the vibrations and looked worryingly at Pieter, "What is it?"

"Enormous beast. Noise loud make," answered Pieter, and for the first time, Isobel detected a hint of fear in his voice. "Show me," said Isobel, wanting to know what it was.

Pieter and Mirra glanced at each other and nodded simultaneously, "Okay," said Pieter, "Come now. Much dust. Noise loud."

Isobel limped along, as quickly as she could, following the others. As they approached the tunnel entrance, the grinding noise drowned out every other sound. It was so deafening Isobel couldn't even hear herself think. Her shield had sealed the tunnel perfectly, not allowing any dust into the tunnel. Isobel closed her eyes, concentrating on the noise, "I've heard that sound before," she shouted but the others didn't hear her. She spun around on her good leg and pointed to the others to go back down to the dining room.

The noise diminished as they made their way back to the dining room.

Mirra said, "What is it Isobel?"

"That noise sounds so familiar, but I can't quite... wait a minute, I know what it is!" Isobel looked directly at Mirra, and asked, "I really can shoot arrows out through my shield, can't I?"

"Yes. You asked that yesterday."

"Sorry. I forgot. I can do this," she said, glad to be doing something positive. "Let's go." Picking up her bow and arrows, she limped back up the tunnel. She was already moving towards the tunnel entrance before Mirra and Pieter had a chance to ask what was going on.

Isobel spun around and said, "Come on. Let's see if we can stop that noise."

Mirra raced to catch up, "Wait! What are you thinking of doing?"

Isobel smiled wickedly, "You just wait and see."

They followed her to the end of the tunnel and Isobel loaded up an arrow, took aim and let go of the bowstring. TWANG. The arrow went right through the shield. "Good," she said aloud, now certain of what she was going to try.

The Commander couldn't believe his eyes when a white arrow emerged from the thick cloud of dust. His disbelief quickly changed to panic when it headed straight toward him. He only just managed to dive out of the way and watched the arrow hit the tent and explode. A ball of fire consumed the tent and everything in it.

Just as he managed to get back onto his feet, another white arrow burst through the cloud of dust. He dived to the ground again but this time there was no need to worry, as the arrow climbed upwards until it reached the top of its flight path. He watched in disbelief as the arrow turned over and fell, disappearing into the cloud of dust. A flash of white sparks followed a loud explosion and another plume of dust billowed upwards and outwards. Despite the deafening explosion and the choking dust, the yellow beast continued to eat feverishly into the rock face.

"Someone is trying to kill the beast," the Commander yelled over the noise, to his aide, "There is nothing we can do about it."

They both stood watching helplessly, knowing they had failed.

Isobel was now talking to herself. "I must have just missed," and released another two arrows in rapid succession, this time at slightly different angles. As the arrows left the bow, she instructed them where to go.

Everyone was watching, waiting for the outcome. The Commander, the aide, and the soldiers of the dark army stood watching as one white arrow, followed by another appeared through the shield, looped upwards, fell down and vanished into the dust again.

The first white arrow hit the rotating teeth of the beast and bounced off, with no damage. The second white arrow hit what Isobel was really hoping for, the fuel tank. A thunderous explosion indicated that it had ignited immediately. Huge yellow flames shot skywards and the mushrooming cloud of thick smoke and dust cast a dark shadow over the surrounding landscape. Flames completely engulfed the beast. At the entrance to the cave, the shield protected Pieter, Mirra and Isobel from the force of the blast.

Outside the cave, the blast knocked everyone over. Picking themselves up the Commander and his aide found that they were the only ones left watching the fiery remains of the yellow beast. All the soldiers had run away, disappearing into the darkness as the Commander and his aide, stared, stunned at the destruction of their plans.

It was now quiet in the tunnel now except for the occasional crackling and hissing from the burning beast. Isobel was smiling, delighted with her success.

Mirra asked in amazement, "How did you know what to do?"

"Once I recognised what it was, it was easy. Anyhow, what's a machine like that doing here?"

Pieter asked, "What's a machine?"

"That thing out there, —it's something we have at home."

Isobel collapsed her shield and walked out into the open. The heat radiating from the burning machinery was intense, forcing her bring her hand up to shield her face. Fortunately, she was upwind from the burning wreck and just caught the occasional whiff of burnt oil, fuel and rubber. Pieter screwed his nose up at the unusual smell and looked around cautiously. "Come now. Back go. Danger about."

Isobel was feeling pretty chuffed with herself and had forgotten there could be another attack at anytime. "I just wanted to see this," she said, pointing at the burning machine, "All right, Pieter. Let's go back inside." As they walked back into the cave, down to the dining room her shield took up its position in the cave entrance.

She sat down at the table with mixed feelings. On the one hand, she was happy with herself for thwarting the dark army's attempts to get into the cave, but she was concerned for her friends out there in the darkness and apprehensive about what might happen next.

CHAPTER 39

TAKEN

Hamish woke up to find he and the others surrounded by Ebrags. The surviving Ebrags had reached the watchtower late last night. The square tower was three stories high, and the huge, silver grey blocks of stone gave the tower its distinctive colour. A narrow internal staircase wound its way up to the top, from a large windowless room at ground level, where everyone was sleeping. Hamish managed to climb over the sleeping bodies without waking anyone and walked outside. The sunrise was eerie. From outside the watchtower, he could see the veil of darkness hanging from the sky like a long, dark, silk curtain. Light on one side, dark on the other, "I bet our science teacher wouldn't believe this," he muttered. Hamish heard a noise behind him and spun around quickly. Thankfully, it was only Marcus.

"For a moment there I thought it was the Scragitch again," he sighed in relief and smiled at his friend.

Marcus was intrigued, "What is it our science teacher wouldn't believe? You shouldn't mutter as loud as you do, you know," and patted his friend on the back.

"Didn't think I was. I was just thinking about that," pointing at the wall of darkness. "I just can't get my mind around it."

Marcus laughed, "Sometimes there doesn't have to be a reason, Hamish."

The boys sat down next to each other, silently studying the strange sky.

Imagen came up behind them, "Both of you lost for words for a change?"

"No. Just thinking," said Marcus.

Hamish, who had been thinking about their adventures, asked, "How exactly did we get here?"

"I'm not sure Hamish. There is one thing I am sure about, and that is we are in Dad's game. How else can you explain the fireballs, the shields, or the rock light? These sorts of things could only exist in a game, and... remember the gatekeeper's story. He told us about the eclipse and the death arrows. We found out about them when we were playing the game in Dad's study, and then when we came here, everything is the same."

"I get it, but it's still pretty hard to believe."

"I agree. I reckon we've been lucky so far. We have to prepare ourselves for anything that might happen. Rosie read Dad's instruction booklet but she could only make out bits and pieces of the how the game works."

"What are we going to do now?"

"Well, the first thing to do is to go back and see the gatekeeper. He had something else to tell us. I just wish I knew what it was."

Marcus turned to speak to Imagen, "How far to the City of Light?"

"It is about half a day's walk from here."

"Good, I want to get back to the gatekeeper today." Marcus thought for a few moments and glanced down at his watch before speaking again, "Let's wake Rosie and have breakfast before we leave."

"You don't have to worry about me, I'm up," came Rosie's voice from behind them. Rosie had walked down to find out what Marcus and Hamish were talking about. The Ebrag leader followed behind her with his two aides.

Rosie sat down next to her brother as they continued talking about what they were going to do. She glanced across at the veil of darkness and said to her brother, "I'm glad we're on this side of that."

"Me too," said Marcus. "That's not a place I want to be with all those strange creatures lurking around."

Hamish left the twins to talk and walked downhill towards the veil of darkness. The two Ebrag aides scurried after him.

"What a great day, my Marcus. When do we leave?" said the Ebrag leader, who then scratched his head.

Rosie and Marcus grinned at each other.

"Soon," said Marcus.

It was then that Rosie noticed Copia's absence and asked Imagen, "Where is Copia?"

Imagen didn't want to worry her, but during the night both Copia and he had heard what they thought was a loud explosion coming from the direction of the crystal mines. "She went back during the night to be with Mirra and Isobel."

Rosie, already worried about her friend, became more anxious with this news and asked, "Why? What's happened?

"Don't worry about…" Marcus started, then noticing what Hamish was doing, and yelled, "Don't do that, Hamish!"

When Rosie saw what Hamish was doing, she was horrified, "Stop him, Marcus."

The twins stood up in unison.

Hamish was jumping in and out of the veil of darkness. Marcus yelled at him again. "Stop mucking around."

"Stop worrying will you!" said Hamish, as he stood half in and half out of the darkness and light.

Rosie stood still as an, eerie, yet familiar, feeling spread through her. Immediately, she glanced down to find her necklace glowing brightly. Now she feared the worst.

Marcus felt it as well, "This is not good," he said to Rosie. "Get back up to the watchtower." Marcus was angry with Hamish and strode purposefully towards him.

Hamish ignored his friend, and continued to act like a fool standing half in and half out of the darkness, half-cold, and half-warm.

Marcus demanded, "Hamish. Get out of there. NOW!"

"Oh, stop worrying." Marcus couldn't call out quickly enough as he saw the dark clothed arm surround Hamish's waist. The creature grabbed him and whisked him away into the darkness.

The two Ebrags immediately went to rescue Hamish, and they too found themselves captured by robed and hooded creatures and were carried off into the darkness.

Marcus screamed out, "NO!" and raced across to the spot where Hamish had stood only moments before. "Hamish. Hamish," he yelled out angrily, and stuck his head through the veil separating light and darkness. Marcus couldn't see a thing.

Hamish almost died of fright when several creatures dragged him off into the darkness. One of them slipped a smelly, dark hood over his head as another expertly tied his hands behind his back, before he had even had the chance to struggle. Two of the creatures dumped him unceremoniously into the back of a cart. Moments later, he groaned as another two bodies crashed up against his. "Who are you?" he whispered to them, wishing he had been more cautious.

He recognized the Ebrags as one of them started talking.

"Be quiet or that will be the end of you," said a shrill, high-pitched voice from the front of the cart.

The three captives lay groaning as they bumped into each other and the sides of the cart, which had departed at high speed and was now taking them further away from safety.

Marcus stood at the edge of the darkness, furious with Hamish for not listening. Whilst angry he was also worried, and yelled out in frustration, "Why don't you think Hamish? Why?"

He wanted to chase after Hamish, but didn't know which way to go. In the darkness, he caught a flash of green off to his right. Marcus recognised the deadly threat instantly, but the arrows were flying towards the others. "Rosie," he shouted urgently. Then he saw another flash of green. Marcus glanced briefly at Rosie and was pleased to see her shield take shape, but the Ebrag leader stood out in the open, totally unprotected. As the first arrow exploded on impact with Rosie's shield, Marcus selflessly threw his shield at the Ebrag leader. The shield wrapped itself around the tiny creature, just as the arrow smashed into the place where he stood, knocking the Ebrag over. Marcus twisted around, to see another arrow. This one was rocketing directly towards him.

He tried to move but his feet were like heavy concrete blocks, stuck in one spot. He called out for help, but knew no one could save him. There was no way his shield would return in time to protect him. His throat was dry, his heart pumped furiously in his chest and a cold sweat broke out on his forehead as he stood there, unable to move. Marcus saw the green trail of sparks spitting out from behind the oncoming arrow. "Sorry Rosie," he tried to shout but there was only a croaky whisper as he closed his eyes and put his left hand up in front of his face, waiting for the inevitable to happen.

Rosie couldn't believe the roller coaster ride of the last couple of minutes. She had felt the danger to herself, then joy when her shield appeared immediately in front of her, and then Marcus had saved the Ebrag leader.

Now she watched helplessly as Marcus stood totally unprotected and facing extreme danger. She collapsed to the ground as she sensed Marcus' thoughts.

She cried out weakly, "No." Rosie felt sick, and was just about to close her eyes when her mouth dropped open in surprise.

A bright blue glow surrounded Marcus, and she cried out happily to her brother, "Open your eyes."

Marcus wasn't aware he was glowing. With the arrow only metres away, a warm sensation suddenly surged through his body. At first, he thought the death arrow had struck him. He heard Rosie telling him to open his eyes, which he did, cautiously, one by one. Instant relief spread over him like a wave, but now he faced a new problem.

In front of him, only millimetres from his hand, a death arrow hovered, quivering and spitting out green sparks as it tried to propel itself forward. The arrow drew the warmth out of his hand and fizzed as it hung before him in mid-air. There was such a terrible, rotting smell emanating from the arrow, he felt sick from the stench. He didn't dare take his left hand down. Reaching around with his right hand, he touched the freezing cold shaft of the arrow. Grabbing hold of it, he tossed it back at his attackers. Throwing it with all his power, the arrow headed back in the opposite direction before exploding in a red and green flash.

Rosie raced down to her brother, embracing him with sheer joy, "You're alive!

"Thanks, Sis," he said, as he stood shaking, "I thought I was finished."

"So did I," she said and then noticed the crystal was missing from around his neck. "Hey, your crystal's gone."

Marcus reached up to feel for himself, when Imagen and the Ebrag leader arrived beside them.

"It hasn't disappeared Marcus," said Imagen, "You have become one with your crystal. You are one of the fortunate few. From now on, you will be able to use the full power of the crystal, which is now inside you."

Somewhat confused, Marcus asked, "What do you mean by that?"

"Lift your hand to throw," said Imagen.

He did as instructed, and as his hand reached the highest point in the throwing action, a fireball instantly appeared. Lowering his hand, the fireball disappeared. Instinctively, he reached for the pouch of firestones only to find it had disappeared as well. "Wow!" he said. "How is this possible?"

"Because deep down you truly believed you could do it," said Imagen. "That is the only way you could have stopped the arrow. You are now ready to fulfil your destiny. We need to continue our journey."

Marcus particularly concerned about his friend, asked, "What are we going to do about Hamish and the two Ebrags?"

"As I told all of you when you started playing the game, each will make their own decisions. He chose his way. You have chosen yours."

Rosie thought Imagen's comment was unfair and said so, "Hang on a minute. They kidnapped Hamish. It wasn't his choice."

"Yes, he was kidnapped. However, he was impetuous and suffered the consequences of his actions. He didn't take the game seriously enough."

"I agree," said the Ebrag leader, who surprised everyone with his reply, "The Hamish has chosen his own path, My Rosie. Thank you, My Marcus, also, for saving me. I will be forever in your debt."

"That's okay," said Marcus, who couldn't think straight and was seriously worried about Hamish. He also knew he couldn't go running off into the darkness to find someone who could be anywhere by now. However, he was also aware of the importance of returning the key to the gatekeeper. Annoyed and frustrated Marcus walked away from the others. He stood staring at the incredible veil of darkness for several minutes, wondering how this was going to finish. Marcus didn't want to dwell on it for too long and made his decision quickly. Spinning around, he walked purposefully back to the others, "You're right. We best be going and return the key to the gatekeeper." He continued walking back up to the watchtower.

Rosie followed her brother and Imagen, and the Ebrag leader tagged along behind her.

CHAPTER 40

THE CITY OF LIGHT

Marcus and the others reached the outskirts of the City of Light just after three o'clock in the afternoon. They had walked at a reasonable pace for most of the day, and the twins were hungry, hot and tired. Even though they felt safe walking in the bright sunlight, the gloominess caused by the veil of darkness, which was always in sight, cast a quiet unease over the group.

The Ebrag leader was disappointed to see the condition of the city, "What a beautiful and magnificent city it once was. It has not been cared for in a very long time," he said, with great sadness in his voice.

Weeds choked the garden beds that edged what once had been busy paths. Thick, thorny vines grew wildly, twisting up the sides of buildings ... hedges, once neatly trimmed, were a rambling mess. Scattered throughout the courtyard and streets of the city, clumps of trees of all shapes and sizes, grew up through the cracked cobblestones. There was no denying the original beauty of the buildings, all constructed from white marble.

"What devastation," said Rosie, as she sat down at the base of a large shady tree. Marcus sat next to her and asked Imagen, "I thought someone said that the City of Light was never in the dark zone caused by the eclipse."

"It isn't, but it sits right on the edge of it, as you can see. That is why the dark army had never tried to take the city before, until Lord Theda came along."

"But they did during the last eclipse, didn't they?"

"Lord Theda is not really one of the dark army. He is originally from another world. Before he arrived, the creatures living on the dark side of the world took part in horrible and evil activities in the darkness but never did they come out into the light. Remember the light reveals all, and these creatures do not wish for others to see them. For each horrible deed done in the darkness, a corresponding change in their physicality occurs. Their appearance is a reflection of their thoughts and deeds. Lord Theda was able to talk, or more likely threaten, them into coming out into the light, which they detest."

Rosie asked, "So what happened when he fled?"

"As you know, Dalastar's weapon was more powerful than Lord Theda had ever planned for, and it pushed his army back into the dark zone. They have never re-emerged into the light, not even the Commanders he brought with him from other worlds. We are not sure what happened afterwards, but we believe the weapon made them less tolerant of light. However, Lord Theda has been able to communicate with them in some way, and promised them he would return, which, as we now know, he has."

"Oh, great," sighed Marcus, vaguely wondering what the future would reveal.

Imagen continued, "Dalastar and Phoebe are not with us, so it is up to you two to defeat him this time. Marcus, you know this, don't you?"

Deep within him, his stomach clenched with nervous tension. At the same time he felt a strange feeling of self-belief from another source which overpowered the nervousness. Marcus surprised himself and his sister with his response, "I know and I'm ready." Rosie looked at him in disbelief and was just about say something when Imagen said, "You will need to go with your brother."

Rosie looked at the other three in shock, "That was when we were playing the game, not now we are in it."

"You cannot escape it, Rosie. It is your fate. Remember, we warned you at the beginning, and as you chose to play, you must live with the consequences and finish the game."

Rosie reached up and felt her crystal and sapphire necklace still hanging around her neck. She looked directly at Imagen and was about to ask him something when he spoke to her.

Imagen had seen the question in the small round face glaring back at him, even before she asked it.

"Rosie. You do not truly believe in yourself. For you to complete your journey there cannot be any doubts."

"All right then," said Rosie. She had had enough, and stood up to vent her anger at Imagen, pointing and shaking her finger at him. "I have been sucked out of my house into a tunnel of swirling light; nearly drowned in a freezing cold lake; and picked crystals that were really weapons. I was almost dragged into the water by an enormous underwater beast. I have been shot at with death arrows on several occasions and nearly had my friend eaten by a wild savage beast. All I want to do is go home." She sat down on the ground in a huff, breathless from her angry outburst.

"I am sorry you feel that way. You and Marcus chose to play the game. You must complete it if you want to return home. That is the only way. Whatever you think or want to do, this is your destiny."

"Don't bring my destiny into it anymore! I'm sick and tired of this destiny stuff."

"Rosie, we will be with you," said Imagen. "You need to help your brother."

"Yes bu... bu... but," stammered Rosie, feeling completely trapped by the situation.

"Come. We will speak with the gatekeeper and I'm sure you will finally understand what you can do." Imagen started to move on.

Reluctantly, Rosie stood up slowly and followed the others.

As they made their way through the city, Marcus remembered the story told to them by the gatekeeper. "That must be the tower," he said, as he looked up at the highest building in the centre of the City of Light.

"You are correct. That is where Phoebe and Alexandria held the weapon that pushed back the dark army."

Rosie felt a strange tingling sensation from her sapphire necklace.

She thought, "What's this all about?

Marcus was curious as he asked with a solemn tone in his voice, "Where are all the people?"

Imagen stopped and turned around to face the boy. "There is no one left," he said. After a moment's pause, he continued, "Everyone in the city was murdered by Lord Theda. Only a handful escaped. Remember what the gatekeeper said: 'their souls lie around the gatekeeper's garden and in the streets of the city where they were massacred.'"

Marcus immediately regretted asking the question, "I remember but I didn't think everyone was killed."

"Yes. It is a horrible thought. Come, we don't have far to go."

Imagen lead the way when Rosie stopped suddenly and Marcus, who wasn't paying attention, walked into her.

"Watch out," Marcus grumbled. "What is it?"

She pointed towards the courtyard and whispered, "The trees, Marcus. We've seen them before." Although only a gentle breeze blew, the trees, dotted randomly over the courtyard, twisted their trunks and branches aggressively at them. The twins heard the creaking and groaning of branches as the trees tried to reach out to them. They took a step backwards.

"They will not hurt you, Rosie. You have the crystals. Reach out to them," said Imagen.

Rosie moved cautiously towards the closest tree and ran her fingers through the leaves. A long thin branch wrapped around her hand and arm and squeezed her gently. Rosie started crying as a feeling of complete and utter sadness surged through her. Shocked at what she felt, she went to pull her hand away but stopped at the last moment. She had never experienced such a deep sense of sadness but she also sensed that the trees in the courtyard wouldn't hurt them. The memory of her father doing the same thing over a week ago flashed through her mind. "I've seen this before Marcus," she said, and with both hands unconsciously stroked the branches.

She didn't get the chance to explain because suddenly the eerie, yet now familiar feeling chilled her to the bone. She glanced down to find her necklace glowing and in a very low voice said, "The dark army is here."

"I know," said Marcus. "I can feel it as well."

The Ebrag leader, sensing Rosie's unease grabbed her by the hand. "Quickly. We need to hide," he yelled and scurried away dragging Rosie with him.

"No," Imagen shouted, but the Ebrag Leader had run off with Rosie so quickly he didn't have a chance to stop them. "Come on, Marcus let's follow them," said Imagen, extremely annoyed with the Ebrag leader.

The soldiers of the dark army entered the courtyard just as Marcus and Imagen disappeared down the alley, following Rosie and the Ebrag leader up the stairs into a first floor apartment.

The noise of troops marching on the cobblestones echoed around the courtyard. Marcus crawled out onto the balcony, being extremely cautious to keep out of sight, and peered over the parapet. "They are circling the tower."

Rosie asked in a whisper, "How many of them?"

Marcus tried counting them but there were too many to count accurately, "Lots, I don't know, I can't see all of them."

Rosie trembling with fear said loud enough for Marcus to hear her, "That's bad."

Marcus had another peek over the parapet and told her what was going on, "They've formed a solid wall of soldiers and …"

Rosie wanted to see, and sneaking up beside Marcus peered over the parapet.

What she saw made her gasp in surprise, "Their faces are terribly … oh no, distorted, they're hideous!"

Imagen came up behind the twins, "They've arrived earlier than we expected. The good thing is they don't seem to be climbing the tower yet. We need to get you into the tower before Lord Theda arrives. Otherwise, it will be too late. Marcus, use your shield to close off the entrance, and make it invisible. Can you do that?"

Marcus nodded.

"This is vitally important Marcus. The tower must not fall into his hands."

"I understand," said Marcus, as he focused on the tower entrance, and put his right hand up in front of him. A white gossamer mist swirled around his outstretched hand, forming a small white ball before it slipped over the balcony, glided across the courtyard, and stopped in the middle of the tower entrance. It then vanished. The shield was in place, ready for action, but most importantly, Lord Theda wouldn't be able to see it.

CHAPTER 41

THE TOWER

Imagen stood on the balcony looking across at the tower and then asked the twins, "How are we going to get you two into the tower?"

Rosie puzzled, asked, "Why? What about the gatekeeper?"

"I'm afraid it's now too late for that," said Imagen.

"We need to be there Sis," said Marcus, resting his hand on her shoulder. "I don't know why but I can just feel it's the right thing to do." Rosie sensed her brother's confidence. It gave her a renewed belief they would succeed. Looking directly into his face, and with a slight nod of her head, she agreed to the challenge.

The twins faced Imagen. "Watch this," they said in unison.

Marcus twisted the face of the watch then pushed the glass down. The orange mist swirled around the twins, disappearing into Rosie's crystal and Marcus' chest. Taking hold of Rosie's hand, they descended the stairs down to the alley. Imagen and the Ebrag leader followed, unaware of what the twins were up to, and then stopped dead in their tracks when the twins simply walked right through the stone-wall of the adjoining building.

Imagen and the Ebrag leader exchanged looks of amazement, "I didn't know they could do that," said Imagen. Imagen thought back to the crystal mine and smiled, "So that's how they knew. Very good."

The Ebrag leader asked, "What is very good?"

"What they have done is good. Come. We will watch from the balcony," said Imagen. "And see what unfolds."

Rosie and Marcus travelled around the courtyard without incident. Every now and then Imagen could see one of the twins elbow or shoulder stick out as they made their way. Thankfully, no one else saw as the twins followed the walls of the buildings and garden beds around the tower, and slipped through the tower wall appearing in the foyer. The loud pop surprised the twins as Rosie finally broke contact with the stone. Fortunately, the thick walls stopped anyone from outside hearing the noise. Smiling at his sister he said, smugly, "How simple was that?"

Rosie agreed, "Mmm, that was but don't be too smart. This is not over yet."

"I know Rosie," he said, this time with a worried look. "We do have to be really careful."

Beautifully carved white marble stairs spiralled up the inside wall of the tower, right to the top of the building.

"The stairs here are like the ones in the gatekeeper's staircase, Marcus."

"It must be nearly three storeys high," he said, as they climbed to the top. Marble railings ran around the rooftop, and like most buildings in the City, were exquisitely hand carved.

A large dome of brown polished marble sat in the middle of the roof. Rosie tried climbing to the top but slipped off a couple of times before managing to perch herself on the middle of the polished dome, "This must cover the entrance to the caverns. There isn't anything else up here. But how would you move it, it looks so large and heavy?"

"Knowing a little about the people that lived here, they would have thought of some way of doing it, but let's worry about that later," said Marcus, twisting the glass cover of his watch back to normal.

Lord Theda strode arrogantly into the courtyard just as the twins reached the top of the tower, and commanded, "Let me through." One of the trees closest to him in the courtyard flung its branches angrily at Lord Theda. A small branch managed to wrap around his ankle as a huge reddish-green fireball appeared in his hand. With a flick of his wrist the fireball blazed its way through the foliage, wrapping itself around the trunk of the tree like a dressing around a wounded limb. The branches of the tree turned inwards trying to extinguish the fire attacking it. It looked as though it may succeed when the tree burst into a ball of flame before vanishing in a puff of smoke. The sickly smell of burnt flesh filled the courtyard before the breeze whisked it away. Without looking at his attacker, Lord Theda pointed to two soldiers and ordered, "You and you go and check what's up on the tower."

Access to the energy crystals was at the top, and Lord Theda knew he had to control the tower to get his hands on them. The last time he had stood here, Dalastar had stopped him from reaching the tower. This time he knew he wouldn't fail. Reports of the white shield from the forest were disturbing but he wasn't going to let this stop him getting what he had come for. The human child he had captured near the watchtower confirmed Dalastar was definitely here. He wasn't going to take any chances.

Lord Theda watched impatiently as the two soldiers walked cautiously towards the tower entrance, "Hurry up. RUN or else," he ordered angrily.

The threat in the order caused the two soldiers to immediately charge towards the entrance. As they came to the entrance, they stopped suddenly, as if they had run into something solid, and bounced backwards, out into the courtyard. A brilliant white flash exploded outwards as the two soldiers hit the ground groaning in agony.

"NOOOOOO," screamed Lord Theda and then cursed, "Damn him!" and with sheer rage, threw a reddish-green fireball at the entrance, with great power and anger. Red and green flames and white sparks showered over everyone in the courtyard. The noise from the explosion boomed outwards from the centre of the City. A gentle wind cleared the smoke away to reveal a white shield blocking the entrance to the tower. Lord Theda's cold black eyes locked firmly on the shield with the fire breathing panther emblem brilliantly emblazoned on the front.

On the top of the tower, Marcus, collapsed to the ground, groaning in agony as he wrapped his arms across his chest as the fireball struck the shield, "That hurt."

Rosie helped him sit up, asking, "What happened?"

Marcus groaned again as another deep sharp pain in his chest took his breath away, and yet another explosion echoed around the courtyard. He felt as though someone had punched him savagely in the chest and this time it brought tears to his eyes.

"He's testing us out," said Rosie, seriously worried about her brother.

"Yes." He groaned again as he sat up and rubbed his chest again. An idea popped into his head, "We need to fight back," he said, smiling mischievously.

Rosie looked at her brother, "What are you suggesting...? Ah, now that's a good idea."

Nobody crossed Lord Theda. He went into a furious rage and hurled another fireball. It spat out reddish-green flames born of anger and hatred as it flew, powerfully and accurately, towards the white shield.

Lord Theda stared in astonishment when the shield simply swallowed up the fireball. Acting like a large safety net, which absorbed the force of the fireball, it flicked the fireball out faster than it had come in. It flew back quickly at Lord Theda, forcing him to react with haste.

Lord Theda had just enough time to put his shield up to protect himself. The force of the explosion lifted him off his feet, throwing him backwards. The red shield flickered on and off a few times after the blow. Its holder was furious and, consumed by anger, unleashed another fireball at the white shield, unaware Marcus had thrown his own fireball down the staircase just moments before. The fireball followed the curvature of the stairs down the inside of the tower, passed through his shield and shot out the entrance.

Marcus raced over to the edge of the tower arriving just in time to see the two fireballs collide and explode a few metres in front of Lord Theda. The explosion knocked everyone off their feet, scattering bodies all over the courtyard. Rosie peered over the edge as well.

Two of the deformed creatures helped a struggling Lord Theda to his feet. Only one other had stood up to him before. The reports were obviously correct. Dalastar was here, but how could he flush him out. Lord Theda knew this wasn't going anywhere and smiled wickedly as he quickly regained his composure.

Marcus ran back to the top of the staircase and threw another fireball just as Rosie fired off a white arrow, both aimed at the middle of the dragon-emblazoned red shield. Stunned by the unexpected impact, Lord Theda saw the next fireball hurtling towards him. He was about to deflect the blue ball of flames when he also caught sight of the approaching white arrow. It was too late. The twins timing was perfect, fireball and arrow striking at the same time. The force of the impact knocked Lord Theda off his feet for the third time. His red shield gave a flicker and a large chunk fell off, immediately disappearing into the ground.

The twins peeked carefully over the parapet. The scene below them was one of complete chaos. Lord Theda struggled to his feet. The blast had knocked many of his soldiers over as well, their weapons and shields strewn all over the courtyard. Lord Theda grabbed one of his Commanders by the throat and whispered menacingly in his ear, "Go and bring that blasted child and those other creatures to me, NOW!"

"Yes Master," croaked the Commander, who was finding it difficult to speak. The Commander saw the fury of the green and red flames burning in Lord Theda's eyes, "Our master will not accept failure. Now go," Lord Theda commanded.

The Commander, coughing and holding his throat, headed off in the direction of the Commissioners' building where Hamish and the two Ebrags were imprisoned.

Another Commander approached Lord Theda nervously, "What are your orders?"

"Death arrows over the top," Lord Theda ordered, pointing to the top of the tower. "It will stop them attacking us."

"Yes master." The commander barked the order, "FIRE ARROWS!"

Wave after wave of death arrows rained down on the twins.

The twins could do nothing to stop the attack and sat patiently, hands covering their ears, under the protection of Rosie's shield. The deafening noise continued as the arrows exploded on contact with the stone floor near the twins. The sky above them turned green, as death arrows continued to fall out of the sky, ricocheting off the purple shield. The attack continued for a couple of minutes and stopped for a few seconds. This small break allowed the twins to fire off arrows and fireballs in return, but they were soon hiding under the protective purple shield as the barrage recommenced. They were taking no risks. "We'll just have to wait patiently," yelled Marcus over the noise. "Until this attack stops."

Rosie simply nodded.

CHAPTER 42

DESTINY

The incident involving the purple shield at the crystal cave was a nuisance, creating unexpected delays to his plans. The white shield standing in his way was a more pressing matter to deal with. Something was going to have to happen soon, he thought, otherwise the stupid creatures making up this army would probably run away in fear and return to the darkness forever.

The Commander whom Lord Theda had nearly choked earlier returned with the captives. The arrow attack on the tower stopped when the commander pushed the three hooded and heavily bound creatures violently into the centre of the courtyard.

"Finally," Lord Theda yelled triumphantly, and walked over to the captives, "What have we here?" He taunted those in the tower, as he lifted the hoods from the captives, one by one.

Hamish stood in the courtyard, heavily bound. His body ached from the rough ride in the back of the cart. He was still angry with himself for not listening to his friend and fearful of what might happen to him and the two Ebrags. Now they were standing before the monster he had heard about.

Lord Theda called out, demanding, "What's a human boy doing here, Dalastar?"

Lord Theda walked around behind Hamish and rested his hands on his shoulders, "Where are you Dalastar? Look what I have," The lack of response from Marcus only fuelled Lord Theda's anger.

Lord Theda was furious with the delay to his plans and screamed out, "Dalastar. You should have hidden them better than that."

The attack from the death arrows had stopped and Rosie took the opportunity to peer down into the courtyard below. Her heart sank when she saw who had appeared in the courtyard. Marcus knew straight away that something was wrong and peeked over the parapet. His heart skipped a beat when he confirmed with his own eyes who was in the courtyard. Marcus was angry with Hamish for getting himself into this mess and despaired when he couldn't think of a way to save his friend.

Lord Theda walked over to the entrance to the tower and called out again.

"Dalastar, look what I have. Maybe you want them back." He flung three death arrows in rapid succession, so quickly they arrived on target before each of the captives had time to blink. The tips of arrows stopped short of them by only millimetres, hovering just in front of them.

"Dalastar, it's your choice, it's either you or your friends," he taunted at the top of his voice. He clicked his fingers and one of the death arrows continued on its way to its target. There was a flash of green, and one of the Ebrags vanished forever.

Hovering in front of Hamish's face, the chilling frostiness of the arrow made his nose ache. Even worse was the disgusting stench of death emanating from it, which made him feel sick to the stomach. All hope of escape instantly evaporated. Before the Ebrag next to him had vanished in a flash of green, he had already been shaking with fear. Now he felt his knees start to buckle and it took every ounce of strength he had to remain standing. He had hoped for a miracle when the Scragitch had him, now he was praying for one.

Rosie and Marcus turned away, horrified at what they had seen. Marcus cursed under his breath.

With tears streaming down her face Rosie asked, "What are we going to do now?"

"There is only one thing I can do Rosie," Marcus said, standing up and placing his hand on her shoulder. "I must go down and face him and save Hamish."

In astonishment, she started to say, "No, there must be some other ... !" when an encouraging wave of confidence from her brother took her by surprise. An idea came to her and standing up she said, "Listen to me." Telling her brother about it quickly, she asked, "Are you ready to give it a try?"

He liked what he had heard and saw her resolve harden, and said, "Good."

She still didn't really want him to go and said, "Be careful. Remember what Imagen said, you are one with your crystal.'"

Lord Theda called out again, "Come and face me, Dalastar, you coward."

"Here goes," Marcus said before racing down the stairs. He stood on the inside of his shield for a few seconds with his heart racing and breathing rapidly. With great trepidation he stepped through his shield and out onto the steps to the tower. His right leg started shaking uncontrollably and he couldn't summon up the courage to look directly at Lord Theda.

"You're not Dalastar," said Lord Theda, slightly puzzled, "Who are you?"

Marcus ignored the question and walked cautiously sideways, concentrating on Lord Theda's hands. His throat was dry and scratchy as he spoke up, trying not to sound nervous or scared, "Let my friends go."

"And why should I want to do that, young warrior?" Lord Theda asked. Pausing for a moment, he pondered, "You look familiar." Then it came to him. "Yes. You're Marcus Saunders, aren't you? Dalastar is your father. You have done well so far. I see you are very much like your father."

Marcus was confused, "What's going on?"

Rosie felt her brother's confusion as her mind skipped quickly over all the snippets of information she had gathered. This confirmed all her thoughts and in that moment, she understood. Her parents were Dalastar and Phoebe. Rosie was about to communicate this to her brother, when a high-pitched grinding noise distracted her from behind. Spinning around quickly to see what it was, she watched apprehensively as the large brown marble stone moved slowly, by itself, across the roof of the tower. She saw what she thought was a passageway under the stone. Then the stone stopped. Rosie had nowhere to hide and stood waiting in fear, briefly forgetting her brother. Amazingly, a familiar face appeared from the hidden passage.

The gatekeeper came to her, "Are you okay, my dear?"

When she spoke, the relief was apparent in her voice. She told Delostyek what they had planned to do.

The gatekeeper rested a hand on Rosie's shoulder, "I know my dear. I have been waiting for you and your brother to return. I heard the explosions and came to see what was happening. Marcus must do this himself. Many creatures have reported to me that he has learnt his skills extremely quickly and is very competent. He must now fulfil his destiny."

Rosie didn't like the sound of that but knew the gatekeeper was probably right. "You must stay here and do what you planned with your brother. In any case you cannot go into the courtyard until he removes his shield from the entrance."

Marcus stood before Lord Theda struggling to remain calm, and said with a brave voice, "My father is Peter Saunders." Confusion and anger took control of his actions and he chucked a fireball at Lord Theda. Lord Theda raised his damaged red shield quickly, easily fending off the fireball, letting it explode harmlessly behind him.

"So Dalastar sends a child to do the work he is too afraid to do himself," Lord Theda mocked. "So Marcus, where is your cowardly father hiding?"

"My father wouldn't hide from anyone," he said and threw another two fireballs in rapid succession. The red shield flickered slightly easily deflecting the fireballs.

"This is really a waste of time Marcus. Stop these foolish attacks or one of your friends will perish."

A death arrow appeared magically in Lord Theda's hand, and with a powerful flick of the wrist, he hurled it towards Marcus. Marcus didn't flinch and simply raised his hand in front of him. Everyone, including Lord Theda stared in disbelief as the arrow ground to a halt. It hovered just millimetres from Marcus' hand. Grabbing the arrow by the shaft, Marcus immediately flung it back at his attacker. For a moment, Lord Theda stood, stunned to see his own arrow returning to him, and only just managed to protect himself with his shield. The death arrow exploded loudly on impact with the damaged shield. To the great surprise of Lord Theda, his shield simply disintegrated into thousands of tiny fragments that fell, bouncing on the cobblestones, before the ground quickly swallowed them up.

Rosie and Delostyek had been peering over the parapet and saw everything. Delostyek turned to Rosie with a smile on his face. "That young man has learnt a lot, hasn't he? I don't believe it."

Rosie smiled briefly, "Well, you're not the only one."

"How about we help him?" the gatekeeper suggested.

"How?" asked Rosie.

"As I said do as you agreed with your brother. Once you have saved your friends there is something important you need to do."

The gatekeeper gave Rosie very specific instructions. She reached down and held the pendant her father had given her in her hand. "You're joking," she whispered, staring at the gatekeeper in disbelief.

"My dear, I am telling you the truth. Time will prove I am right; you need to believe me, for soon you will see it with your own eyes. You will know what to do. Quick. Make sure your bow and arrows are ready," and then the gatekeeper left her alone and descended the staircase to the courtyard while the large brown marble dome moved slowly back into the centre of the tower.

Marcus shielded his face from the explosion, losing concentration for a brief moment. Four strong hands grabbed him from behind and skilfully bound him with ropes so quickly he didn't even have time to struggle. Unable to move he kept both eyes fixed firmly on his enemy. For a short moment, he thought he was able to read Lord Theda's angry mind, feeling the knot in his stomach tighten. The hatred coming from within this monster was too frightening to comprehend and he stopped immediately.

Lord Theda spat out the words, "You will not ruin nearly one hundred years of planning. Who are you to think that you are better than I? This will teach you that I will not be stopped" and he hurled an enormous fireball at Marcus. The fireball was more than just flames; it bulged and dripped with all the rage and hatred Lord Theda could cram into it. Bright angry red and green tongues of flame dripped from the ball, as it flew towards the boy.

Marcus stood, unable to move his arms or legs, as he watched the fireball fly towards him. For a few moments, his thoughts were all over the place until he remembered Imagen's words to him, 'the crystal and you are one.' Quickly and calmly, he refocused his thoughts and recovered his shield from the tower entrance.

Everything happened at once. Rosie unleashed two white arrows, one after the other, from the top of the tower. They crashed into the death arrows, which still hovered before Hamish and the remaining Ebrag. With the arrows destroyed, the Ebrag moved quickly. Managing to wriggle his arms free, he pulled a dagger from underneath his tunic, and within a matter of seconds, cut through the ropes setting himself, then Hamish, free. The Ebrag threw Hamish over his shoulder, and raced away before anyone could react.

As this was happening, Marcus' shield formed a complete sphere of protection around him. Microseconds later Lord Theda's fireball hit the white shield with tremendous power and the deafening pulse of energy from the explosion knocked everyone in the courtyard to the ground. The massive ball of green and red flames transformed into long searching fingers, encasing the sphere, savagely searching for a flaw, looking for a way in, to attack the life inside. The force of the blast lifted the sphere off the ground and caused it to spin backwards until it came to rest against a wall. Marcus felt as though he had been in a tumble dryer, and he didn't move until all the green and red flames had finally disappeared. Heavily dazed and sore, he was happy to be alive. A short familiar figure now stood over him, reached down, and helped him to his feet, cutting his bindings with consummate skill.

"You are now free, my Marcus," said the Ebrag leader.

Lord Theda saw his opportunity and started to move to the tower entrance, only to find a tall figure standing in his way, "So, Lord Theda we meet again, in slightly different circumstances. You will not get your hands on the energy crystals."

Lord Theda flicked back the hood exposing his face.

Marcus recognised Andrew immediately, "So Rosie was right," he said, as he watched the gatekeeper and Lord Theda argue.

Lord Theda turned to Marcus, "So Marcus, this surprises you. Your father knows all about what I can do," Lord Theda now boasted defiantly, "You will never capture me, Marcus. Your father failed and so will you. I am too good for both of you."

Lord Theda swore loudly when the intensity of the light changed dramatically from the yellowish glare of the late afternoon to an intense bright blue. It caused the soldiers of the dark army to shield their eyes immediately. A powerful wave of light followed. Bursting outwards from the top of the tower instantly it knocked the soldiers off their feet, leaving them stunned and confused on the ground. Seconds later, another even more powerful pulse of light, surged outwards from the tower. The second wave lifted the remaining creatures out of the courtyard, carrying them all the way back to the veil of darkness. It cleansed the City as if a strong wall of water had swept through, washing all the rubbish away. Great waves of light continued to pulse outwards from the top of the tower.

Lord Theda stood in the courtyard, angry and bewildered, and yelled out, "Not again. How can this be?"

"You are alone again, Lord Theda," called out Delostyek, "Your army once again has been defeated. Now it is your turn. You murdered my family. The family I loved is no longer here because of you. You shall pay for your evil deeds."

"You old fool," Lord Theda yelled back, as he fired off a death arrow at the gatekeeper. A purple shield quickly appeared in front of the gatekeeper and stopped the arrow.

Delostyek pulled out his purple crystal to launch his own attack against Lord Theda. However, Lord Theda was quicker and unleashed a powerful fireball directly at Delostyek. The gatekeeper deflected the fireball easily but before he could fire off an arrow of his own, Lord Theda sprinted off in the direction of the gatekeeper's garden. He came to a grinding halt. Before him, Marcus stood defiantly, blocking his way.

A tiny spot of brilliant white light to the left of Lord Theda caught Marcus' attention. It expanded rapidly into a swirling circle of light, which he recognised immediately. It was as though Lord Theda knew it was coming and he smiled confidently at Marcus. Marcus could do nothing to stop Lord Theda diving towards the whirlpool of light.

The gatekeeper was determined not to let this monster escape. "NO YOU DON'T!" yelled the gatekeeper and fired a purple arrow at Lord Theda, hitting him in the right leg. Lord Theda's leg buckled underneath him and he crumpled to the ground. There was no explosion this time, just a hideous haunting scream that echoed off the walls of the courtyard. A purple mist surrounded Lord Theda for a few seconds then vanished as he thrashed around on the ground groaning in pain.

Marcus watched in shocked dismay as a strange reddish-green mist emerged from the twisting, pain-racked body on the ground. A vile, nauseating odour, drifted across the courtyard. Marcus almost puked as he caught a whiff of the pungent stench and immediately covered his nose. Terrified, he watched in disbelief as a distinctive bright red outline intensified around the shapeless rising mist. As the creature grew larger, tiny red and green flaming balls of fire multiplied rapidly, deep within the creature. In a matter of a few seconds, there were thousands of them, blazing way. There was no way he was going to approach the intimidating creature and took a couple of steps backwards as it grew. Hissing menacingly, it now towered over him, and spat at Marcus with a spray of flaming spittle.

His shield responded quickly forming a perfect sphere of protection around him. Instinctively, he covered his head against the attack and heard the sizzle of flames hitting the sphere as they tried to burn their way through the protective layer. Marcus felt the full force of the attack as the creature unleashed all his anger and fury.

Before anyone could move, the shapeless creature headed swiftly towards the swirling whirlpool of light, and vanished. Then, as quickly as it appeared, the wormhole disappeared in a brilliant flash of light, followed by a thunderous boom. The terrible screaming stopped, and peace and quiet returned to the courtyard.

Marcus relieved the danger had gone, stood visibly shaking from the experience, turned towards the gatekeeper and swore, "Damn. Where did THAT come from?"

CHAPTER 43

THE SAPPHIRE PENDANT

Rosie watched as the Ebrag leader cut Marcus free, and was just about to rush down the stairs to help her brother, when a brilliant beam of light shot out from the middle of the marble dome straight up towards the sun above. She stared in disbelief at the powerful beam of light. Remembering the gatekeeper's instructions, she followed them exactly and placed the sapphire pendant into the light beam. A brilliant bluish-white light radiated outwards in every direction from the top of the tower.

Rosie shielded her eyes from its brilliance, feeling the warmth, as the energy flowed through her body, making her glow bright blue.

Taking a step backwards she watched in awe as the stones in the pendent grew to three times their normal size, ready to burst free of the silver bands at any moment. A great pulse of light mushroomed outwards in all directions. The pendant hung in midair beating like a heart, each beat releasing powerful pulses of light that continued to flow out like giant waves into the world beyond the City of Light.

After the last powerful pulse of light erupted from the tower, Rosie put her hands under the pendant, catching it as it fell. The release of energy had deflated the stones and returned the pendant to its original size. She slipped it over her head and was surprised to find the other crystal necklace had now disappeared. Happy she had completed her task, she raced down the staircase to be with her brother. Rosie reached the entrance to the tower just as the gatekeeper stood above the groaning body of Andrew.

The gatekeeper reached down to touch the arrow. When he did, the arrow vanished leaving behind a purple mist that spread slowly over Andrew's body. Finally, it reached his head and disappeared into his eyes.

Andrew lay on the ground curled up in a ball, pale and shivering. Tired and confused he stared up at Delostyek through glazed eyes. Struggling to speak, he whimpered, "What happened?"

"You were caught up in a nightmare, my friend," said the gatekeeper, "We will do what we can for you."

Marcus didn't want go anywhere near Andrew. However, a nod from the gatekeeper told him it was all right. Andrew fixed his eyes on Marcus.

The first thing Marcus noticed about Andrew was that his eyes had changed. They were no longer cold and dark. The fiery flashes of red and green were gone.

Andrew grimaced, "I'm so... so very sorry, Marcus. I know we've only met a couple of times but

I couldn't stop him..." Marcus, desperate to hear more, jumped backwards as Andrew vanished in a purple flash.

Marcus looked solemnly at the gatekeeper, "Where did he go?"

Delostyek shrugged his shoulders, "Once Lord Theda has invaded a body for a while there is little chance of survival."

Marcus heard a familiar voice call out joyously to him and spun around quickly. "You're safe! I'm so glad," said Rosie, before embracing her brother with a huge affectionate hug. "You were so brave."

Still shaking from seeing Andrew disappear, he said, "I didn't feel it." Marcus stood quietly as he reflected on the extraordinary events that had occurred in the courtyard that afternoon. He blamed himself for the death of the Ebrag and the escape of Lord Theda.

Marcus wanted to be by himself. When he noticed the Ebrag leader scurrying over towards them with Imagen following behind, he didn't feel like talking.

Looking nervously at the Ebrag leader he said regretfully, "I'm so sorry that I couldn't save your aide."

Shaking his head vigorously, the Ebrag leader was straightforward with Marcus, "The leader of the dark army is an evil and ruthless killer. It was not of your doing. Lord Theda killed him. When I return to my village, we will honour him. He was a brave Ebrag."

However, right now Marcus couldn't see it any other way.

Rosie sensed the turmoil caused by the mixed emotions racing around inside her brother's head.

By this time, Hamish and the other Ebrag had made their way back to the courtyard. Hamish rushed towards Marcus and happily embraced his friend, tears streaming down his face, "That was totally awesome. You were brilliant." He embraced Marcus again, very much relieved to be alive.

The boys stood, hands on each other's shoulders, smiling at each other, "It might have seemed that way, but I've never been so scared in my whole life."

Everyone talked among themselves. However Marcus wandered away from the others and sat down at the base of a tall shady tree. Naturally, he was happy to see his friend safe and deep down felt very pleased with himself. Nevertheless, much had occurred and many things were weighing heavily on his mind.

The Ebrags cleaned up one of the apartments surrounding the courtyard and organised something to eat. Whilst the others were eating, the gatekeeper, leaning awkwardly against the window frame, looked out through the glass at Marcus, who was still sitting by himself.

"You need to explain the rest to him, Delostyek," said Imagen. "He has the right to know."

"You're right," said Delostyek, as he slipped quietly out of the room and walked across the courtyard to Marcus.

"Can I talk with you, my boy?"

"Yeah. Sure," said Marcus, as he opened his eyes and glanced up at the gatekeeper. "I'm thinking about the Ebrag who died. If only I'd gone down earlier, he might still be alive."

"We have already talked about this. That was entirely Lord Theda's fault, my boy. You did everything you could. How could you know what he was going to do?"

"That's easy to say. I still feel bad about it."

"Marcus, Lord Theda has killed many people and does not value life as you do. Truly my boy, you did nothing wrong. You should feel proud of what you did."

Rosie noticed the gatekeeper talking to her brother, went over, and sat down next to them.

"I am really proud of you two," said Delostyek. "You worked together and you have learnt a lot about yourselves and each other. Marcus, your loyalty to your friend was impressive. That is a very important trait to have. Going down to face Lord Theda alone was a very brave and courageous thing to do."

"I was going to free Hamish even if it meant Lord Theda caught me instead."

"Yes my boy. I saw that. Lord Theda is very powerful. He can control the energy in the red crystal and the death arrows were his creation. When did you know you could defeat him?"

"When his shield disintegrated I knew he was in trouble. While I was staring at him I caught a glimpse of what he was going to do, just before he threw the fireball at me."

Rosie and the gatekeeper were shocked to hear this and glanced at each other briefly.

Delostyek was worried but tried not to show it and asked, "Did you feel anything when this happened?"

"Yes," he said, puzzled. "He was very angry, but he was also scared at the same time. That doesn't seem to make sense."

"Yes, well the anger was to be expected," said Delostyek. "You ended Lord Theda's journey. As strange as it may seem, you probably felt Andrew's fear."

Marcus shuddered at the memory of reading Lord Theda's mind. Even though it was only for a split second, it revealed the chilling ruthlessness and pure evil that powered Lord Theda's malicious actions. "What sort of creature can do that sort of thing, Delostyek?"

"Lord Theda is from a predatory and parasitic race from the furthest parts of the universe. They are a race of unselective parasites that invade, and take possession of the bodies of others, and suck out every ounce of energy created by their host. Eventually the host dies and he moves on to another. When he first arrived in this world, he had managed to invade a person here who knew of the existence of the crystal weapons in the miners cave. Somehow, he managed to gain access to the miners' cave and steal the red crystal, we still don't know how but somehow he did. It is similar in power to the crystals that are now within you. Rosie, I mean you too. You have become one with your crystal, just like your brother."

Surprisingly, she didn't ask any questions. Rosie already knew and simply reached up with her right hand to touch the sapphire necklace still hanging around her neck.

The crystal necklace she had received in the miners cave had vanished after she had finished her task on the tower.

Delostyek, expecting a question or comment from her, paused for a moment and when she didn't respond, continued. "Lord Theda managed to unleash the power within the crystal and transport it from victim to victim. Lord Theda is the most senior Commander from the planet Sarappia. We understand he reports to a ruler who is an absolute dictator and who, many tell us, is utterly unforgiving about failure. This is the second time Lord Theda has failed to take the energy crystals from under the tower in the City of Light. He may try again. We must be vigilant and watch for his return, for next time it may not be so easy."

Marcus remembered when Lord Theda called out his name, "How did Lord Theda, sorry, I mean Andrew, end up here then?"

"I am sorry to say I cannot answer your question, just as I don't know exactly how you arrived here Marcus. All I can tell you is what you already know. Lord Theda escaped from here many years ago, and Dalastar and Phoebe followed him. Their paths must have crossed somehow in your world.

Marcus looked up at the gatekeeper, saying, "That swirling light he disappeared into, that's what brought us here, did you know that?"

"That may be, my boy. But as I have already told you I don't have an answer for you."

"Where did Lord Theda go to?"

"I don't know, my boy." There was a deep sadness in his voice as he continued, "I fear we will see him again."

"Fine", said Marcus, feeling bitterly disappointed, "Until I saw Andrew's face I thought we were part of a game. He was in business with our father. Now I don't know what to think."

"Do not blame him, Marcus," said the Gatekeeper. "Lord Theda must have invaded his body many months ago, and could be the reason you are here now. For many years your father has been working on a way to transport himself here but so far as been unsuccessful. We discovered that while the gate in the octagonal room is closed, the portal in your father's house would not work properly. We have however been able to use it to keep in touch with each other. The game you started playing was interactive because the portal allowed the Imitators to use your thoughts to copy you. Nothing physical could or would pass through the portal, only your thoughts. As you know now, something went wrong. We still don't know how it happened, as we have not been able to speak with Dalastar for nearly three days. All we know is that you two, and the others and Lord Theda all arrived here at the same time, in this world, unexpectedly. We had so little time to teach you all the skills you needed but in the end you two learned them yourselves."

Marcus wondered about Lord Theda's shield, "Why was his shield destroyed by the death arrow."

From what Imagen has told me, Lord Theda's shield flickered when your fireball and Rosie's arrow hit his shield at the same time. The cumulative power of your weapons in combination with his own death arrow was the final straw, and broke down the energy flow to the shield. It couldn't sustain further attacks and collapsed.

Rosie sat there, wondering, and asked, "How do you stop a creature like that?"

Delostyek shook his head, "There is only one way and it is very dangerous." The gatekeeper remembered many of those who had tried and failed, including Dalastar's father. He was just about to mention it to the twins but at the last minute, decided to spare them from the gruesome details. It was best to leave it to their father to discuss it with them in the future. There was, however, one thing he could tell them.

"There is one mineral, which will stop him. We call it Oridium. It's very rare and extremely dangerous."

Rosie asked, "Why's that?"

"Firstly, my dear it must be handled in the proper way—to touch it without the right protection results in instant death. Secondly, the only known location known is in the caves at the base of the dark mountain. It is a cold and very dangerous place. It's too hazardous to try and I warn you not to think too much about it. Anyway much more will be explained when we speak to Dalastar."

The Gatekeeper realised he had already said too much. These two had already excelled at their first contact with Lord Theda and the gatekeeper was mindful they still had much to learn.

Rosie, on the other hand now wanted to know more. She tried hard and used all the skills of persuasion she had to extract more information about the Oridium. The gatekeeper kept on changing the subject, which infuriated Rosie. When she knew he wasn't about to give her the answer she wanted she gave up and asked, "Delostyek?"

"Yes my dear."

"Where are we exactly?"

"You are on the planet Agarutu, trading centre of the universe."

Marcus looked with disbelief at the gatekeeper, "Excuse me."

"Well, it was once the centre of the universe," continued the gatekeeper, smiling at him. "And it will be again. Dalastar tried everything in his power to return the key but nothing worked. He had to get the key back to me and we thought maybe if you played the game, an opening may appear and the key would return to me. Anyway, it worked, but not in the way we ever expected. Now that you have returned the key, other people and traders will be able to return here to the City of Light. The City of Light will now return to its former glory. Now Marcus, I believe you have something that belongs to me," said the gatekeeper, relieved he had brought the conversation to this point.

"Yes. Of course," said Marcus as he reached into his pocket and pulled out the tiny key. The light glistened off the tiny object as the gatekeeper took it from the outstretched fingers. Tears of joy ran down the gatekeeper's wrinkly face and his face glowed with happiness, "Come it is time to eat and rest."

Marcus and Rosie stood up together and the gatekeeper walked with them, his hands on their shoulders, as they strode across the courtyard.

Rosie had a terrible thought and stopped in her tracks, "Isobel! I'd forgotten all about her."

"Imagen told me that Mirra and Copia will bring her back," Delostyek informed her. "I am sure she will be looking forward to seeing you again."

Happy with this they walked across to where the others were eating.

CHAPTER 44

VICTORY CELEBRATIONS

After destroying the machine and surveying the damage she had caused, Isobel, Pieter and Mirra all returned to the dining room. The miners gathered around her clapping and cheering. Great quantities of food appeared on all the tables in the dining room. Pieter stood up and bellowed, "Quiet!"

Everyone stopped talking immediately.

"Cave safe. Thanked be Isobel." Pieter raised his mug, "Protector Crystal Caves!" he roared loudly. The whole room erupted in one singularly loud cheer.

Isobel, red-faced with embarrassment, was still sitting at the table when Mirra whispered in her ear, "Stand up, but don't say anything."

"Okay," she said, nervously, standing up to face Pieter.

Pieter called to his wife, "Magda bring special thing you."

Magda appeared from the back of the room carrying a small bag. She stopped in front of Isobel, reached inside the bag and held up the small glistening object for all to see. She reached forward, placed the object in Isobel's hand, and backed away. Isobel couldn't believe what she saw. The pink diamond, perfectly carved into the shape of a panther, dangled alluringly at the end of a fine gold chain. Isobel held it up to the light. It sparkled with all the colours of the rainbow as it reflected the light from the cave. The disappointment of losing the other crystal necklace after destroying the machine vanished as she quickly placed the pendant around her neck. Tears of delight streamed down her face.

She looked uncertainly at Mirra, not knowing what to say.

"Just say thank you. That will be enough," she whispered to Isobel.

Isobel, overcome by this show of kindness couldn't help herself and lunging towards Magda gave her a huge hug and whispered, "Thank you."

Pieter's turn to be embarrassed came seconds later as Isobel threw her arms around his neck and hugged him.

Everyone cheered again and then sat down to enjoy the food together. Eventually the celebrations died down and everybody went to their dwellings for the night. The Elders allowed Isobel to collapse her shield. The dark army had not attacked again. Everyone felt that the danger had passed.

It had been just over six hours since Isobel had destroyed the machine, when Copia arrived at the cave. Isobel was sound asleep as Copia listened to Mirra and Pieter describe the events of the last twelve hours.

When they had finished, Copia said, "It would appear the dark army has failed this time. We should take her to be with the others."

Mirra agreed, "It is a long walk. She will not make it with her sore ankle."

"Cart her take. City of Light," said Pieter. "Come now. Leave soon. All day take."

"Good," said Copia.

The journey to the City of Light, whilst scenic, was rough and uncomfortable. Isobel bounced around in the back of the cart hour after hour as Pieter and Slvad drove the cart hard. She arrived in the City of Light, sore and weary, late in the day. Everyone was delighted to see each other, and after all the joyous greetings and welcomes, they shared their stories of their adventures.

Isobel described her time with the cave miners.

Hamish and Marcus sat silently through her story. When she mentioned the yellow machine, the gatekeeper became particularly interested.

"Just go over that again, please Isobel," said Delostyek.

Isobel repeated her description of the machine to the gatekeeper.

"Thank you, my dear."

"Delostyek?

"Yes?"

"What's a machine like that doing here?"

The gatekeeper sighed deeply before answering," I guess Lord Theda must have brought it here from another place. That's something I need to investigate further and discuss with Dalastar."

Rosie asked her friend "Weren't you scared?"

Isobel shrugged her shoulders, "I was a little, at first, but the cave miners were kind. I also had Mirra to help as well. Oh! I almost forgot. Look what the cave miners gave me for destroying the machine," she said, showing her pendant to Rosie.

"That's out of this world," sighed Rosie.

Isobel looked at her friend and pulled a wry smile, "Very funny, Rosie."

They talked for a little longer when the gatekeeper said, "It is now time to go."

They chatted all the way to the gatekeeper's courtyard. The tunnel of vines and bushes opened wider as they walked through.

A handrail of purple lights lit the staircase as they descended.

The gatekeeper raced down ahead of the others, anxious to open the gateway to the universe. Rosie and Hamish were still walking in the door, when, with the precision of a watchmaker, Delostyek inserted the tiny key into the first of the two enormous locks, and then the other. For the first time in many years, both locks glowed, softly at first and then bright purple, spitting sparks out on to the floor. They all heard the latches click open. The door groaned and creaked, opening slowly at first, and then once it had gained momentum, moved more freely, revealing a dark hole behind. Absolutely no light emanated from it at all. For the gatekeeper, it brought back the memory of his wife and child and those who had passed through it. Delostyek appeared to be in another world when

Marcus approached him, "Excuse me, Delostyek, I need to know a couple of things."

"Well ask, my boy."

"Why did you appear behind me when I was fighting Billy and Fred?"

Marcus saw the answer to his question in the gatekeeper's smile, "Everyone needs a little help sometimes, don't they?"

"I thought you said you couldn't leave here?"

The gatekeeper looked down at him and winked, "I am the gatekeeper and sometimes I break the rules when the need arises. Anyhow, it was not as it appeared. And your second question?"

Rosie and Marcus had discussed how the gatekeeper had appeared suddenly in the tower and had come up with only one possibility.

"Why didn't you tell us about the secret passage to the tower?"

"You don't miss much, do you?" replied the gatekeeper, without really answering the question.

"Marcus my boy, there are many secrets here in this chamber and this world. As you explore more of it, you will learn these things yourself. It is now time for you to leave and return home. However, before you go I need to speak with you alone. Come." Together they walked across to the other side of the room and started talking quietly together. Hamish and Isobel sat on the ground, while Rosie crept closer towards her brother to listen, but Imagen shook his head, making her stay where she was. The gatekeeper blocked Rosie's attempt to read her brother's mind and when she couldn't, was more than a little miffed about it.

"There are some things that are better fixed by time," said the gatekeeper, smiling down at Marcus, "Imagen tells me you know about the power of the watch."

Marcus nodded and quietly told the gatekeeper what had happened.

"You deserve to be shown something else," It didn't take long for the gatekeeper to give Marcus the instructions he needed. Before returning to the others, the gatekeeper placed his hands on Marcus' shoulders and looked straight into his eyes, warning him, "This knowledge is a powerful tool. You must not tell anyone about the things I have told you. You must use them wisely. This is very important."

"I understand," then did as the gatekeeper had directed him.

The usually tolerant Rosie, tired and dirty, was particularly annoyed that she wasn't included in the conversation and just wanted to know what was going on. She finally lost her patience with both her brother and the gatekeeper and went to interrupt their discussion. This time however, the gatekeeper turned his head towards her, shaking his head from side to side. Rosie understood the gatekeeper's thoughts immediately and didn't say another word, and quietly sat down on the floor next to Isobel and Hamish. After another minute or so, Marcus re-joined his sister and friends as the gatekeeper advised everyone it was time for them to return home.

Imagen, Copia, Mirra, Pieter and Slvad said their goodbyes to the twins and their friends.

The Ebrag leader came forward, saying, "Goodbye my Marcus and Rosie. Goodbye, my Hamish and Isobel."

Rosie reached down to hug the Ebrag leader, but he scurried away and hid behind the gatekeeper. Realising he was embarrassed; Rosie thanked him for his bravery. The Ebrag leader, peering out from behind the gatekeeper, remained silent for the first time in many days, sad to see these four creatures depart.

There were no more good-byes. Marcus joined the others at the gate to the universe and they all took the step into the darkness together, which immediately whisked them away. A few seconds later, they found themselves standing in complete darkness, in the middle of the computer room they had left a few days ago.

CHAPTER 45

GAME FINISHED

The familiar smell of the study welcomed them home.

Marcus took a couple of paces towards the light switch and turned it on.

Hamish was happy to be back and said, "At least we finished that game."

Isobel agreed. Whatever they'd been through Rosie was glad it was finished as well. Their eyes quickly adjusted to the light. Isobel was the first to notice that something was wrong. Shocked, she said, "Everything's back in place. This is too weird."

Somewhat puzzled herself, Rosie said, "I can see that. What's going on?"

Isobel sucked in a deep breath as she stared in disbelief at the clock hanging on the wall. She tapped Rosie on the shoulder, and then in a soft voice said, "Look at the clock."

Hamish turned around to see what the girls were talking about and saw it as well. Three pairs of eyes focused in on the clock, each in complete shock. It read Friday 14th June, 10.49pm.

Isobel said, "It says we are back before we've left. That's impossible."

Hamish, just as confused as the others, said, "Something's wrong, here Rosie."

Rosie spun around and glared at her brother, who was trying to keep a straight face. However, she had the sense not to say a word. You knew didn't you, she thought.

Marcus simply nodded his head and put his finger up to his mouth to indicate to Rosie not to say a word. She wasn't happy about it, and sort of understood. She knew Marcus would explain it to her later, after the others were gone.

Marcus spoke softly but firmly to his friend, "You have to be quiet, Hamish. Otherwise someone else will hear you." Then he said to the others, "You lot stay here, and don't make a sound."

While Rosie and Isobel talked quietly to each other, Hamish noticed the large book sitting on the cable of controller number four and gently pulled the cable from under the book. Marcus caught a glimpse of Hamish fiddling with something and growled quietly at his friend, "Don't touch anything Hamish. Can't you just leave things alone for once?"

"I haven't done anything," the whispered reply came.

Marcus was just about to say something else to his friend when he heard someone running up the stairs then stop. Fortunately, he was standing next to the light switch and quickly turned it off. The footsteps stopped for a few moments and then continued up the stairs. Carefully, he opened the door and slipped through the narrowest of gaps, closing it behind him.

The gatekeeper had warned him that they must not run into themselves, because it would seriously complicate everything. When the gatekeeper first told him what was going to happen he was sceptical. However, Delostyek had told him clearly to prepare for it. Isobel and Hamish were not to know that it was Marcus, through the watch, who controlled the current situation. Rosie would find out, but the others were never to know.

Marcus heard laughter in the television room at the other end of the house. Good, he thought, right where they're supposed to be. He heard the other Marcus coming back down the stairs and managed to sneak back into the computer room without being seen, or heard. He called the others who were standing in the darkness, over to the door, "Quickly, we have to get out of here. The others will be here in a minute."

Hamish asked, "Which others?"

"Us. You. Isobel. Rosie and me. I'll explain later. When I say so, follow me and keep quiet. We are going straight upstairs to Rosie's room," he instructed them. "We can't bump into ourselves."

Marcus put his ear to the door, listening for when the footsteps reached the bottom of the stairs and ran along the hallway to the television room.

"Right, let's go," he said in the softest of voices and opened the door.

Isobel and Hamish lead the way with Rosie next and Marcus last. Marcus bounded past Rosie up the stairs and half pushed Isobel and Hamish around the landing of the staircase. Rosie just made it around the corner as the four children from the television room walked past the bottom of the staircase. The four on the staircase stood perfectly still.

When Rosie stopped on the landing, the floor creaked beneath her. She held her breath and didn't move a muscle as she heard her own voice from the hallway below say, "I thought I heard something. It's probably nothing," and the other four children walked past, unaware of her presence. Her curiosity got the better of her and she snuck back down the staircase to peek into the hallway, only to see the door to her father's study close behind the others. "Hope you enjoy the journey," she whispered, smiling and almost laughing at the thought.

After Rosie went back down the stairs, Marcus pushed Isobel and Hamish into Rosie's bedroom and told them to be quiet, as he waited impatiently for Rosie to come into the room. Rosie opened the door quietly and closed it behind her, only to have her brother grab her by the arm, "Where have you been?" he asked angrily.

"Let go. I just took a peek at the others."

After his discussion with the gatekeeper, Marcus was keen to ensure the other children had not seen them, and asked his sister, "Did they see you?"

"No," she said, "Why?"

"It's important."

"No. They didn't see me."

Isobel asked, "Who didn't see you?"

"You, me, Rosie and Hamish. We have come back in time Isobel. That's why the study is like it is. The others downstairs are us. Only they're in our past. The gatekeeper said they had to play the game exactly like we did. They're down there now doing what we did. I can't explain it. All I know is the gatekeeper wanted us to come back early."

Rosie didn't say anything, as she knew her brother must know the reason.

"I've already asked you once." Isobel demanded, "What is going on?"

She wasn't the only one. Marcus saw Hamish was just as determined to know.

"Look, all I know is the gatekeeper said 'when we get back here we had to make sure they played the game, just as we did.' That meant we couldn't bump into ourselves when we got back." He told me it was better this way, that's all I can tell you."

"Rubbish," said Hamish. "You're not telling us what's going on."

"You have to keep it down," said Marcus, worried about waking his mother.

Rosie tried to read her brothers thoughts but found she couldn't. The harder she tried the more he resisted.

Marcus felt her efforts, looked across the room at her and shook his head, they cannot know, not just yet.

Rosie wasn't happy but understood her brother and suggested to everyone, "Listen. How about we go down and grab something to eat."

She knew Marcus well enough to know he wouldn't tell anything to anyone.

Reluctantly the others agreed, but they both told Marcus they weren't happy.

"Perhaps we should change out of these clothes first," said Rosie.

Marcus, now happy for the chance to do something other than explain what had happened, said, "That's a great idea. Come on Hamish let's go."

Hamish was angry and pushed the door with a little too much energy and it slammed shut.

"Great," Marcus whispered angrily to his friend.

Hamish snapped back, "Sorry. I didn't do it on purpose."

"Right. Quick we'd better get into bed."

The twins' mother awoke with a start as the door banged shut. She rolled over in bed and looked at the clock. It was now after past eleven o'clock. Right, she thought, angry at being disturbed. Hopping out of bed, she grabbed her dressing gown and stomped her way across the bedroom, opening the door just in time to see Marcus' door close. Wasting no time, she barged into her son's room, turning on the light, "What's going on in here Marcus?" she demanded.

Marcus pretended to be asleep in his own bed, while Hamish did the same in the spare bed.

However, his mother wasn't having anything of it, "Marcus, I know you're awake, so stop pretending and tell me what's going on!"

He rolled over and peered up at his mother, his face half hidden under his doona, "Nothing Mum, we were just talking to Isobel and Rosie."

"Hmmm," she said. "Well that's it. No more talking and no more noise. It's time for sleep. Do you understand me?"

"Yes Mum."

"I mean it Marcus!"

"Yes. Okay. Good night."

Helen withdrew from the room and switched the light off before closing the door. Unseen by anyone, a fine pink mist settled over the boys as it had done to Isobel and Rosie moments earlier; both boys dropped off to sleep moments after the light went out. When she peeked into Rosie's room, she found the girls sound asleep. Good, she thought. Now I can get back to sleep. She smiled and said softly to her sleeping children, "I'm looking forward to a quiet couple of days this weekend." She hopped back into her own bed and switched off the light.

THE END

ABOUT THE AUTHOR

Being avid readers, my wife and I spent a significant amount of time reading to, and encouraging our four children to read and enjoy a wide variety of literature. As a parent with a creative and imaginative mind, I made up numerous stories, which the kids loved to hear. For many years, I attempted to start writing but kept putting it off. It was during a performance review that someone asked me to express some personnel goals. I stated I had always wanted to write a novel.

Challenged to do so I started that very afternoon, bought a notebook and began writing on the one-hour journey home on the train to Ballarat. Six months later, I had finished the first draft. Apart from the challenge of writing a novel such as "Finish the Game." There are a number of themes running through the story. The children learn that the actions they take or the decisions they make can have serious consequences on those around them affect. Secondly, the book is about trusting others and helping each other to defeat Lord Theda. The main character Marcus does this. When at great danger to himself, he decides to stand up to Lord Theda to save Hamish. Only as we stand together can the problems we face be defeated. The final aspect is persistence. Marcus and Rosie realise to get home they have to Finish the Game. The journey is not easy and filled with danger but they stick at it despite the difficulties and their personal doubts.

Writing this novel has given me a special freedom from the normal things we do on a day to day basis. Apart from the obvious tedium of typing, it is relaxing to allow my thoughts and ideas to roam about, doing whatever they like, not bound by the rigid walls of the business world. There are times at night after writing, I dream the scenes and the live the adventure. I have enjoyed the journey of writing the original draft and constantly learning as I went through the editing and rewriting process. The most rewarding aspect of the whole process is to be able to improve the story and the give the characters their own personality.